# SET AT ODDS

# SET AT ODDS

## STORIES OF THE PARTITION AND BEYOND

Prafulla Roy

Translated from Bengali by
John W. Hood

SRISHTI PUBLISHERS & DISTRIBUTORS
64-A, Adhchini
Sri Aurobindo Marg
New Delhi 110 017
srishtipublishers@forindia.com



First published in 2002 by
Srishti Publishers & Distributors

ISBN 81-87075-77-5
Rs. 250.00

Cover design by Arrt Creations

Printed and bound in India by
Saurabh Print-O-Pack, Noida

## CONTENTS

# TRANSLATOR'S INTRODUCTION

What was once known as 'India' is now three countries: India, Pakistan and Bangladesh, a subcontinental division that is the direct result of the Partition of India that came with Independence in 1947. The Partition may have satisfied certain political and ideological egos in the early stages and given at least temporary comfort to those who feared the consequences for minority communities in a free India. However, it is sadly evident that if the basic intention of Partition was to dispel tension and obviate the potential for further disputation and conflict, then it has been a monumental failure. In their little more than fifty years of independence India and Pakistan have been at war three times, while continuing tension over the rightful identity of Kashmir, in particular, keeps relations between the two countries in a worrying state of ongoing stress. As East Pakistan, Bangladesh experienced violence and oppression while being in one way or another kept under the thumb of West Pakistan and, after a crippling war of liberation in which India became heavily involved, attained its independence in 1971. Since then, Bangladesh has been involved in on-going border and immigration disputes with India. Looming ominously over what has become a miasma of mistrust, blame and counter-accusation is the nightmare reality of the continuing enhancement of the nuclear capabilities of India and Pakistan, while in all three countries the extent of poverty is immense as is the expenditure on defence.

In the contemporary world it would seem that the politics of divisiveness have a more ready appeal than the politics of cooperation. *Realpolitik* is rooted in rivalry, the demonising of the necessary Other, and the quest for profit at the expense of one's competitors. This is not to say that politicians and those who devise their platforms are without morals, but that their morality is often limited by a philosophy determined by notions of Us to the exclusion of Them.

The necessary conditions of difference in which such a *realpolitik* may thrive are to be found in every human society. Indeed, diversity is a necessary social and cultural base on which the advancement of ideas may prosper. However, such social and cultural differences may also be exploited to nurture the divisiveness that will give rise to leaders whose egos may be gratified by their over-powering in one way or another those, characteristically distinct from them, who are perceived as their rivals. Minority groups may also be exploited for their distinctiveness and demonised not as potential rivals but as scapegoats, or even used as smokescreens. Religious differences, for example, have little social or political significance for most ordinary people, but they may very easily be exploited by leaders who see political advantage in social discord. During the Freedom Movement in India, egos were continually being made, unmade and remade, but despite the best efforts of even a humanitarian giant like Mahatma Gandhi, the politics of difference determined the nature of the freedom that India would attain, and more than half a century later continue to thrive in the partitioned subcontinent.

Arising out of the major – though not the only – aspect of difference in Indian society and culture came the Two-Nation Theory that held that there were such fundamental, irrevocable differences between the Hindu and Muslim communities that the only way for peaceful coexistence between the two with the attainment of independence must be in separate nationalities. The Two-Nation Theory was espoused most vociferously by Muslim leaders, especially Jinnah, who promulgated the fear that the Muslim minority would suffer at the hands of the Hindu majority in a free India. There were also devout and scholarly Muslims, such as Maulana Abul Kalam Azad, who vigorously and cogently opposed the Two-Nation Theory. Azad and his ilk were the apostles of the politics of cooperation; they were admired by many and ignored by most. Capitalising on the easily fanned fear and mistrust among a largely illiterate populace in a politically and economically long repressed society, the proponents of the politics of divisiveness won the day.

The victory, however, came at an appalling cost. In the initial months of relocation alone, millions were killed, often brutally and with abominable bravado; rape was unrestrained; homes were burned; property was looted. No community bore all the guilt, and all were victims in one way or another. Sadly, the blood-letting did not stop. In India, the beautiful state of Kashmir became a focal point for terrorism and international conflict; communal carnage flared again, notably against Muslims in the 1960s, against the Sikhs when Indira Gandhi was assassinated, and, a few years later when the Babri Masjid was destroyed, between Hindus and Muslims throughout the subcontinent. In Pakistan, the Mohajirs, or immigrants from India, had for long been the subject of often bitter antagonism from the established community. The majority Bengali population of East Pakistan endured various acts of repression by the national government in West Pakistan, resulting in violent demonstrations, riots and, ultimately, civil war. Even after liberation, the new government was ousted by the simple and efficient process of assassination in a military coup, while fundamentalist groups continue to pose a threat to Bangladesh's peaceful, democratic and secular development.

It is easy to count the dreadful cost of all of this as bureaucrats and newspapers do, in statistical terms. But what does it actually mean that a certain number of people were shot by pro-government troops or butchered by another community in a property dispute or murdered by neo-fascists wanting to cleanse their society of the Other? And who is to blame for all the carnage that emanates out of the politics of difference?

The answer to the first question lies most vividly in human memory, even with its propensity to fade, and not much in history books, with their preoccupation with political processes and statistical evidence. The answer to the second question might easily point the finger at governments or political parties or ideological organisations, but there is no escaping the fact that a communal riot, for example, involves communities which are made up of ordinary men and women. Such ordinary people have little time for ideology; they are too concerned with keeping their jobs, making ends meet for their families, and living in peace. Here is the basic irony, for being lured into extremist action in fear of a supposed threat, they are, in effect, bringing about the destruction of that which they would so ardently defend.

The Partition of India dissected the country in two places; a large hunk was carved out of the northwest and became West Pakistan, while a less large territory was carved out of the east, predominantly from Bengal, and became East Pakistan, the subordinate wing, in effect, of the new Muslim state. All but one of the stories in this volume that have direct relation to the Partition are concerned with the Partition in the east. Three of the stories are set during the Partition itself, the rest emanate from it in one way or another. Underlying this range of stories is the notion that the history of Partition and the politics of division that brought it about is a history that will not confine itself to the past. The flames that were fanned by the proponents of separatism in the decade prior to Independence have still not gone out and from time to time flare up in some belligerent act or pronouncement that evokes communal hostility and violence, while the foreign policies of the nations of the subcontinent would seem to underline their prevailing mistrust of one another.

The breakup of Bengal was aggravated by some characteristically regional problems. There were, as in the west, innumerable acts of savagery associated with dislocation and resettlement, particularly in people's having to come to terms with the apparent absurdity of winning freedom and then losing their homes. Calcutta, in India's West Bengal, absorbed hordes of Hindu refugees from the east (as did various parts of the states of Assam, Tripura and Bihar), while Dhaka and other cities in the new East Pakistan were forced to accommodate masses of Muslim refugees from West Bengal as well as from Bihar and the eastern parts of Uttar Pradesh. These non-Bengali refugees were for the most part Urdu-speaking and by their language, at least, set themselves apart from the Bengali-speaking majority, while those who had opted to go to West Pakistan were soon embraced by an unwelcome chill there. The national government of Pakistan, centred in the western wing, declared Urdu to be the national language in both West and East Pakistan; in the eastern wing, Bengali would be reduced to the status of a second language, despite the fact that Bengalis made up more than fifty percent of the population of Pakistan as a whole. Thus, incipient Pakistani nationalism came into confrontation with a centuries old pride in Bengali culture and East Pakistan became a battleground once again, this time in the cause of the cultural interests of the majority Bengali population against their new national government.

What were seen to be further discriminatory policies against East Pakistan and its Bengali population in particular were enacted by the government in West Pakistan, gradually alienating the national affections of the eastern wing to the extent that civil war became inevitable. With massive economic and military aid from India the eastern province established its independence in December, 1971, and became the new nation of Bangladesh. However, national unity and civil harmony were not the results of liberation. While the dramas of political intrigues and military coups were acted out on one level, the social fabric was being frayed by tension between the exultant Bengali population and the minority Urdu-speaking population who felt that they had been abandoned by Pakistan to the hostility of the Bengalis. A great many of these people sought to migrate back to India, but could do so only illegally, so giving rise to a major point of contention between the two countries. As the politics of divisiveness came again to the fore with the rise in India of the Hindu nationalist Bharatiya Janata Party, certain right-wing Hindu groups, especially the Bombay-centred Shiv Sena, took up with a vengeance the cudgels against many hapless Muslims in the city whose name would be changed to Mumbai as a gesture of Hindu cultural assertiveness, and those who could not prove their Indian citizenship with valid documentation were summarily deported. Predictably this antagonism was countered by a wave of violent retaliation by certain Muslim extremists. The situation was horribly exacerbated after the demolition in December 1992 of the Babri mosque in the town of Ayodhya, believed by many orthodox Hindus to have been the birthplace of the legendary hero, Rama. The reaction to this carefully orchestrated act of destruction was explosive and reverberated throughout the subcontinent in acts of hostility against Muslims and Muslim institutions and against Hindus and Hindu businesses and temples in Bangladesh and Pakistan; years after, at the turn of a new century, the tension between bigotry and reason continues.

This simplified piece of potted history is intended only as an introduction to the stories which follow and to provide a basic context for them. No matter how history is written, we frequently have to be reminded that what captures the interest of historians has ramifications for ordinary people, usually too ordinary to feature other than as statistics in the columns of newspapers or as generalisations in the pages of history books. Literature can often go a long way in sharpening our perspective on the past, and Prafulla Roy's stories focus on the anonymous, ordinary people who bore the brunt, in one way or another, of the grand designs of those who sought to create history.

Thus, in the first three stories, all set close to the time of Partition, the focus is on little people. The first story in the collection, *The Boatman,* is Prafulla Roy's first short story, and sees an east Bengali boatman, caught in the midst of a microcosmic version of the greater communal hostility with its attendant atrocities, forced to lend his hand to the universal blood-letting that characterises the times. *One King Goes and Another King Comes* is a much more peaceful story, looking at the momentous political transformation in east Bengal from the point of view of one of its least important citizens. Whether it is east Bengal governed by the white saheb, or East Pakistan governed by the brown saheb, life goes on unchanged for the humble people, battling with nature simply to eke out an existence. *The Island in the River* is based in the unrestrained terror perpetrated by thugs taking up any excuse to indulge themselves, but the outcome of the story is a salutary reassurance of the enduring power of natural justice and morality.

The Bangladesh War of Liberation excited passions on both sides of the boundary between the two Bengals, not the least of which was the passion for the Bengali language and its cultural tradition, seen to be threatened by the policies of the government in West Pakistan. The Bengali language was saved, as were other kinds of freedom, with the liberation of Bangladesh. In *The Dream Train,* an aspect of the patriotism evoked by that war is presented from the viewpoint of someone on the western side of the border, a young man whose family had left their village in East Pakistan – idyllic as he remembers it in his dreams – for Calcutta – not at all idyllic as he experiences it – some ten years after Partition. (Many Hindus stayed on in their erstwhile east Bengal, only to be made more uncomfortable and less secure as more and more Urdu-speaking refugees came into East

Pakistan from the Indian states of Bihar and Uttar Pradesh, as we may note in *The Father.* These people were at best neutral to Bengalis and, given the experiences that drove them from their homes, hostile to Hindus.) Built on the sadness that comes out of the life of a poor family trying to survive in Calcutta, the story touchingly depicts the pathetic irony of a man whose patriotism for the land of his birth is smothered by that very battle for survival.

After the foundation of Bangladesh the Urdu-speaking minority, clinging to the blind faith that planes would be sent from Karachi and Lahore to take them to Pakistan, came to feel, now that they no longer had their privileged language status, less and less secure, and many of them decided to return to India. Although most of the older ones among them were actually born in India, they were now citizens of a foreign country and therefore unable to return legally to the land of their birth and their forefathers. *Unlawful Entry,* while describing the hardships faced by illegal immigrants desperate for a home that would genuinely accommodate them, also raises the issue of national identity, once so easily lost when an Englishman drew lines on a map, now so easily achieved, apparently, when unscrupulous politicians seek to use refugees as pawns in their own less than honest quests for power.

Muslims throughout India were drawn once again into the turmoil of communal hostility during the frenzied lead up to the demolition of the Babri Masjid and in the aftermath to that most widely publicised act of destruction. In Bombay, particularly, where the politics of divisiveness had enjoyed a resurgence, the violence was particularly devastating, but hostility was let loose all over India, so prompting a wave of anti-Hindu violence in Bangladesh and, to a lesser extent, Pakistan with its negligible Hindu population. It is important to note, however, that the vast majority of people appalled by what many perceived as the mischief of fanatics were Hindus, while the vast majority of those who suffered the violence, the arson, the looting and the killing were, needless to say, ordinary working people who could ill afford the luxury of religious extremism. The helplessness of little people in the face of a frenetic mob, and the brutish bigotry and rapaciousness of the mob itself, is chillingly depicted in *The Destination.* Similarly, in *For a Little While,* the basic humanity of humble people, bereft of home and livelihood and made weak by hunger, is set in relief against the raucous voice of bigotry; yet loud as that voice may be, it proves no match for the quiet voice of reason and the generous heart of humanity. Roy's sense of reality is persistent, however, for the seemingly happy ending of both stories is only an illusion, the reader being left with a disturbing uncertainty about how things may have turned out after the final sentences.

There follow three stories in which the Partition and its ramifications are seen in retrospect. The one story set in the context of the western partition, *Where there is no Frontier,* looks back after fifty-one years at the social turbulence of the Partition, the essential arbitrariness of which is reflected in the unnatural, lasting division of a family. The context is the continuance of grudge-bearing and the commonness of ignorance and bigotry, but these negatives are tempered by the force of reason and simple compassion throughout the story and eclipsed by the ultimate triumph of repentance and forgiveness. *The Father* is also retrospective, recollecting the horrors of a once happy world turned upside down. It too ends in a spirit of celebration when the coolness of reason allows the recognition of simple human worthiness to shine through the clouds of orthodoxy and bigotry. *The Foreigner* sets out to be a story of a reunion of a group of boyhood friends, separated by the Partition, but develops into a somewhat bitter account of the rise of self-interest over altruism. There is an element of pathos in *Roots,* in which members of the younger generation are depicted as glorying in what they see as their historical self-sufficiency, uninterested and therefore cut off from the lives and the wealth of experience of their grandfathers. There is a poignant irony in the fact that the two old men, for all the awful upheavals in their lives, have had a richer experience of the world than what is likely to be experienced by their materially much more fortunate grandchildren.

The final story is set against the zeal with which the Mumbai police were imbued after the Babri Masjid conflagration in rounding up and expelling illegal immigrants. While the desire of any state to minimise illegal immigration is understandable, the kinds of 'evidence' that might entitle a person to this or that nationality might sometimes be questionable and inconclusive. But what does, in fact, make a person a national of a particular state? In most countries of the world, particularly the politically comfortable developed world, the answer is self-evident. It becomes a lot more complex in the light of the Partition of India that allows, for example, a Bangladeshi national to have been a Pakistani national and before that to have been an Indian national without ever having set foot out of his own village. Add to that the complications emanating out of dislocation, resettlement and migration and the question of identity can become perplexing. The issue is first raised in *Unlawful Entry;* it is developed in *Stateless* to the baffling extent where an innocent and helpless man, born in a country that no longer exists, becomes something of an ethnic yo-yo.

If we are to believe the champions of the politics of difference, then it would seem that Hindu and Muslim are like Kipling's East and West, inevitably destined never to find mutual accommodation. However, there are several stories here that suggest that even amid the frenzy of hostility, communal distinctions can easily – indeed, naturally – be transcended. In *The Boatman,* Fazal has no hesitation in shattering his own dream in order to protect a helpless young woman. That she is not of his community and that the man he kills is, should be of great significance to the reader, yet it is of no significance at all to him. His recognition of human need overrides communal distinction and even self-interest, but his gallantry comes at the price of his own cherished dream of the future. However, it is significant that Fazal is not presented as some kind of knight in shining armour – he is throughout the story nothing more than a humble Bengali boatman.

This first story is typical of all the stories dealing directly with communal conflict in that it focuses on basic human goodness rising above the excesses of communalism. Indeed, in these stories cross-communal sympathy is an ever present counter to the forces of destruction and, more often than not, expressed without any recourse to forethought by the characters who shine by it. *The Island in the River* has as its background the standard extravagances of violence stirred up by the irrational, frenetic espousal of a cause's slogans rather than any thoughtful commitment to the details of whatever substance that cause might have. Out of a horrible experience of rape a young Hindu woman is left for dead on an island in the Meghna where she is cared for unstintingly and without a word of complaint by a family of Muslims so poor they can barely survive. The ultimate power of innocence is symbolised in the newborn child and its use as a righteous weapon against the forces of greed. The gentle manifestation of simple humanity that forms the pinnacle of *For a Little While* is carefully shown by the writer to exist in its own right, making the passing tirade of communal invective quite irrelevant to its articulation. The exchange of houses fundamental to *Roots* might be seen by a cynic as a conveniently civilised means of effecting communal separatism, but it is clearly the intention of the writer that it be recognised as the basis of cooperation that animates the mutual acceptance of the two old men and of their young adult grandchildren.

The Partition of India had its roots to a large extent in notions of perceived threat, particularly as pertaining to a Muslim minority in a Hindu-dominant independent India. It might well be argued that the hardships created by the Partition were immensely greater than any that its proponents sought to avoid. The horrors are well documented in history books, in literature and in cinema, but what is prominent in the stories of Prafulla Roy is more the moral lessons that emerge from this calamitous experience. Clearly the politics of divisiveness have brought out time and time again the worst in people. Roy, however, is keen to note that its worst articulations have also been known to bring out the best in people. While communal divisiveness may well give rise to violence and atrocity, there are many who know or have come to realise both the absurdity of the hatred and hostility and the fact that violence can never have any positive effect. It is people such as these, prominent in Roy's stories, who initiate the bridge-building and lead the quest for harmony. However, there are stories such as *Stateless* and *The Destination* that also offer a sobering reminder of the persistence of the anti-people forces in society and imply a gentle warning to the reader who would seek to look at present reality, at least, through rose-coloured glasses. Indeed, much of the relevance of all these stories lies in their reflection of the persistence of a partition mentality in contemporary society where such notions as homeland, mother tongue and identity are so often given an exaggerated significance.

Prafulla Roy was born into the family of a small businessman in a village in Dhaka district, now in Bangladesh, in 1934. By the time he started writing at the age of nineteen he had lived through some of the most momentous events of Indian history and experienced at first hand many of the bleaker realities of the Indian condition. He was still a boy when the country was partitioned, a calamitous event for all Bengalis but more so for a Hindu family living in what was to become the Muslim state of East Pakistan. The Roy family stayed on in Dhaka for some time after the Partition, but in 1950 were faced with no alternative but to flee to Calcutta, forsaking all their belongings and property. They arrived in Calcutta destitute, and in 1951 moved to Bihar in a desperate quest for work and survival. The following year they returned to Calcutta and the young Prafulla Roy started to write what would become, by the end of the century, the first of a projected thirty-odd volumes of collected works.

The indelible experience of Partition and, to a lesser extent, of rural poverty in India, have become salient themes in Prafulla Roy's short stories and novels. Although he writes in Bengali, one of the major regional languages of India, his extensive travelling – mostly on foot – throughout the country and the Andaman Islands has imbued his work with an interest and a socio-cultural appreciation that are more national than regional.

Interpreting his country with a broad, all-India appeal has been a major factor in the popularity of his works among filmmakers and the makers of telefilms; such major filmmakers as Buddhadeb Dasgupta, Tapan Sinha and Biplab Ray Chaudhury have on a number of occasions looked to the stories of Prafulla Roy for material. Many films based on his works are in languages other than Bengali, and some of his writings have also been translated into other Indian languages. Moreover, Roy is widely recognised as a powerful and imaginative writer, a master story-teller who creates depth out of ordinariness, simplicity out of complexity, and whose direct, undecorated language lures the reader into confrontations with reality that are profound, moving, and sometimes quite disturbing.

Generally Roy's interest lies with unremarkable people, people caught helplessly on the treadmill of poverty or in communal hostility or in confrontation with the brazen assertion of power by the strong. In many of his stories his characters are marginalised, and often their interest lies in their unusualness. The seemingly inconsequential world of ordinary people, isolated and exquisitely drawn on a small canvas, is in Roy's short stories endowed with an extraordinary vibrancy. And while so many of his characters are helpless against overwhelming circumstances, there is a special strength that he is able to evince from the fellow-feeling and mutual support that many of them find in the experience of a common plight. Communalism, casteism, territoriality and simple selfishness are shown as fundamental to the denial of social harmony, yet ordinary individuals find some degree of strength in their mere mutual experience of them. Sentimentalism is avoided by the genuineness of the writer's compassion and by the essentially gentle and balanced disdain he shows for the powerful, the privileged and the unscrupulous. Prominent in these stories is an underlying faith in the power of simple humanity and its natural values to prevail in the midst of mistrust and hostility. This faith is given cogency from the writer's many years of having lived among the people who find their way into these pages and having shared much of their experience, along with an extraordinary balance between his sense of realism and his natural compassion. His economy of expression and the tightness of his construction, enhanced by the simple and logical structure of the various narrative and poetic elements in his stories, serve to respect that realism and to endow with no more than appropriate pity the wellsprings of compassion.

A translator would ideally like to translate every word of his text and have no words of the original language in his work, but this is not possible. A lot of words belonging to Bengali and/or Hindi – such as *chapati, sari, lathi, ghat* – have found their way into the Oxford English Dictionary and therefore are used here without any explanation. The names of many trees, flowers, birds and fish, given their essentially regional nature, are untranslatable into English, as are certain food items, especially sweets. Bengali has a much more extensive and formalised nomenclature for personal relationships than is the case in English, and where such terms are used it is hoped that their sense is made clear by the context. It is possible to translate the Bengali names of months, but it is a venture doomed to clumsiness because of the calendar difference that has the beginning of a Bengali month occurring halfway through a month in the Gregorian calendar. Hence, the Bengali names have been preferred, though in some stories with a metropolitan context English names for months are used by the characters. A list of Bengali months and seasons has been given.

# MONTHS AND SEASONS

The traditional calendar has the year starting in mid-April. All months start in the middle of a Gregorian calendar month and end in the middle of the next one.

| | |
|---|---|
| Baishakh | April – May |
| Jyaistha | May – June |

| | |
|---|---|
| Asharh | June – July |
| Shraban | July – August |
| Bhadra | August – September |
| Ashwin | September – October |
| Kartik | October – November |
| Agrahayan | November – December |
| Poush | December – January |
| Magh | January – February |
| Phalgun | February – March |
| Chaitra | March – April |

Bearing in mind the variations that prevail throughout such a vast country, a rough guide to the seasons would see summer in force from Baishakh to Bhadra; autumn from Bhadra to Agrahayan; winter from Agrahayan to Magh; and spring – often a very warm one – from Magh to Baishakh.

# THE BOATMAN

*majhi*

Passing through the thick green water-weeds the Raynabibi canal flows in a straight line like the parting of the hair of a royal princess and surrenders itself into the Dhaleshwari river. Near the canal were groves of coconut and betel-nut trees, and it was there that Fazal drew close in his single-oar ferry boat in the dim light of the soft Ashwin dawn. His eyes peered through the grove of *karamacha* trees a little distance away to the side the canal, then he caught a glimpse of the tin-roof, bamboo house in the midst of the betel-nut grove. Perhaps Salima had forgotten her promise of the previous evening.

Fazal waited for quite a while, then he took up the oar. If he did not reach the market at Sirajdigha soon, the other boatmen would have taken his share of all the passengers. He was just about to push off when he heard a soft sound like a billowing wave coming from the Raynabibi canal. Then, passing a tall coconut tree, Salima appeared, issuing a peal of giggles that seemed like music harmonising with the waves.

Fazal did not look, but sat with his back turned towards her. His face was darkened by a shadow of resentment at her being so late.

Salima came right up to the prow of the boat. This fine-bodied, vivacious Salima, her eyes flashing like diamonds in the first light of the morning, was like a soft vine, but her tongue could be very sharp.

"Isshhh! You're not angry again! Seeing you like this makes my body burn as hot as a chili."

Fazal said nothing.

"What's the matter?" Salima demanded. "Turn around."

Fazal did not turn around, nor did he say anything.

Salima then said sternly, "I don't like your sitting with your back turned to me like that. You're angry for nothing, aren't you? I've thrown dust in the eyes of my father to come to you. Day and night he keeps watch over me. If only you knew the trouble I've had. After he'd got up, he went into the yard to smoke for a while, and only when he'd gone off to the paddy-fields was I able to come to you."

Fazal turned around then. Having heard a reasonable explanation for Salima's lateness the cloud of annoyance dissipated and his face lost its sour look. He said, "You won't have to play hide-and-seek with your father for much longer. I'll have everything fixed up in three or four days. I've saved six score and ten rupees. Another ten rupees and that'll make seven score. I should get ten rupees from the boat today. The Hindus are fleeing their homes and the country, so there'll be quite a few fares. Then I can put seven score rupees in the hands of your father and take you to my house. So. Now I have to be going."

"No, no. You can't go yet," said Salima. "I've gone to so much trouble to come here. If you've got a couple of minutes, there's something I have to say." A shadow fell over her face.

"Your father is such a miserable bugger. He'll take the seven score rupees and then count them one by one before he'll let his daughter go. I'm off now. Come again in the evening."

"All right, then. I'll come in the evening. I won't be late again."

"No. Don't be late."

Something suddenly occurred to her, and she said, "Just one thing –"

"What?" Fazal's eyes looked questioning.

"Last night Kasim Ali from Nabipur came to my father with money. The son of Satan wants to marry me. I chased him away in tears. And before that Aibuddi came from Basail, and before that there was Habib Mian from Giriganj. I chased them all away. But I can't keep on doing it for much longer. You know my father. If he gets some money in his hands, he's likely to lump me with anyone any day. Apart from that –"

"What?"

"I don't like being alone any more. My heart is becoming very restless."

Fazal was highly amused. He said, "Is it, now? You want to become a bird and fly away?"

Salima was embarrassed. "I don't know what," she said.

Fazal said nothing immediately. He thought for a bit, then changed the subject. "Don't worry," he said. "Kasim Ali, Sikim Ali – no one is going to be able to pinch you from me. Tomorrow I'll settle with your father. Now I have to go." He waited no longer, but pushed off with the oar and took the boat into the middle of the Raynabibi canal. Then, as he drifted along, he took up a boatman's song:

> A sprightly girl of sixteen years
> has now turned seventeen,
> and keeps the morning star
> captive in her sights.

The girl who kept the morning star of his dreams was enchanted to hear his song in praise of her youth on that beautiful morning. Fazal's sad tune drifted away as his boat kept to the blue line of the canal and then became a dot in the distance.

The evening had now become quite dark and the lamps were

burning in the boats at the Sirajdigha ferry ghat. Flickering in the darkness under the awnings at the market were the countless orange flames of the kerosene lamps of the various local stall holders. From a distant trader's boat came the peaceful, solemn sound of a boatman offering his prayers.

Fazal had spent the whole day ferrying passengers for a total of seven rupees. Having delivered his last passenger he was now bringing his boat into the ghat on the river. He pushed the pole firmly into the mud in the shallows very close to the bank and tied it up securely with the heavy rope. Then he lit a kerosene lamp, took out the cash from its secret pouch tucked into the waist of his lungi, and counted it rupee by rupee. In total there were six score and seventeen rupees. He was still three rupees short of his required amount of seven score, a total which he had hoped to achieve today. So now he would have to wait one more day.

The Hindus had been leaving their old ancestral homes as fugitives and heading for Calcutta, so under the circumstances it should not have been at all difficult for a hire boat to fetch five to ten rupees in a day. Fazal was confident that he would make that by tomorrow, though this morning he had assured Salima that tomorrow he would satisfy her father with the seven score rupees. Now that would not be possible, but it definitely would be the day after. Having waved one hundred and forty rupees in cash before the face of Salima's father, who looked like an old polecat, he could then finalise all the arrangements for bringing Salima to his house.

Sometime back Salima's father, whining like a vulture, had said,

"You want to marry Salima! Put seven score rupees in my right hand and I will give the girl away with my left. And just remember this. You'll have to bear the full cost of the wedding."

Indifferently Fazal had said, "I already have four score rupees. I'll give you that now and the rest after the wedding. In the name of Allah."

Salima's father was very mindful of the outstanding amount, which was like stars in the sky – you never actually hold them in the palm of your hand. And so, just as indifferently, he said, "I'm not in the business of giving credit, Mian. I'll settle only for cash in full."

"All right. In that case give me a month's time to come up with the money."

"If someone else comes with the money in the meantime, I'll fix the girl's marriage with him."

Fazal slowly got up, turned from Salima's father's ugly face and went back to his boat in the canal. Fazal resolved that no matter what it took and however soon it had to be, he would come up with the money.

From that day he had saved his rupees one by one. In order to realise the dream of his youth, he had sweated and toiled, plying his boat without rest as he ferried passengers to various places – Delbhog, Sabhar, Basail, Sonarang – in the riverine region of Bengal. His days passed like a storm in which there was no concern for time or exhaustion. Singularly intent on setting up a home with Salima, Fazal pursued his toil, rigorous in his preparations to realise his dream of bringing Salima into his house. Now, having counted his money he put it back in the pouch which he fastened inside the waist of his lungi. He kept his money as close to his body as his skin lest even one rupee should go missing. He would not spare anyone who tried to snatch even a paisa and would chase him to hell as he would a wicked spirit.

Only three more rupees, and he could marry Salima. Picturing that lovely dream day, Fazal sang in a soft and drowsy voice:

> I have drunk the wine of your dark eyes
> and have become excited,
> and I have drunk the wine
> of my bride's first-flowering youth.
> How can I dispel
> the melancholy of my love?
> I will kiss her eyelids
> and offer to her lips sweet betel leaf.

Absorbed in his song, Fazal suddenly remembered the promise he had made at dawn to meet Salima again in the rustling coconut grove at evening. So he got up to be on his way, but just as he did there came the voice of a passenger.

"Hey, boatman, are you for hire? Who is it there? Fazal Majhi, is it you?"

The voice was familiar. Fazal turned around and saw Yachhin Shikdar standing close to the water's edge, and right behind him was the burka-covered figure of a woman, very probably the Mian-saheb's wife.

Next to the ferry ghat was a permanent jetty that had been built for launches. Right now a launch from Narayanganj was approaching, and the whole area was pervaded by the strong glow of its searchlight. Fazal asked, “Where do you want to go, Mian-saheb?”

“Ishmail Island,” answered Yachhin.

“I can’t go that far now. It’s got very late. Come tomorrow morning.”

Yachhin was impatient. He took hold of the prow of the boat and said, “No one wants to go this late. But this is urgent. You take me, and I’ll make it worth your while.”

Fazal tried to be interested. “How much will you pay?”

“Five rupees.”

“Five rupees – phuu! Why don’t you and your wife spend the night under the awnings in the market, and in the morning you can both swim to the island!”

He had already wasted a lot of time. By now the night would certainly have darkened around the face of Salima, who would be counting the time as she waited among the rows of rustling coconut trees.

Yachhin then grasped the prow of the boat even harder. “I’ll pay seven rupees, then. But you must get me to Ishmail Island tonight.”

Fazal replied, “What’s seven rupees! Why don’t you save your money and lie down, and forget about Ishmail Island for tonight. Now let go. Come on, let go!”

“How much do you want, then?”

“You’ll have to pay me ten rupees, Mian-saheb. That’s quite reasonable.”

"Ten rupees!" and he let out a cry of horror. "Now we've become Pakistan, you've all become high and mighty."

Quite disinterestedly Fazal said, "If you agree to the fare, get into the boat. Otherwise, let go of the prow. I've got things to do."

"This is extortion," Yachhin muttered. "All right, you'll get your money. I'll pay you ten rupees."

Fazal seemed not to have heard the first part, but there was no mistake about the rest. He said, "Now you're talking sense. You and your wife sit up on the decking there."

No sooner had Fazal said this than Yachhin Shikdar grabbed hold of the hand of the burka-covered female figure behind him, and immediately she gave a suppressed yet intense cry, saying, "No, no. I won't go. Let me go, I beg of you."

Yachhin's voice came as a subdued roar. "You'd be stupid enough to reject a comfortable life for a troubled one? I'll treat you like the grand-daughter of a prince. I saved you from that crook Kiramat who would have dragged you off with him. Wouldn't it be better to be my principal begum than live in hell with him?"

Her suppressed cry now became quite heart-rending. Yachhin was taken aback by it and he pressed his rough and heavy hands over her mouth. "Shut up. Shut up or, so help me, I'll kill you." From the tone of his voice there was not the slightest doubt that he might indeed do something violent.

The searchlight of the ferry-launch had turned the other way and now the glimmering surface of the Dhaleshwari looked like black glass. In the darkness Yachhin's eyes flashed like those of a snake.

Fazal now focussed on what he could see and hear. Abruptly he said, "You know, Mian-saheb, your wife doesn't seem to want to go to Ishmail Island, does she?" He sounded suspicious.

Yachhin leaped towards the boat and said in a low, hushed voice, "She's just a child. She's crying at leaving her father for her husband's house. It's nothing, boatman, it's nothing."

"Oh. I thought there was something else."

Ignoring Fazal's words, Yachhin virtually lifted the female figure onto the decking of the boat and straightaway there came from under the cover of the burka a cry to pierce the firmament.

His voice shaky and apprehensive, Fazal said, "Mian-saheb, I think you should go tomorrow morning."

"Now I'm depending on you. All right, then. I'll pay you fifteen rupees. But don't delay any longer. Get a move on. I have to get to Ishmail Island tonight."

Fifteen rupees! Didn't the man say that? With the sail set to catch the north wind they would reach Ishmail Island long before dawn. Steering with a firm grip on the oar Fazal would have nothing more to do than to try to see Salima's face in the gaps between the stars in the sky, and in return he would get fifteen rupees! He could settle Salima's dowry of seven score rupees and lie down happily with another twelve tucked away in the waist of his lungi. The very thought of it filled his heart with joy.

By now Salima would be waiting expectantly in the coconut grove, but he could do nothing about that. Tomorrow morning, before the eastern sky was tinged with pink, Fazal would amaze Salima's skinflint of a father by thrusting the dowry money under his nose, and within the month he would marry Salima and take her to his house. He was a simple man, Fazal Majhi, and for a few minutes his mind was overflowing with the joy and wonder of Salima.

A little later Fazal checked with Yachhin. "How much will you pay?"

"Fifteen," Yachhin answered.

Fazal was quite sure that he could have squeezed out a bit more even, but that would not have been right. He had at least some scruples.

So Fazal did not delay. Leaning on the oar he pushed the boat to the middle of the river and the fast, ever-flowing current of the Dhaleshwari. The darkness pervaded everywhere and the dim light from the hazy moon gave the Dhaleshwari a ghostly look. The waves slapped against the hull of the boat.

Fazal held the oar firmly as he steered, looking up at the sky streaked with cloud, between which the countless stars flickered like fireflies. As he watched, he started thinking of Salima again and his thoughts made him feel strangely intoxicated. Truly his life would be worthless without her. At present his bed in that two-room house seemed as cold as the touch of a dead snake. He felt very lonely, and in his joyless solitude he would lie awake the whole night just thinking of Salima. However, after delivering his passengers to Ishmail Island tonight, he would set sail straight for Salima's father's house. Excitement seemed to run through his veins as his blood surged and his heart quickened.

The boat was now moving quickly with the stream. Fazal kept a firm hold on the oar as he started to sing:

> Youth washes over the body of my love like the tide.
> A lotus opens up and dances in my tears of joy.
> O, my love, let your face be the moon
> and I will be its veil.
> You are the light of my eyes,
> and I am but collyrium.

He stopped suddenly as an intense shudder ran through him. He sat there anxiously, intently listening to everything. It seemed that a frenzy was starting to flare up inside the canopy. Fazal discerned hints of a struggle and a nasty feeling of unease swept through him.

Like a snake hissing Yachhin Shikdar spat out the words, "Shut up! Shut up, or I'll strangle you!"

"All right. Go ahead, then. Either kill me or let me go. Or I'll jump into the river – "And then the female voice was suddenly stifled.

Then Yachhin laughed hideously like a burial ground jackal. "Would it be so easy to die? I'll kill you bit by bit if you like."

This exchange between Yachhin and the woman hit Fazal with all the furore of a storm.

As the boat skimmed over the fathomless stream of the Dhaleshwari, the wind suddenly started to gust wildly through the reeds and the coconut groves on the bank. The struggle in the canopy abated for a while. Having been preoccupied with what was going on between Yachhin and the woman, Fazal gradually let his mind wander, and as he cast his glance towards the countless stars spread out across the sky, again he tried to think of Salima.

Fazal felt immense satisfaction thinking about how, before the rooster's crow in the morning, Salima's father would have a look on his face like that of a dumb bull when Fazal would wake him and thrust the seven score rupees dowry money under his nose. Of course, Fazal was not absorbed by thoughts of Salima's father for very long, as little by little his dream of Salima became more and more lifelike. Her dark eyes, her lithe and shapely dusky body and her coloured striped sari all helped to represent her wonder to him.

But the dream was broken.

From inside the canopy came the tearful, helpless female voice. "Take me to Calcutta. Be like a godfather, I beg at your feet."

Yachhin tried to stifle his hideous laughter. "Not your godfather, you bitch, but I wouldn't mind being the father of your son. Now shut up. In winning you I had to suffer a few spear wounds from your husband."

The weird combination of Yachhin's laughter, the dark and rolling Dhaleshwari, the indistinct darkness, the sounds of wave and sail, and the whistling of the wind gave rise to a terrible sense of foreboding that gradually increased in its intensity, as though millions of demons had risen up from the depths of the river and, spreading themselves across the horizon, were breaking into horrible laughter.

Fazal felt very frightened.

There was another burst of Yachhin's demonic laughter, and he said, "Stop whimpering so much, you trollop, or I'll really put an end to you."

The woman's voice now sounded desperate. "Do it! Then I'll be free. You killed my husband."

"So I killed your husband! And how much longer would you have had any taste for that old man? Now you can set up a home with a new husband. Regenerate yourself!" And Yachhin immediately burst into raucous laughter.

There then came from under the burka such an inhuman scream, a cry to rend the heavens, that Fazal could not imagine it coming from the burka-clad woman. Immediately following the cry he heard the woman's voice, "Don't touch me! Don't touch me! Isn't it against your morality to lay hands on me like that? Please send me to Calcutta. Don't touch me – ah! –"

"Huh! Thinks she's the goddess Sati! 'Don't touch me!'" And so Yachhin went on.

Then a new struggle began inside the canopy and the boat started to rock on the waves so much that at any moment they might all go under. Just as Fazal was about to say something, the woman screamed piercingly again and cried, "Save me, boatman, save me! I'm in terrible danger!"

Her plea penetrated Fazal's whole being.

There was only the infinite sky overhead, the whistling wind around them, and the rolling river underneath. Apart from the two passengers, there was no one anywhere. The dream of Salima had long been wiped from his mind as now Fazal's blood started to boil and his eyes flashed like those of a tiger. He felt suddenly electrified as he cried out threateningly, "Mian-saheb!"

And even before his cry was heard he was already reaching under the right side of the cross-beam for his sharp fishing spear, all the while keeping a strong hold on the oar with his left hand. Up until now the shadowy sky and the flickering stars had evoked in him a tender longing for dreams of Salima, but now who could say what terror accompanied that longing?

At Fazal's cry Yachhin Shikdar opened the flap of the canopy and came and sat on the decking, while at the same time the woman seemed to lurch out and the boat listed on the rolling waters. Again the woman gave a terrible cry as she shouted, "Save me, boatman, save me! I am the wife of a weaver's family. They killed my husband in the riots. And now this –"

There seemed to be something unearthly in the woman's voice, a sound that set Fazal's nerves on edge. His reaction was instinctive. Unwittingly, even to himself, Fazal hurled the spear. It did not miss its mark; indeed, before Yachhin knew anything about it, it was stuck in the man's ribs and he let out a deathly scream.

The boat was now considerably lighter as Yachhin's body swirled about in the deep waters of the Dhaleshwari. Fazal washed the spear and set the boat back on course. The woman seemed paralysed with fear. Her fingertips tingled as though the blood would burst from them and her eyes gaped.

Calmly, as though nothing had happened, Fazal asked, "Where do you want to go?"

She mumbled indistinctly, "I have no one here. They all fled in the riots. My husband was killed. I have a brother-in-law in Calcutta. I'd like to go there."

Fazal asked nothing more. He simply turned the boat and pointed the prow in the direction of the Tarpasha steamer ghat. Soon they were running with the current again, listening to the lapping of the waves and the whistling of the wind.

Just as the eastern sky was becoming tinged with the faint light of dawn, Fazal fixed the bamboo pole into the Tarpasha steamer ghat and secured the boat with the rope. The young woman was still sitting motionless on the decking of the boat as the first rays of dawn shone over her face. As Fazal caught a glance of her like that, he thought for a moment that she resembled Salima.

Countless people had gathered at the steamer ghat. Now fugitives, they were all leaving their homes in this country.

Fazal took the young woman up to the ticket office. "Give me your money," he said, "and I'll get your ticket for you."

The woman hung her head and told him that she had no money at all.

For a moment Fazal just stood there, saying nothing. Then he thought of the secret pouch tucked away at his waist containing the price for that wondrous dream of his youth. He hesitated for a moment as he wavered inside. Then he resolutely turned his back on his own dream as he pushed into the vast sea of people and purchased a ticket to Calcutta.

In the meantime the steamer's whistle was sounding. Fazal placed the remaining money he had after the purchase of the ticket in the young woman's hand and said, "Keep these few rupees. All these people are now boarding to go to Calcutta. Will you join them, then?"

"I will, but this money –" The woman hung her head in extreme humility. A few seconds later, when she raised her eyes, she could see no one. By some strange stroke of magic the boatman was nowhere to be seen.

What was Fazal thinking about as he returned to his boat at the ferry ghat? Salima? No. The young widow of the weavers' family, who had lost everything? No. Was it the thought that if he could not produce the one hundred and forty rupees dowry money in three or four days, Salima's father would arrange to have her married to someone else? Not that, either.

He was thinking of the blood-smeared spear of the night before, the image of which danced ceaselessly before him. And before setting up his home with Salima under some shady tree on the bank of the Dhaleshwari, how many times in the cruel dead of night would so many other Yachhins come to his boat? How many times?

Fazal remembered that the spear had not been sharpened for many days. He would sharpen it today until it gleamed like silver.

# ONE KING GOES AND ANOTHER KING COMES

## *raja jai raja ashe*

One morning Rajek was sitting on the east wing veranda, tapping his foot. He was wearing a green and yellow striped lungi and a net-weave singlet. Now, at seven in the morning, he was doing his hair, spreading it out like a peacock's tail and then parting it, with a very large-tooth comb. His heart was bathed by waves of happiness; indeed, not only today but for quite some months the rivers of joy had been welling up inside him.

Like the east wing the north and west wings were very spacious. There was a corrugated tin roof, wall posts of *shal* timber, and a polished cement floor. There was a spacious courtyard beneath where Rajek was sitting; on one side of it were rows of paddy-stacks, on the other a *shiuli* tree. Beyond the courtyard was some low-lying land covered with thickets of *pithkshira* and *sonal* trees. Then there was the pond and beyond that were the paddy fields. During the monsoon the pond flooded out over the paddy fields and there was no discernible distinction between them, and this was the case at present.

It all resembled the domain of a king, with so many big rooms, the large courtyard, the pond and the ninety *kanis* of land with its two crops. And now it was all Rajek's. Yet eight months ago . . . Oh, that was a very different story.

It was early in the month of Ashwin. The sky, washed by all the rains of the month of Bhadra, was still in its wonderful shade of blue with clusters of clouds floating aimlessly across it. The *shiuli* tree in the courtyard had begun to flower before the advent of autumn and was still blooming. As the sun rose, its light permeated everywhere like molten gold. From somewhere or other two *mohanchura* birds flew onto the roof of the north wing and rubbed their beaks against one another in love play. All around, everywhere one looked, autumn was manifest in all its splendour.

Rajek was lost in thought as he looked out towards the paddy field, tapping his foot. For some months now he had sat like this every morning on the veranda of the east wing, aimlessly staring. It was a kind of luxury, a precious indulgence.

Far in the distance a boat was coming, rending the surface of the waters over the paddy field. It could only just be seen – the round canopy, the gleaming dark boatman and the rise and fall of the punt pole. Every morning, so many boats going this way and that would break the glassy surface of the water over the paddy field. Rajek was not at all concerned about where this particular boat might have been heading, for in the gentle, pervasive sunshine of Ashwin he saw nothing, not even the pair of *mohanchura* birds dancing or the clouds drifting in the sky. Rajek was absorbed in his own thoughts, with the long story of his own thirty years.

Oh, what a life it had been! Just eight months ago it would have been quite inconceivable that today he would be sitting in a net-weave singlet, parting his hair and tapping his foot, bathed by the river of joy. Yet had the country not been partitioned and had Baikuntha Saha and his family not left this village of Chhiptipur, fortune would never have been so kind to him.

However, the story had not ended, for there was also the extraordinary matter of the boat that had now crossed the pond over the paddy field and was coming to moor at the ghat. Rajek frowned and sat upright. He could not imagine who might be visiting him at this hour of the morning, but he did not have to wait long to find out. Soon someone got out of the boat – none other than Torab Ali, the richest man in Chhiptipur.

Torab Ali had two hundred *kanis* of land growing three crops, countless ploughs, fifty or sixty head of cattle, and some forty or so boats. He had twenty five or thirty day labourers toiling the whole year through, and rice, jute and lentils all grew in abundance on his land. About eight months ago Rajek, too, had been one of the day labourers at the house of this esteemed and worthy head of Chhiptipur village.

Torab Ali was not only a prosperous householder, but he was also a man much given to luxury. Even in this early morning he was quite immaculately attired in a silk lungi, a finely embroidered panjabi and suede leather slippers, and he had had his hair and beard blackened. As he came closer, Rajek could see the fine line of collyrium under his eyes and smell the intoxicating aroma of attar.

Had Torab Ali come to visit him? At first Rajek was not sure, although there could probably be nothing more amazing in all the world than a man like Torab Ali coming to visit him. Rajek sat there stunned for some moments, then suddenly he leaped to his feet and breathlessly ran down to the ghat. Wringing his hands, he said very reverentially, "Oh, Mian, it is you!"

Teasing out his beard with both his hands, Torab Ali offered a slight smile and said, "Ah, I have come to visit you."

Oh, Allah! Rajek could hardly believe his ears! Like an echo he said, "Come to visit me?"

"Yes, to visit you."

Rajek could think of nothing to say.

Softly Torab Ali asked, "Are we going to stand at the ghat, or will you escort me to your house?" His tone was quite intimate. Rajek had known Torab Ali since his childhood days and had never heard him speak like this.

Rajek felt quite abashed. Eagerly he said, "Come, please come."

While he was taking Torab Ali up to the house, Rajek was bothered about where to seat him and how to entertain him. He immediately ran and spread out a woven grass mat on the veranda; not happy with that, he rolled it up and went and fetched a small wooden stool.

Torab Ali did not sit down, though he was touched and pleased to see Rajek bustling about attending to his comfort. He said, "No need to fuss, Rajek. I'll sit down later. First let me see your house."

Rajek looked at Torab Ali with a flash of suspicion in his eyes. Had the man come so early in the morning, in fact, to see his house? Who could say what really was in Torab Ali's mind?

Torab Ali ventured to read the look of suspicion on Rajek's face. Gently teasing, he said, "Don't worry, I won't seize your house. You can keep all your things."

Seeing Torab Ali's beaming face Rajek could hardly say no, though with mounting doubts and suspicions he nevertheless showed him around.

Having had a good look at everything, Torab Ali sat down squarely on the stool. "Do you have any tobacco?" he asked.

Rajek had indeed thought it proper to offer tobacco but, with his mind clouded in misgiving, he had forgotten. He ran straightaway and prepared some.

Casually drawing on the hookah Torab Ali said, "So Baikuntha

Saha has put you in charge of the house?"

The man's intentions were not fully clear to Rajek who, almost holding his breath, answered, "Yes."

Pointing in front of him Torab Ali said, "That pond also is Baikuntha Saha's, then?"

"Yes."

"And the land on the other side of it?"

"That too is his."

"How much land is there?"

"Ninety *kanis.* "

"Then you are in charge of it all?"

In an indistinct voice, Rajek said, "Yes."

There was silence for a little while. Torab Ali drew lazily on the gurgling hookah a dozen or so times and puffed out the smoke. Then he said, "Baikuntha Saha and his family left the village eight months back, didn't they?" It was obvious that the man knew a lot.

In the same indistinct voice Rajek said, "Yes."

"Where did they go, do you know?"

"I heard that they'd be going towards Calcutta."

"Have you had any news?"

"No."

"No letter?"

"No."

Torab Ali said nothing for a while, frowning and seemingly given to thought. Then he asked, "What do you think?"

Rajek did not understand the question. "About what?" he asked.

"Do you think Baikuntha Saha and his family will come back?"

"How would I know?"

Torab Ali seemed not to hear what Rajek said. Very much to himself he muttered, "I don't think they'll come back."

Rajek said nothing.

Torab Ali went on, "If Baikuntha Saha and his family don't return, then his land, house, pond – everything – will become yours. Not *will* become, *has* become!"

Again Rajek said nothing.

Torab Ali went on for awhile fishing for information about Baikuntha Saha and his great wealth. Then suddenly he said, "Now let me tell you why I have come."

Rajek held his breath. Barely audibly he said, "Why?"

"I want you to come and have lunch with me tomorrow."

A burst of thunder would not have startled Rajek as much. Torab Ali, the most wealthy, the most respectable, the most honoured householder in Chhiptipur, in whose house Rajek had worked as a day labourer not that long ago, had come in person to offer him an invitation to lunch. Rajek tried to say something, but not a sound came from his mouth.

Torab Ali pushed himself up with his hand and said, "That's settled, then. Come at midday tomorrow."

Unconsciously, as though in a dream, Rajek nodded his head.

"Don't forget, now," Torab Ali said. "We'll be eagerly expecting you." And so saying he was on his way across the spacious courtyard, through the wood of *sonal* and *pithkshira* trees and down to the ghat at the pond. A little later his boat crossed over the distant paddy field and out of sight.

Rajek went on sitting there for quite some time after Torab Ali had left, and then it occurred to him that he should have seen the man to the ghat. But never before had he been so surprised and bewildered, nor had he ever been so frightened.

Torab Ali had come to see him and had extended an invitation to come and eat with him at noon the next day. It all seemed so fantastic. That he should not only visit a man like Torab Ali but be entertained by him was something utterly inconceivable. How his life had been changed by Baikuntha Saha's leaving the country!

As he sat benumbed on the veranda of the east wing on that Ashwin morning, Rajek let his mind drift into memory.

What a life his had been! After losing his parents when he was little he used to go like a puppy from door to door in Chhiptipur for two mouthfuls of rice. He would go to the houses of the Mridhas, then to the Sardars, then to the Khans, but most often he would go to the Hindu quarter. Sometimes he would get something, other times nothing. In those days all he knew was the constancy of hunger.

When he had grown a little older, Rajek started to realise that he would not always survive on the compassion of others, nor would it be respectable to try. So he found some line and some fish hooks, and with various kinds of bamboo he made a fish basket and wove a net. That marked the beginning of the second stage of his ongoing battle with life.

In this country there is water all the year round. If the canal should run dry, there was always the marsh, and if it dried up, the river would be full. Rajek would go off with his hooks, his net and his basket to the canal or the marsh or the big river two miles away. Whatever fish he caught in his ceaseless endeavour from morning until evening, he would take to the Inamganj market. Once evening had fallen and he had sold his fish, he would go to the poor Muslims' quarter of Chhiptipur and cook some food on someone's oven. After eating, he would bed down on their veranda.

Rajek toiled in the waters the whole year through, though from time to time he worked as a day labourer in the houses of others, harvesting paddy or planting jute. For the greater part of that time he would work for Torab Ali. In the months of Poush and Magh when the paddy was harvested he would go through the fields gleaning whatever grains the farmers had missed and poke into mouse holes to retrieve the grains taken by field-mice. This kind of harvest might last him for half a month.

His relentless struggle of a life went on in the wetlands for virtually the whole year, for indeed he did not get to spend many days on dry land. Being in water for almost twelve months of the year his skin had become cracked and flaky, his hair and beard were matted and tangled and his eyes grew dull. He had ruined his nails by clawing through mud, and suppurating ulcers had formed where his fingertips had rotted. At that time there was but one colour before Rajek's eyes day and night – the colour of hardship, endless hardship.

Oh, what a life Rajek's had been! As the seasons turned for thirty years, how had time passed? Rajek could hardly say.

One morning when he was up to his waist in the stream wielding his net, he noticed a large crowd of people gathering on the ground in front of the school. A band dressed in coloured clothes played music, then speeches were made in full voice. Finally, a new silk flag was raised.

With dull eyes Rajek looked towards the school ground. Later on, in the evening, when fireworks were being let off, he could not stay away. Venturing among the crowd he asked, "What's all this show for? Why the fireworks?"

From somewhere in the throng came a contemptuous voice. "Where've you been, you idiot? Let's have a look at you." A man looked him up and down thoroughly, then said, "Oh, well, who other than our Rajek could ask such a thing? In the water all the time his senses have washed away. Haven't you heard anything about –"

"Cut out the claptrap and just tell me what's going on."

The man explained that this was indeed a special day for the country had become independent – not only independent, but on this day Pakistan, which many had dreamt of, which many had fought to the death for, had been proclaimed. It was not just another day in the year, but it was different from any other ordinary old day in ages and ages. Nor was it an occasion for mere formal shaking of hands but one for a passionate embrace of welcome into this brave new nation. This was why there were so many people, this was why there were fireworks, this was the reason for so much exuberance.

Rajek stood among the crowd in the school ground until late into the night. It was all so bright, so lively, so exciting, so colourful – he kept thinking how much he loved it all. But the enjoyment would last but one night, and the next day he must take up his basket and wade again through the canal.

About a year had passed since that momentous occasion. Then suddenly one day in the month of Kartik, while Rajek was setting out his wicker fishing trap in the putrid waters, he heard that Chhiptipur village was breaking up. The Gosain family had sold up all their property and gone to Calcutta. The Bhuimalis had gone after the Gosains, then one by one the Baruis, the Kumors and the Yugis had left Chhiptipur virtually empty.

All his time in the water had made Rajek quite dull to experience. After all, who stayed in the village and who left was no real concern of his. His one and only worry day and night was how to reap from the water his living silver harvest.

The grand celebration of Independence, the Partition, the break-up of the village, all had little impact on Rajek, who scarcely had the time to think about such things. Indeed, he had so much to do merely to survive that he had no interest in anything else. However, he could not keep his back turned on the world for very long.

One cold noon in the month of Magh Rajek was wandering through the fields gleaning grains of paddy when all of a sudden the elderly Baikuntha Saha appeared in front of him.

Rajek asked, "Have you something to tell me, Mian?"

Baikuntha Saha nodded his head.

"What is it?"

"We're leaving the village."

"Where're you going?"

"Calcutta."

"When'll you come back?"

"I'm not sure that we will."

Rajek said nothing more.

Baikuntha Saha went on, "I need to talk to you about something."

"What?"

"When we go to Calcutta, I want you to look after our house, our land and our pond. In return all the rice and jute harvest will be yours. If we ever return, then you give it all back. If we don't return, then the whole lot will be yours."

Baikuntha Saha and his family did, indeed, leave, and their immense wealth and property fell into the hands of Rajek who, for eight months now had not had to go out into the waters and wetlands in order to eke out a living. Now he had become quite comfortable in his new circumstances. Now used to ease and contentment, he had done with broken nails and rotting feet. Now his flaky skin had taken on a gleaming smoothness, and his hair was soft and wavy. And now he had developed a taste for luxury; these days he would not be seen without his silk lungi, his net-weave singlet, or his *kalidar* panjabi, nor could he do without his scented oil.

Rajek had been thinking a lot recently about how fortuitous the Partition and the departure of the Sahas had been. How his luck could have gone otherwise! His face reflected all this happiness, and the days passed well. But why, of all the people in Chhiptipur village, should Torab Ali have suddenly chosen to visit him? And not only to visit, but to invite him to eat with him! Who could tell just what that man might have in mind?

Torab Ali had issued an invitation and there was no way of refusing it. The next day Rajek sat thinking from morning until noon, pacing back and forth trying to see into Torab Ali's intentions. Then, somewhat mechanically, he took a bath, put on a brightly coloured lungi, panjabi and suede slippers, and got into the boat.

Torab Ali's house stood like an island at the top end of Chhiptipur village, an imposing brick-built edifice. The house, which accommodated many people, was made up of countless rooms and covered a very large area.

By the time Rajek reached the paddy field the Ashwin day was well advanced and bathed in golden sunshine. No sooner had the boat approached the ghat than Torab Ali came running. In a voice of warm welcome he called, "Oh Mian, you have come! I was worried that you had forgotten."

Rajek was dumb to give reply. In former times Torab Ali had used contemptuously the inferior form of 'you' and had addressed him with the familiarised form of his name, 'Rajeika'. Only yesterday he had used the inferior pronoun. So what had happened overnight that now he used the respectful form of 'you' and called him 'Mian' instead of Rajeika? Such changes were too much for Rajek.

"Come, come," said Torab Ali.

Saying nothing, Rajek got out of the boat. As Torab Ali started to lead him towards the house, he asked, "Why are you so late?"

Choking on his voice, Rajek mumbled something incoherently.

Torab Ali went on, "I waited for a while, then I thought, if you didn't come, I would have to send someone to your house."

Struggling to articulate the words, Rajek said, "You came to me yesterday. How could I not obey you? I have only one head to lose."

Torab Ali smiled and said nothing.

Once they were inside the house, Rajek was seated with great ceremony on a dazzling white carpet amid men and women of various ages, and a crowd of children stood in front of the door. Sherbet, paan and tobacco were brought in.

Rajek started to sweat. He could not forget how only eight months ago he used to work here as a labourer, harvesting the paddy from the fields and retting the jute. But Torab Ali and his household had forgotten – at least, it seemed so from their cordial reception and hospitality. It was as though he were an honoured guest in this house.

Torab Ali said, "The food will be a little while yet. There are still one or two dishes to attend to. Have some sherbet, Mian."

All the other members of the household agreed. "Yes, have some," they all said. So with trembling hands Rajek raised his glass of sherbet.

After the sherbet, tobacco was prepared. Torab Ali took three or four draws of the hookah and offered it to Rajek, who diffidently raised his hands and shook his head. "Oh no, no. No, no."

Torab Ali almost forced the hookah into Rajek's hand. "Oh, take it, Mian, take it. Why be so bashful?"

With his head bowed, Rajek muttered indistinctly, "Not in front of one so senior and respected! No, no."

"What do you mean, 'in front of one'? Take it, take it."

After much protestation Rajek turned coyly from Torab Ali and took a few quick draws of the hookah, then turned back again.

After taking sherbet and tobacco, they began to chat – about the Partition, about the break-up of the village, jute and paddy, the recent rains – all the usual things. But the greater part of the conversation was about Baikuntha Saha and his wealth and property.

And so most of the day passed in talk. By the time the sun had sunk low in the western sky, word came that lunch was ready.

Torab Ali got up eagerly. "Oh, the time has got away from us! I have caused you great discomfort, Mian."

"No," replied Rajek. "There has been no discomfort."

"Come, then. Come and eat."

The dining room was in the inner part of the house. Torab Ali had gone to a great deal of trouble, having arranged for five or six kinds of fish, meat, rice custard, *patkshir*, big bananas, and very thick and creamy yellow milk.

Rajek was not alone, as Torab Ali and several of the older men of the house sat down to eat with him. The subject of Baikuntha Saha came up again during the meal and there was some discussion of whether or not he and his family would come back. Rajek, of course, had nothing much to say at all. He was so overwhelmed that little more than a mumbled "Hm," or "Huh," came from his mouth in answer to Torab Ali's questions.

Rajek went on eating, his head down. Just as he raised his head to reply to one of Torab Ali's elderly uncles, Kamran, the daughter of Torab Ali, was seen standing at the window on the other side of the room. She had golden skin like undried turmeric, strong facial features with soft, tender lips, and ringlets hanging over her small forehead. She was like a princess out of a fairy story.

It was very likely that the girl had taken a quick glimpse of Rajek and, when seen by him, gave a sweet and bashful smile and hurried away. Of course, it was not the first time Rajek had seen Kamran, for he used to see her often when he was coming to work as a day labourer. How haughty that girl was, with her conceit and her upper-class arrogance, as though the earth had been made just for her! At least, that is what they all said about her, as she treated ordinary people like flies. But the Kamran who could now smile like that was someone quite different.

After they had eaten they went to the outer room, but it seemed that no sooner had they sat down on the carpet than evening fell. "I must go now," said Rajek.

Torab Ali made no demur. "All right, then," he said. "But do come again." And he took Rajek down to the ghat and saw him into the boat.

It was now very dark, and millions of glow-worms were glimmering everywhere, and the playful breeze of Ashwin blew in desultory gusts. As the boat made its way over the paddy field, Rajek thought about the whole business – Torab Ali's warm amity and his generous hospitality – and tried to fathom the point of it all. Could there be a trap in all of this? Could it be that he wanted to seize the estate of the absent Baikuntha Saha?

Having once accepted an invitation, others kept on coming right through until towards the end of Kartik. Every three or four days Rajek would be summoned to Torab Ali's house on one pretext or another. And just like that first day, every time he was welcomed fondly.

Rajek noticed that recently Kamran had not been present. When sitting down to eat or while chatting, she would be seen once or twice, just for a moment, at the open window. When he and others used to come to the house as day labourers eight or ten months earlier, the proud girl would walk about amongst them all quite unabashed, flaunting her beauty and conceit. But Rajek could find no reason at all for Kamran's recent behaviour. In his ocean of thoughts he could not find the shore.

At last the mystery was solved. One morning at the beginning of the month of Agrahayan Torab Ali came to Rajek and said, "There is something I need to discuss with you, Mian."

On all the many previous occasions when Rajek had been invited to the house, Torab Ali had entertained him lavishly. They had talked only about this and that and nothing in particular, but this time Rajek could guess that his host had something of great import to say, and had just been waiting for the opportunity. It was this thought that had denied Rajek his sleep, as though a sharp thorn were piercing his chest whenever he lay down.

Who could tell what it was that Torab Ali had to discuss? Rajek just looked at him, holding his breath. Torab Ali said, "You have seen my daughter, Kamran, then?"

Not knowing what the man was getting at Rajek simply nodded

his head in bewilderment.

"I want you to marry her."

Rajek leaped to his feet, startled. "But you are such an important man –"

"So what?" Torab Ali asked.

"You are such a rich man and from such a noble background! But I used to come here as a workman. To marry the daughter of such a man – oh, no, no."

"Forget about having been a workman, Mian. Now that you have wealth and a grand house you can forget everything about when you were nothing. You've got all that land of Baikuntha Saha's, his entire estate. How can you ever be a little man? You've come up in the world, Mian."

Hesitantly, Rajek said, "But –"

"What, then?"

"If you give your daughter to me in marriage, what will your kinsmen say or do?"

"No bastard'll do anything. They wouldn't dare. Besides –"

"What?"

"I can't see my daughter being so greatly happy anywhere else. Who other than you has ninety *kanis* of fertile land and such a fine house? There is no one of the kind. At least, I've never heard of him."

It was all so utterly unexpected, so unimaginable. All Torab Ali's fussing about, his amiability, his warm hospitality, were all for making Rajek his son-in-law. Borne along on the waves of fortune, Rajek said, "In that case, you do what you think best."

After a moment's thought Torab Ali said, "I think the marriage should be celebrated once the paddy has been harvested."

Rajek said nothing. He just sat there, his head bowed.

Torab Ali went on, "So that's that, then. I must go now."

Even after Torab Ali had gone, Rajek still did not get up. As he sat there, he started to think how fortuitous the Partition of the country and Baikuntha Saha's leaving the village had been! Otherwise, how could he have been so lucky?

Harvest time started in the middle of the month of Agrahayan. The paddy was brought from the fields, winnowed, then dried out in the sun and stored until the end of the month of Magh. Then Torab Ali came again. "The harvest is over," he said. "Now let us call in the mullah and his lot."

Pinching his nails, Rajek said, "Whatever you wish –"

Considering the situation, Torab Ali said, "What day is it today?"

"Wednesday."

"I'll send for them at noon on Saturday. You come to my house then. I'll tell the clerics also to come then and fix the wedding day and settle the matter of bride-price. I'll send a boat to bring you to my house."

Rajek said, "There's no need to send a boat, I can go and –"

Torab Ali did not listen. Emphatically shaking his head, he said, "This must be done properly. How could I not send it? Have you no sense of honour?"

After Torab Ali had gone, time seemed to stop still for Rajek and an unrestrained excitement ran through his veins making him constantly restless.

Nevertheless, Thursday came and went, as did Friday. From early on Saturday it seemed that time had indeed stopped, that the sun had risen much later than on other days and would not get moving! Whereas it would take one hour for it to cross the road, today it seemed to take ten times as long. Rajek paced back and forth, looking out at the distant fields. He had lost count of the number of times that morning he had looked out at the fields on the other side of the pond. Of course now, in the month of Phalgun, there was no water in the fields, but beside them there was a big canal which ran straight into Baikuntha Saha's pond and along which Torab Ali's boat would come.

The time dragged until at last it was one o'clock, and precisely then did Rajek catch sight of the round canopy of the boat in the far distance. Immediately a storm blew up inside his chest like the haphazard, unregulated drawing of a bow across a stringed instrument. This was not the usual two-oared craft, but a peacock-shaped boat had been sent to take him to his fairy princess!

Rajek watched as the boat approached the ghat on the pond. He stared, unblinking. He wondered whether or not to go down to the ghat. But then Rajek leaped up in a flash. Had he been struck by a thunderbolt he could not have been more startled. He trembled as though his blood had started to run cold. In the last two or three months he had not even dreamt of the man who was now getting out of the boat.

Not only Baikuntha Saha, but another man got out with him. From his dress and appearance he seemed to be a Muslim. He was about sixty.

Baikuntha Saha took his companion straight from the ghat to the house. He was very happy to see Rajek, saying, "It's good to find you at home, Rajek. I was worried that I might miss you. How are you? Are you in good health?"

Rajek just stood there like one struck by lightning. All he could say was, "It's you, Saha Mashay!"

Baikuntha Saha said, "Yes, it is me. But I could not let you know I was coming. The opportunity suddenly arose and here I am."

"Where have you been?"

"Many places. Calcutta, Bangaon, Dattapukur, I can't name them all. Finally we settled in Murshidabad." While he was talking he remembered his companion. Addressing him, he said, "Sit down, sit down, Amin Saheb. Rajek, bring out a stool for him to sit on. And prepare some tobacco."

A stool was brought and Amin Saheb sat down. Baikuntha Saha also sat down on one side of the veranda. Then they started to chat, about the state of the country, about who was still in the village and who had gone, and so on. Baikuntha Saha asked one question after the other and Rajek, emotionally enervated, answered listlessly. Then, after a lot of chat about one thing and another, Baikuntha Saha came to the main point. "So you have kept the house and everything in good order?"

It was not clear why, after such a long time, Baikuntha Saha had suddenly returned to the village or why he had come back on the very day on which Rajek's marriage date was to be fixed. Occupied by these thoughts Rajek said, "You can see for yourself how I have kept it all."

Baikuntha Saha got up straightaway and beckoned Amin Saheb. "Come, come. You saw my land when we arrived, but now come and see the house."

Baikuntha Saha took Amin Saheb around and showed him everything. Rajek, however, did not accompany them but remained sitting, steeped in worry and anxiety. He felt as though a husking-pestle were being pedalled inside his chest.

After all this time Baikuntha Saha had not, indeed, brought anyone from his family but only Amin Saheb, who was not a man of these parts – if he were, Rajek certainly would have recognised him. What was Baikuntha Saha's connection with this Muslim gentleman? When they arrived, Baikuntha showed him the land, and now he was showing him the house. The whole business was a mystery to Rajek. He could make nothing of it.

A little later the two of them returned. As they sat on the veranda, Baikuntha Saha asked, "How does the house look to you?"

"It's fine," Amin Saheb replied.

"Do you like it, then?"

"Yes."

While talking with Amin Saheb, Baikuntha Saha suddenly remembered something. Quickly he turned to Rajek and said, "My goodness, I have not introduced you to Amin Saheb. He is from

Murshidabad, a friend of mine." And to Amin Saheb, he said, "And this is Rajek, a most reliable man. When we left the country, the whole responsibility for the estate was placed on him. You can see how carefully he has looked after it all."

Amin Saheb said nothing, but just nodded his head.

After this introduction Baikuntha Saha said, "You see, Rajek, I am not returning to this country. So do you know why I have brought Amin Saheb?"

Rajek nodded, but he had no idea.

Taking a good look around him, Baikuntha Saha said in a somewhat suppressed voice, "I have made over my entire estate as a gift to Amin Saheb. Actually, do you know something?"

"What?"

"Amin Saheb will not stay in India, so he has made over as a gift to me all his estate in Murshidabad, and what is mine in Pakistan, I have given to him. It's called in English 'an exchange'.

Just as Rajek was about to say something in reply, Torab Ali's two boatmen had come and were standing in front of him. One of them said, "Come, Mian Saheb. Come quickly. We're running a little late."

Having heard that Baikuntha Saha was to exchange all his wealth for Amin Saheb's, Rajek could not conceive of how he could possibly go now to Torab Ali's house, despite all the preparations. Simply, he could not get his thoughts together as the two boatmen started to press him. Suddenly Rajek remembered Torab Ali's big-heartedness, his generosity and his hospitality. He thought that Torab Ali had gone so far in the matter of the marriage that he could not now back out.

As though in a trance Rajek got up. To Baikuntha Saha he said, "You both sit for a little, Saha Mashay. I have to go out for a while." And he went and embarked with the two boatmen.

The splendour of the occasion could be seen as one approached Torab Ali's house. The clerics had by now come. There were no guests present from any but the most important homes in Chhiptipur – the Sardars, the Mridhas, the Khans and the like.

The excitement was noticeable when Rajek entered. Much rose-water had been sprayed all about and the place was redolent with attar. There was paan, there was tobacco, there were sweets. All about there was chatting and joking, and laughter swelled on all the colourful and joyous talk. But Rajek seemed not to hear or see anything. He sat, bewildered and benumbed.

Torab Ali noticed Rajek. Today he was in an excellent mood, beaming and radiant. He could not resist a little banter with his future son-in-law. He sat down close to him and asked, "Why so down in the dumps today, Mian? What is the matter?"

Mechanically Rajek replied, "Baikuntha Saha came back today."

Torab Ali was startled. "Baikuntha Saha has come back?"

"Yes. He brought a friend with him, Amin Saheb. He is making over all his estate to him."

For a moment the whole room stood still. After some time Torab Ali said, "In that case, what's the point of a wedding? We must accept what Allah wills. It is fortunate that Baikuntha Saha has come today. If he had come after the marriage – "As he spoke, he got up onto his big feet and went inside the house.

A little later the guests all left one after the other. After sitting for a long time in the empty room, Rajek also left.

After that the days came and the days went. Again Rajek took his wicker basket, his net, his line and his hooks and went into the waters of the canals and marshes and streams, and again in autumn he scoured the fields to glean grain. Again his feet started to crack, his fingers started to rot, and his skin started to flake off.

Nowadays, as Rajek goes about in search of fish and particles of grain, he thinks to himself, "The country was divided into two and the Sahas and the others left the village. One king goes, another king comes."

# THE ISLAND IN THE RIVER

## *char*

The four-oared boat swept through the reeds and was brought to a stop by the muddy sand of the island. It was deep into the dark last hours of the night, and all the stars were hidden by a screen of thick, black clouds. Over the rough waves of the Meghna a feverish whimpering drifted off towards the obscure horizon.

One of the boatmen said, "We haven't done the job properly, Tamiz. And if Dhala Mian finds out, he'll set fire to our house. I'm frightened too that he'll probably stop our supply of paddy seed. Then how'll we have any harvest?"

Tamiz sat in the boat, his hand firmly holding the rudder, casting a vacant glance over the dark, starless sky. As soon as he heard this, he burst out angrily, "You're inhuman! Anyway, how will Dhala Mian know? He's not here. No, no, my hands won't murder this girl. Besides, she's pregnant. We'll just put her down here on this island and leave her to fate."

"I'm not so sure. I'm really scared." The boatman spoke almost inaudibly.

"Oh, look, your fear's pointless. I know that. You're not so much frightened of murdering the girl as of leaving her alive." Tamiz sounded extremely annoyed. He paused for a moment, then said, "No. We must be gone. It's almost daybreak. Bring her out from under the awning."

After they had put the pregnant girl down on the island's soft soil made smooth by the rains and bordered by the reeds, the boat quickly drifted far off to merge with the thick darkness.

The girl's name was Sukhi. Very slowly she was sinking into unconsciousness, writhing in an unbearable pain which kneaded and twisted the soft flesh of her belly as it moved downwards, as though forcing her innards out of herself. Little by little it spread right through her body, permeating her skin and flesh and bone.

A little later there emerged in the eastern sky indistinct tints like diluted lac, and the gentle rays of the morning started to dance over the waters of the Meghna. From some distant Muslim home came the noise of a flock of chickens.

So far it had seemed that the girl's consciousness had been masked by the black wings of a bat. Everything before her eyes was obscure, but once it had cleared, Sukhi was suddenly gripped by an awful fear. No longer was she alone, for, lying beside her, smeared with blood, was a newborn baby with the morning light playing on its tiny, still eyelids. Surprisingly, it was not crying at all, but just lay silently beside Sukhi, its two soft fists clenched.

One particular night flashed into Sukhi's dim and meagre memory. How long ago had it been? She could not focus on it, and all that she saw now was like flashes of a picture. That night ...

All the houses in the weavers' quarter were ablaze. From the far end of the village came the cries of women screaming desperately, while the deathly sobbing of the children indicated some dreadful calamity. Sukhi was sitting stock-still in her locked house, cringing in terror. Her heart was thumping frenetically and a fierce trembling that she could not stop ran throughout her body which was racked from running the shuttles all day. And now the screaming, the fire, the violent clamour had all together numbed her mind.

What a night! How long ago had it been? In the present dimness of her memory Sukhi could not determine that.

The blaze and the tumult had come right up to her house. Amid the ghastly, raucous laughter, before her loss of consciousness, one familiar voice came back to her ears: "Hey! The gorgeous Sukhi!

What a looker! Let's break down the door and have her – "But then the picture speeded up so that it remained disjointed in the faint uncertainty of her memory.

A year ago Sukhi's life had been very different. She was a childless widow in a weaver's family. All day she would sit at the shuttle weaving coarse cloth and *gamchhas* to be sold by traders at the market. Then she was self-sufficient and had no cause to depend on anyone. But now, as the sands glittered in the soft morning light and the wind rustled through the reeds, rippling the surface of the Meghna and playing with the foliage of the distant *heuli* thicket, Sukhi was taken captive by something as real as the wind and the sunlight – the fearsome fact that she was a mother.

Strangely her heart quickened. She was a mother! And beside her was the little lump of flesh and blood curled up in the cool breeze of the monsoon season. But suddenly her face was hardened by cruelty and she reached out her hand to the baby's throat. At this time there was no one anywhere to see her. She hesitated for a few seconds, then decided – No, no. She would not keep this disgrace.

But just at that moment, from beside the island's half-sunken field where the tops of the paddy shoots waved in the breeze above the water, there came a voice singing a sweet and dreamy song.

> I shall put at your feet all that I bring from the market
> just for your smile, for which my heart burns.
> Have pity on me, and I will give you attar and rosewater ...

So she was not alone on this sandy island! Hearing the song quite clearly she stayed her hand from the baby's throat and, in the gentle light of morning, looked again at this newcomer to the world and was amazed. Nowhere in its face could the crime of Chhadan Shikdar be seen; rather, the baby bore a very clear resemblance to herself.

Sukhi drew back her hand. She put out of her mind her resolve of moments before. She could not kill the baby, just as she had not been able to kill herself over the last nine months, despite the hellish torment since that terrible night. She held her baby close to her breast.

All the while the song came floating on the breeze, and soon the singer appeared near to her. He was a boy of about fifteen, wearing a multi-coloured, striped lungi. With some line and a hook he was wading through the water looking for fish when he caught sight of Sukhi. He stared, dumbfounded, at the bloodstains all about and at the blood-smeared, newborn child. Snapping out of his reverie, he asked, "Who are you? How did you get to this island?"

"You can think of me as a sister. What is your name?" This was the first time Sukhi had smiled fondly since that original night of terror.

The boy's wide eyes did not blink. Coming a little closer, he said, "My name is Ramzan."

Sukhi suddenly contorted in a sharp spasm of pain and in a strained voice she said, "I'm in pain, brother. I'm in terrible pain."

"Wait just a minute. I'll be right back." So saying Ramzan started to run, dropping his line and hooks. His multi-coloured, striped lungi was seen to dash along the side of the *heuli* thicket before it disappeared on the other side of the half-sunken paddy field.

Sukhi did not know when she let her eyelids fall over her lifeless eyes, but she woke up to the sound of many footsteps. Ramzan had brought a few others back with him, among whom was an elderly woman. Her hair was as rough as jute fibre and she had cataracts over her eyes. All over, her skin was wrinkled.

Ramzan said, "Look, Grandmother. Here's what I was talking about."

The old woman peered anxiously through her dull eyes at Sukhi. Sharply she said to the others, "What are you all gawking at? Go on, clear out of here, blockheads. At such a time no men should be around. Elem, go and get a boat. We'll have to take her home."

Izem, Osman and Rustam disappeared behind the *heuli* thicket. Elem and Ramzan ran across the sand bed and then hurried across to the other side of the paddy field to find a dinghy. The old grandmother attended to the blood-smeared baby's cord, and Sukhi, in fatigue and pain, let her eyes close.

Taking the baby up into her lap the old grandmother said, "The baby'll be frozen in this breeze off the water. Oh dear, what a time this girl has had of it. What a fate!" The old grandmother slowly massaged Sukhi's back with her thin and bony hand. A newborn one had come into the world, an age-old cause to celebrate. In such a sacred moment all are equal.

A little later Ramzan brought a boat around the bend in the river. Elem and the old grandmother carried Sukhi to the boat and laid her down in it. Ramzan sat beside her with the baby in his lap. The waves of the Meghna lapped playfully against the boat in the bluish monsoon morning.

Once the *heuli* thickets, the *hijal* trees and a jungle of reeds had all been cleared, a tiny settlement had been established, just a few houses with thatched roofs, homes that were stamped with the mark of their owners' sweat and toil. Sukhi was brought from the boat and put down in one such humble house.

The grandmother took a small coin from an old and tattered wicker basket and whispered, "Hurry up, boy, and go to the other side of the river and bring a little milk."

"But you were going to buy sweets to offer at Imam Phakir's shrine," said Ramzan.

"Go on, now. Don't waste time. Just see how the mother is looking close to death. If I use the coin to save her, it will help me go to heaven." The old woman paused for a moment, then smiled and said, "Hurry along now, and I'll make you something really nice."

Ramzan's face lit up hungrily. "What will you make?" he asked.

"You bring the milk first."

Ramzan and the little boat were tossed about on the waves of the Meghna and soon disappeared into the distance.

When the old woman went back into the house, she said, "What's your name, sister?"

In fear of her identity, Sukhi cried out, "My name? My name?"

"Rest, rest, girl. It can wait till later. Don't be upset, you've just had your baby. If you cry now, your innards'll be in pain and you'll not be able to sleep at night."

The wind whistles freely here where the world is laid bare beneath the boundless sky, and every moment is a struggle between man and nature as the people wage an unending battle for survival.

Today the wind had been blowing wildly, and in the evening Rustam was spreading a bundle of straw over the roof of Sukhi's hut. "Grandmother," he said, "the moneylender wants thirty rupees as deposit before he'll give us the boat. I can't see how we can manage. Within two weeks we have to pay back the money he lent us last year for paddy seed."

"Don't worry about the boat. I'll weave a net by the day after tomorrow and you can catch fish from the canals to sell. How can we repay the paddy seed? Most of it went into the monsoon and the autumn crops, and we've eaten the rest. We can pay back something when the monsoon crop comes up." The old woman spoke slowly and calmly.

Rustam looked dubious. Diffidently, he said, "There's also the money we borrowed to buy the cow and the plough. All that has to be paid back. If it's not, then – "Rustam stopped abruptly.

"Don't worry so, Rustam! Remember what happened a few years ago when the landlord, Dhala Mian – this same money-lender's brother – burned down our homes? Did we die? If we could survive those times, we'll survive anything. Good times will return to us."

This was the old woman's one and only article of faith in their life of dire need, disappointment and hazard, the one and only relief from all their difficulty, her one and only assurance. In her all their hope was restored and solutions would be found for all their problems.

Only a few years back things had been different for them. Their village was where the tops of the trees of the forest mark the thin line of the vast horizon. With their tin-roof house in the shade of *hijal* and coral trees, and a little paddy field, they did not want for much. But in time, whatever hopes they had were shattered like clay plates. Famine came, war came, riots came. Then, on the pretext that they could not pay the rent, the landlord's men set fire to their house. Rahimuddi's pregnant wife and Kasem's three-month-old boy perished in the flames.

Then, one melancholy evening, many people like Ramzan, the old grandmother, Rustam and Osman, rowed across the Meghna to this island. They made their broken life anew on that desolate stretch of land, applying themselves with new strength and spirit, absorbed in the satisfaction of arduous toil.

And into this island life in the Meghna, all of a sudden Sukhi appeared among them.

One day the old grandmother had set the baby on his feet and was gently swinging him. Sitting away from them, boiling the new paddy, Sukhi thought what an uncommon hold on life the child had, able to survive the buffets of wind, water and cold. Amazed, she wondered why. He was a genuine son of the devil!

The old grandmother said, "Your baby's becoming very naughty, sister. Isn't it amazing that he can appreciate affection so much? His father was probably naughty too! I'd really like to meet his father."

A sudden chill ran through Sukhi; her heart thumped and her face set hard. In the mirror of her memory there were images of so many terrible days and nights. She remembered the night when she was sprawled on the ground hearing that lustful, lecherous voice. To think of the days that followed would make her catch her breath and cause her heart to miss a beat. The blood raced through her veins and her skin tightened in terror.

She had been held in a derelict house where, night after night and sometimes during the day, the money-lender would come to collect his interest. Sukhi had told the whole story to the old grandmother, even the money-lender's instructions to Tamiz and Halim: "The bitch doesn't need to be kept alive any more. The day after tomorrow, on the night of the new moon, dump her in the Meghna. No one will suspect anything."

Sukhi had told her everything except the shameful story of the baby's conception. She could not bring herself to say anything about that.

Looking Sukhi in the eye, the old grandmother said in her metallic voice, "I understand, it's a matter of pride. So I should leave off talking about his father? But if he should come to this island, I'd not let him off easily. His wife might have been abducted, but what sort of husband is he that doesn't inquire about her?"

Husband! While secretly she herself burned, Sukhi decided to let the old woman be satisfied with thinking what she liked. She went on sitting in silence beside the paddy vat.

After a month or two the island's monsoon paddy had ripened and was glimmering like gold. The peasants' hard labour, smiled on by good fortune, had filled the green fields with a sweet-smelling charm on these last days of the month of Bhadra.

One day the old grandmother asked Osman, "When are you all going to the fields to cut the paddy?"

"Let another week go by, then we'll see. The north field isn't quite ripe yet." Osman spoke slowly, looking at the land.

In the evening, Rustam returned from the market on the other side of the river. His grandmother had made a net for him and he spent the days catching the new fish in the island's canals; in the afternoons he would take the boat to the Kamala Ghat market and sell the fish to the traders. Taking the old woman's hand and placing in it the three shiny rupees he had taken from the waist of his lungi, he said, "I got some news today, Grandmother."

"What news?"

"The money-lender's men want to take the ripened paddy. The money-lender's really angry about the paddy seed and the money he lent us for the boat and the plough." Rustam spoke in a whisper and looked somewhat apprehensive.

In the meantime, Osman, Ramzan and some others had come and were standing there. Sukhi too had come with the baby. They were anxious, and fear showed on all their faces.

Someone asked, "What's going to happen, Grandmother?"

Another said, "If they take the ripened paddy, there'll be nothing for us to eat. We'll starve."

The old woman reassured them. "You needn't worry about that. I don't think the money-lender or his brother will set fire to the house. Did we die then? Anyway, aren't you men? Don't you have red blood? Would you look tame and stand by meekly if they came across the river to take our paddy?"

Someone asked diffidently, "Will you resist them, Grandmother?"

"We'll fight if we have to. But if you're frightened, then stay at home. I'll face them. My son, Ramzan's father, was killed by that landlord – this money-lender's brother. I'll settle his score myself."

Heatedly, Osman said, "Are you saying we're afraid to die, Grandmother? Aren't we the sons of Muslims? To fight is in our blood! If they come from over there to take our paddy, the money-lender and his men will see just what a fight is!"

Slowly the night became dark, pitch dark. The old woman's pledge before the assembled men – "I will fight if I have to" – had ignited their spirits.

One morning a few days later Sukhi was sitting beside Ramzan, who was dandling the baby in his lap. He said, "Your little boy is starting to look really beautiful. His face is exactly like yours, don't you think?"

Sukhi was a little taken aback. She looked carefully to see if there was any resemblance to Chhadan Shikdar, any trace on his face of the stain of Chhadan, any profane shadow of that original abominable night, and as she looked, a warm smile came over her face. No, there was no hint on that innocent face of the evil of Chhadan Shikdar.

"Oh, no, brother, his face is just like his uncle's," she said.

Sukhi's life had now blended in with theirs on this island. There was only an indistinct memory of a lovely village a long way away where, in a little house, a widow dressed in plain white worked noisily at the loom the whole day long, but that picture now seemed unreal and fanciful. All that counted for her – at least, in the little world of this island – was what they all acknowledged: she was a mother, the mother of a little boy.

A few days later, as the news gradually spread, the insignificant little settlement was quickly startled into fear. The money-lender had come to the island.

It was late in the afternoon. Clouds as black as snakes' eyes were gathering in the sky and the Meghna was getting very rough.

The old grandmother was sitting inside the house sewing a cotton shawl for the baby. Then she went outside and cried heatedly, "Osman, Rustam, you're still just sitting there! What's the matter?"

Just then Ramzan came back from the river. He smiled and said, "Don't be frightened, Grandmother, the money-lender's not coming to take the paddy. He was taking his three wives to some relative's house, but seeing the clouds in the sky they got frightened and took shelter on the island. The Meghna's going mad."

Dubiously the old woman said, "Are you sure that's why they're here?"

"Yes, yes."

In that late afternoon the shadow of the clouds was darkening everything.

Rustam had taken the money-lender and his three wives into the neighbouring hut where they were sitting on small wooden stools.

Sukhi was stunned when she recognised quite unmistakably the money-lender's voice coming from that house, for along with the voice came all the experience of those horrible months. One did not forget Chhadan Shikdar's voice in a hurry, and the bat's wings of that ghastly night again started to flap over her mind and her eyes flared up and blazed fiercely. She woke her sleeping baby, held him to her breast, and went into the hut where the money-lender was.

Chhadan Shikdar was saying, "I'll want the money and the paddy-seed repaid during the monsoon harvest – "but then his voice froze, set still by the sight of the face of the little boy in the lap of his mother, and he trembled in fear.

Tamiz and Halim, the money-lender's boatmen, were also there, and they got up and came and stood beside Sukhi. In surprise one of them said, "You are still alive, Sukhi. That's wonderful!"

"Yes, I am. And look. See how beautiful your nephew is."

The baby gave a sudden smile, and for Chhadan Shikdar that smile had the power of so many cobras about to flare their hoods. Through half-closed eyes he looked at his three wives. The eldest was like a tigress; the second, malicious as a wildcat baring its claws; the third, whom Chhadan had married only recently, young and voluptuous. Had they been able to discern the origins of this baby, all three would have rushed at his throat.

Panic had drained the colour from Chhadan's face. He whispered, "Actually, it won't be necessary to pay back the money and the paddy seed. Now we must go."

Blocking his way and brandishing the baby like a weapon, Sukhi said, "And you can give us five hundred rupees come Sunday."

Mechanically Chhadan said, "Yes. All right." Then he said to Tamiz and Halim, "Get the boat ready. I have to get back to the village."

Tamiz and Halim were destitute boatmen. Chhadan Shikdar would have them murder someone for just a few rupees, but getting their blood-money from him was no easy task. Now all this had come like the sudden swoop of an eagle.

Halim said, "We're not coming right now, Mian."

"When will you come?"

"Sunday. We'll come to get the money with Sukhi. You can go with your wives."

Tamiz took the baby from Sukhi's lap and held him up above his chest. How simply this child had made smooth the way to a consummation!

Now, with their new weapon, they would go not only on the following Sunday, but many, many more times as well.

# THE DREAM TRAIN

*swapner tren*

## ONE

Some thirteen or fourteen years ago Ashok used to have a dream just before dawn. It was a strange dream in which he was travelling in a train through paddy and jute fields that stretched as far as the horizon. Here and there would be a cane grove, some kind of jungle or other, or a wood. As far as one could see the fields were bathed in golden sunshine and flocks of birds were flying overhead, their bodies daubed with the gold of the sun. There were so many different kinds of birds – yellow-beaked blackbirds, bulbuls, cranes, small herons, wild parrots, and many, many more – making it look as though someone had scattered to the winds countless pieces of coloured paper. The clouds were like wisps of cotton wool with the brilliant blue of the sky gleaming between them.

The dream train would bring Ashok to a ghat beside a vast river where a large steamer was docked at the jetty. Along with many other people Ashok would go up the wooden steps to board the boat, but with nowhere for him to sit he would stand on the deck, holding on to the railing.

With a blast from its whistle the steamer would depart, and then only water would be seen. Here and there one might see a clump of water-hyacinths and, in the distance, looking like black spots, numerous passenger boats and cargo boats. Flying just above the waves might be a flock of brown-winged, white-breasted kites looking for a chance to catch in their curved beaks some *kajali* fish or some of the moon-fish that gleamed like silver.

Then the steamer would come to some ghat or other – Rajabari, Bhagyakul, Tarpasha, Lauhajang – and as it approached, numerous one-man snack boats would come from everywhere, offering all kinds of fruit and sweets.

The steamer would go on from Tarpasha and Lauhajang and head towards Munshiganj, and Ashok would know that in a short while he would be getting down at the ghat there and then be on his way to his village of Bajrayogini some five or six miles away, where he would see all his boyhood friends: Rashed, Kamal, Atikul ... and just then a rattling, wheezy voice would wake him up.

The steamer never got to Munshiganj, for the rattling, wheezy voice was always heard before it could. The voice was always his father's.

"Time to get up, son. It's morning already."

In a brief panic, Ashok would sit up. With sleep still hanging on his eyelids he would wonder where he was and would not be able to get out of bed at first, but after a while the dream train and the steamer would fade from his mind and before his eyes would be the three-legged bed (a few bricks had replaced the fourth leg) in an ancient room, with himself sitting amid the grimy covers. None of the walls had any plaster left, and soot-laden cobwebs had amassed up in the corners.

His bed was on one side of the room and on the other side was a clothes rack, next to which were stacked up a trunk, a torn suitcase and a tin box. At the foot of the bed were various kitchen utensils, a cane basket, a broken pitcher and various other odds and ends. As well as all these things the bed where his father and two little brothers, Paltu and Hiru, slept, was spread out on the floor in the little space that was left.

Ashok would see that only his father was up; Paltu and Hiru, their knees doubled up to their chests, would still be asleep. They had always slept like that.

His father would say, "It's gone half-past-five, son. It's time to go out. There'll soon be a terrible crowd at the Employment Exchange."

Ashok would rub his eyes and look at his father, a man who rented one and a half rooms in a tenement in a suffocating alley of north Calcutta, but who once owned three hundred and fifty *kanis* of land in Bajrayogini village near Munshiganj. It was there that he had taken on the headmastership of the village school without remuneration. When he lived in the village, he used to be so wonderfully healthy, so it was painful for Ashok to see his father deteriorating in this north Calcutta tenement. His body had become nothing more than skin and bone, his eyes and cheeks were sunken, and his collar-bone protruded. After leaving his home and three hundred and fifty *kanis* of land, he had wandered about for a year before finding a two-hundred-and-fifty-rupees-a-month job as a clerk in a Marwari firm. After seeing to the needs of a family of seven on that wage, how well could he look after himself?

His father would hurry him along. "You can't keep on sitting there. Go and wash your face."

Without saying anything Ashok would get down from the bed. Beside his father's bed he would pour some tooth powder into the palm of his left hand and go outside.

On the right going out was the tiny strip of a room where his mother and two little sisters, Chhaya and Putul, spent their nights. The girls were never in any hurry to get up, but their mother would have risen already and lit the coal oven.

The sun did not get into this alley, which all year round, in summer and winter, was always under the thick gloom of evening. Lights were lit even in the daytime. Ashok would go out to the tap in the cracked washing area behind the kitchen where ashes, fish bones and all the refuse of the universe were scattered about. A little later he would have a cup of hot tea and a couple of stale chapatis, and then go out.

On some days his father would say when he woke him up, "You must go and meet Mr. Chatterji from the jute-mill. The gentleman goes out by eight. If you don't hurry, you'll miss him."

Ashok would say, "I've been there several times. It seems that nothing's going."

But his father would say, "Go again. Explain carefully our circumstances –"

"I do that whenever I go."

One morning his father had asked, "What does Chatterji say?"

"Nothing much. But –"

"But what?"

"He can get me something if I can raise about three thousand rupees."

His father's eyes had suddenly clouded over. He kept quiet for a few moments, then said, "Tell him that if he gets you the job, I'll pay him the money in monthly instalments."

"He won't give the job without the money first," Ashok had replied.

"Then try just once."

On other days his father would wake him up to say that he was sending him to the house of some big government officer or some member of parliament. So as he went from the Employment Exchange to the house of this one and that, Ashok could never remember that the dream train had stopped coming at dawn.

## TWO

### (i)

Late one night in the month of April some thirteen or fourteen years later, in 1971, the dream train came all of a sudden to Ashok once again. Not only did he see it, but it took him on board and away through the fields that stretched to the horizon and on to the steamer ghat beside the vast river that flowed beneath the brilliant blue sky.

Ashok's jaw was set firm and his face reflected a stern resolve. He was dressed in military uniform,

But as the train approached the steamer ghat, he was woken by the sound of somebody crying. He sat up with a start in the unclear dark and saw beside him, on the three-legged bed in the old house in north Calcutta, his wife, Namita, asleep. She was about seven months pregnant, and her body was racked with illness; there were heavy shadows under her eyes, her unkempt hair hung over her broad forehead, her lips were as lifeless as boiled meat, her eyes were half-closed, and she gaped like a *katla* fish. Her dry and almost flat breasts rose and fell with the rhythm of her breathing.

Only a few years ago this same Namita was a vivacious woman of flesh and blood who kept excellent health, but now her body was little more than the skin covering her bones. In her ten years of married life she had given birth to three children, and now the fourth was six or seven months inside her. As a result she was now wasting away.

The sound of sobbing could still be heard. Ashok got down from the bed.

The room still looked much the same as it had thirteen or fourteen years back. One difference was a tall wardrobe Ashok had bought after their marriage and which stood where the clothes rack had been. The clothes rack had been moved into his mother's room. As before, a bed was spread out on the floor, but Hiru, Páltu and their father no longer slept there. Their father had died about seven years earlier. Hiru had found work in Nasik, and wrote as he felt like it – one letter in six or nine months. The question of his sending money home was never even raised as his connection with home was by but a very thin thread, one that might snap at any time. And Paltu was now in police custody for breaking into the wagons of goods trains.

Now Ashok's three children – Khuki, Mana and Bablu - slept on the floor in place of his father and brothers. Khuki and Mana were well but Bablu was suffering from jaundice. Was it Bablu who was crying? Ashok moved past them and a little to the right to the switch on the wall and turned on the light. He bent down and saw that Bablu was not crying but was sleeping with one leg spread across Khuki's body.

Ashok then realised that the sobbing was coming from the next room. It was his mother who was crying.

He quickly opened the door and went out. He knocked on the door to the narrow neighbouring room and called, "Mother – Mother –"

A moment later the widowed mother, wrapped in a grubby dhoti, stood face to face with her son, tears flowing from her eyes.

Nowadays she stayed in this room with Paltu and Putul. Chhaya was no longer with them, for she had run away from the locality with a young man about two years back.

"Why are you crying, Mother?" Ashok asked.

Wiping her eyes with the end of the dhoti, the mother said, "I suddenly started to worry so badly about Paltu."

Ashok said nothing. Paltu had been in custody for three days. Each day Ashok had gone around trying, unsuccessfully, to have him released.

His mother went on, "Listen. If bail can be raised for Paltu –"

"I'm trying, Mother," said Ashok. "I'm going to see a lawyer after work today." (After so much endeavour, Ashok had been able to get a job as a clerk in a mercantile office.) "Without a lawyer, I don't think he'll get bail."

Saying nothing, his mother went to the tap. After washing her face, she would have to light the oven.

Ashok could not get back to sleep. A little later, as morning broke, he took his bag and went to the market.

A little way down the alley, opposite the bend, was a teashop; there Ashok saw a number of men with newspapers, engaged in heated discussion. Ashok caught a glimpse of some headlines: 100,000 KILLED BY PAK SOLDIERS – DHAKA UNIVERSITY IN RUINS – PLANES BOMB UNARMED VILLAGERS. Seeing them made his blood boil. He very much wanted to join in the fervent discussion in the teashop but he had to hurry to the market and return home to take Mana and Khuki to school. They went to morning school, and Putul brought them home.

After leaving the children at school he would get back home by eight. He would shave and take a bath, have a quick bite and be at the tram by nine-thirty or a quarter to ten. He would have to be at the office at ten.

When he got to the office that day, Ashok saw that all the young men were engaged in a heated uproar over the explosive events in East Pakistan. These days there was nothing but East Pakistan talked about in trams and buses and in roadside cafes. Ashok felt that now he could raise his voice with the other young men in the office, something he had not been able to do in the teashop that morning, but then he remembered the stack of files on his desk and the boss's instructions that they had to be cleared within two days. So without looking around Ashok went straight to his own desk and buried his nose in the heap of files.

A meeting had been called in the office during the afternoon tea break over the east Bengal – or East Pakistan – question. It was decided that they would raise a subscription to send to the Bengali freedom fighters. Some contributed then and there but many were unable to give just yet, among them Ashok. It was already the eighth of the month and by now much of his wages had been spent; the little that was left would have to do for the remaining twenty-two days, and there was no possibility of taking even a penny from that. Moreover, he had to see the lawyer after work. If the lawyer could arrange for bail, then Ashok would probably have to find another twenty or thirty rupees. Who could say how much he might have to borrow that month?

Ashok promised that when he got his next month's wages he would try to make a contribution.

(ii)

Four days later, deep in the night, Ashok once more boarded the dream train, again dressed in military uniform. But before the train reached the steamer ghat, he was woken by a little voice calling, "Daddy – Daddy –"

Ashok sat up, startled, and saw Bablu in tears, his hand pressed against his stomach. He got out of bed quickly and, massaging the little boy's stomach, said, "What's the matter, now, eh? What's the matter?"

"I've got a really bad pain."

The boy had been suffering from jaundice for some days now. His face, the palms of his hands and the soles of his feet were all yellow. The doctor had prescribed some expensive medicine for him. Ashok had kept turning the prescription over in his pocket but had still not bought the medicine. No matter what, he would have to buy it today.

Ashok massaged Bablu's stomach for a long time, and the little boy at last slumped listlessly and fell asleep.

Ashok took two days off from the office, and when he returned he heard that a relief committee had been set up to aid those refugees who had been displaced by Yahya Khan's atrocities and were now fleeing to this side of the border. Ashok's name had been proposed for the committee.

The company management had already donated twenty five thousand rupees to the refugees' relief fund, to be spent on medicines and clothing which would be taken to the border that day at midday.

An exceptionally enthusiastic young clerk said, "You come too, Ashok-da!"

"Me?" said Ashok.

"Yes, you. There's nothing to stop you. Apart from your family you have no particular burden."

This brought a wry smile to Ashok. So he decided that he would go, he would certainly go with them.

But then he remembered that he had not yet bought Bablu's medicine and he would have to go and borrow some money from a friend in south Calcutta. No, there was no possibility of his going to the border with the relief.

(iii)

A few days later the dream train appeared to him again, but before it reached the steamer ghat the sound of a heavy fall caused Ashok to spring up. He quickly switched on the light to see Namita lying on the floor and the room flowing with blood. A feeble whine came in fits and starts from her throat and her sick and frail body shivered in its pool of blood. Apparently she was going to the bathroom when she stumbled and fell.

At first Ashok just stared at her, stunned, his mind totally empty.

Then suddenly he was overcome with an icy chill from head to toe, inside and out. He leaped to the door and opened it. In a choking voice, he called, "Mother! Mother!"

His mother came from the other room, along with Putul and Paltu. (Paltu had been released on bail of twenty-five rupees, raised with great difficulty.)

Then came the doctor and the ambulance, and they went to the hospital. It was after one o'clock the next day when Ashok, not having eaten or washed, got to the office. There he learned that after work that day the staff of his and other offices would demonstrate for the recognition of Bangladesh outside various consulates.

Ashok felt that he would not be able to join this demonstration, for after work he would have to go to the hospital. Before that he would have to buy some medicine for Namita. And before that he would have to borrow, at a steep rate of interest, about a hundred rupees from the office caretaker.

## THREE

Late at night, having raised the money for Paltu's bail, still needing to borrow money for Bablu's medicine, and having gone mechanically each day to the hospital to see Namita, his dream train was not running any more.

For all of his life, Ashok had been embroiled in the great middle-class war of survival. Life could offer him no greater battle than that.

# UNLAWFUL ENTRY

*anuprabesh*

The sun was very late in rising. In fact, the dawn still had not fully broken as the small party came down silently from the main highway onto the side road, stealthily moving in file, like a worm – men and women of two families, of various ages, eight of them in all. In one family was Farid and his grandmother,

Habiba, and the other consisted of Rasheda, her father and mother, her two younger brothers, and a frail, elderly aunt.

The men were wearing lungis or pajamas and shirts, and wore woollen pullovers or were wrapped in shawls; the women were wearing loose-fitting salwar-kameez and shawls. They all carried in their hands or on their heads some item of luggage: a big tin box, small wicker baskets, larger bamboo baskets, cloth bags, various kinds of bundles and the like.

At the head of all of them was Shaokat, a distant uncle of Farid and the general of this small force of pilgrims.

The month of Phalgun was half over, but in this region of Bihar the mood of winter lingered on, especially between the fall of evening and the next sunrise. The moon had set just a little earlier, and throughout the vast sky the countless stars still shone, like silver embroidery. There was not a wisp of cloud anywhere, but there was a pervasive haziness as the light fog blended with the darkness. The cold wind blew like an unseen current, cutting at their flesh.

On either side of the unpaved road were woods and scrub and tall, luxuriant pipal trees, beyond which were open fields. It was not possible to tell whether or not there were any villages, near or far. The entire world seemed bathed in sleep, and a numb stillness permeated all around them as far as one could see.

The ubiquitous fireflies glowed as myriad pin-pricks of light in the darkness. From a hole in the pipal trees came the harsh cry of a woodpecker, shattering the profound peacefulness of the dawn. Also challenging the calm was the constant rasping sound coming from the chest of Rasheda's aunt, Anwara, as she struggled for breath.

In a weak and indistinct voice Anwara would ask, "How much further now, Shaokat-bhai?" And having got the words out she would pant heavily. Here in the open the air was so fresh, yet it was insufficient to the task of reanimating this decrepit old woman.

Shaokat did not slow down at all. He merely looked back once while he kept up his pace. He said, "It's not far. Walk a little faster."

"I can't go any further. I've become terribly weak. It's pitch dark in front of me, I can't see a thing. I'll have to rest for a bit." Anwara's words came with a plaintive whine.

"No way, sister. We have to get there before sunrise and we still have about three miles to go." He looked around as he spoke. "We must cover this stretch of road before the world opens its eyes. We can't afford to have anyone see us."

After that Anwara said nothing more. Her head hung and swayed, but for the life of her she summoned up every last ounce of energy from her weak and worn old body and, like a blind woman groping her way, staggered onward.

Farid was right behind Anwara. On his head he carried a huge tin box, which he held in place with his right hand, and over his left shoulder was slung a big hessian bag. He noticed Anwara nearly topple over as she dragged herself on, and he reached out his left hand to steady her. "Hold on to me as you go, Auntie," he said.

Anwara replied, "You've got all that load on your head. You can't manage it if you have to hang on to me."

"I'll manage."

Anwara walked on, holding Farid's left hand and leaning her weight on his shoulder. She said, "Farid, my boy, do you know what I think?"

"What?"

"I don't think I'm going to make it. You'll have to bury me beside the road."

"Don't talk like that. We'll all get there in one piece. Just be careful where you put your feet."

Anwara said nothing more; only the rattling sound kept on coming up from her lungs. As Farid went along bearing the weight both of his luggage and his aunt, it seemed to him as though an artful sorcerer had spirited them away from the known world and brought them to some unknown, sleeping planet.

Three days earlier the touts had collected two hundred rupees per head to get the eight of them across the West Bengal border, and the same arrangement had again applied on this side, too, each of them having to pay two hundred rupees, not a penny more nor less. From the border they went straight to Calcutta; from there they took a train to Katihar, where they took a branch-line train, getting down in the evening at Kamtapur to wait for Shaokat. He took them some of the way by bullock dray, then, in the middle of the night, they set out on their long, continuous walk. If Shaokat was right, they still had another three miles to trudge.

Farid was twenty-three. He was born in what was then East Pakistan, six years before the birth of free Bangladesh. He had been told that, when India was partitioned in 1947, his grandfather,

Mudassar Ali, and his wife and children had left Bihar for Dhaka. In the dreadful riots in Bihar in 1947 their house had been burned to the ground. Although none of the family was killed, many of their friends were slaughtered. All around them there was a frenzy of arson, murder and bloodshed, piles of corpses, distrust and hatred. It did not seem to Mudassar and his family, caught in this maelstrom of malice, that things would ever get better, and so one winter's night they decided to flee what had been the home of generations of their family for two hundred years, leaving behind them their land and the ruins of what had been their house.

In Dhaka Mudassar Ali did not survive for long, dying within a year of their arrival. His only son, Rahmat, had grown up by then and took on all the responsibilities of the family. They somehow managed to get by in one way or another. From early in the morning until late at night Rahmat worked like a demon for the sake of his family. He scraped together a little money and, by borrowing a little more from others, he started up a ready-made clothing shop; within two or three years the business had developed successfully. He arranged for the marriage of his only sister, Maleka, and also got married himself. Seven years later, his son, Farid, was born.

When, after various struggles with trouble and strife, Rahmat had got his life into some sort of order, he was set back again by two deaths, one after the other: first Maleka died, and then his mother, Amina. Even this grief subsided, but emotionally he had been so bruised that he could not attend as well to his home and family or to his livelihood, and they only barely got by. The house – and Rahmat

– were kept in order by his grandmother, Habiba.

Things went on in much the same way when suddenly the War of Liberation broke out in East Pakistan. Such immense distrust, hatred and malice emerged between Bengali and non-Bengali Muslims, even though they were of the same religion, as had not been seen since the days of the terrifying riots prior to Partition, although the antagonists then had been Hindus and Muslims. Now Pakistan's bloodthirsty army swarmed out onto the roads with tanks, machine-guns and automatic rifles. In the villages and the towns a staunch resistance sprang up, followed everywhere by the sounds of gunfire, the harsh noise of the tanks, the smell of gunpowder, mountains of corpses, rivers of blood, rape, murder, arson, and the distressful cries of imperilled and devastated people.

Rahmat Ali was an extraordinarily simple man. He had no head for the intricacies of politics and was interested in nothing beyond the limits of his diminishing family. However, when the fires blazed all around him, it was impossible for him to get away from the heat. Then one day his shop was set alight and he was brutally beaten, but at least he got away with his life.

Once before, in quest of safety, he had left India and gone to Dhaka. He had a profound commitment to the newly independent East Pakistan, for then it had seemed as though all the panic and fear and uncertainty of life had become things of the past. But now where could he go?

The War of Liberation came to an end and the new, independent, sovereign state of Bangladesh was born. The smell of gunpowder was blown away and the bloodstains were cleaned from the earth, but the malice, suspicion and hostility towards the Urdu-speaking, non-Bengali Muslims continued to simmer.

There was a widespread belief that Pakistan would take the Urdu-speaking Bihari Muslims away from Dhaka. They did indeed take a few, but several hundred thousand remained in Bangladesh faced with tremendous uncertainty. The days passed, the years passed, but no plane or ship came from Pakistan to take Rahmat and his family.

Yet survival was everything. Rahmat had re-opened his shop, but sales were not like they had been before and his income fell dramatically. In the meantime Farid had grown up, passing through school and then college. But just before his B.A. examinations, he was struck down by fever for ten days. Who would pay for more study after this? So Farid left college, not just because of the lack of funds, but also because of the dejection he was suffering from at the time. Even if he could, albeit with difficulty, get a B.A. degree, there would be no guarantee of his getting a job. What future did he have in Bangladesh?

The first seventeen years of independence in Bangladesh passed in a flash. Most of the Bihari Muslims who had gone to East Pakistan at the time of the Partition of India still dreamed that some day a plane would come from Lahore or Karachi or Islamabad and take them away, but there were some people whose faith had started to crack and no longer did they believe in the plane from Pakistan. At night the Urdu-speaking residents of Mirpur would secretly meet and discuss ways of returning to their roots in India. They had learned also that those Urdu speakers who had gone to Pakistan in 1947 had, in fact, met instantly with the hostility of the people already long-settled there and had fallen into disfavour as intrusive alien residents. Riots and killings went on there, too, over a fair share of the bread.

After a lot of discussion they made up their minds. Their ancestral villages in Bihar, a very long way from Lahore or Karachi, were familiar to them and not so distant, but it was generally held that going there would be difficult. To go from one independent nation to another was no easy matter. But whatever the legalities might be, the world still had its black market and its touts were starting to appear in Mirpur under cover of darkness. They explained first to the fugitives where they would have to go. A remote place had been found with no surrounding settlement. However, it would be very dangerous for many to go together, as trouble might erupt should they be seen; they were advised that they would be safe travelling in small groups of eight or ten. The journey would take no more than a few days. Once they had made their decisions, arrangements would be set in motion.

The first group had arrived according to plan fifteen days back accompanied by Shaokat, an astute, versatile, cool-headed man. After that, some two or three families had been coming almost every day. Today it was Farid and company. Rasheda and her family had not been supposed to come today as her aunt Anwara was suffering serious breathing trouble, and it was decided that once she was better they would come with some other group. However, it was because of Rasheda that they had come today.

Long ago there had been some talk and negotiation about a marriage between Rasheda and Farid. That the marriage had never taken place had been due to the uncertainty of Farid's future; he could not even think of marriage until he had managed to get permanent employment. Now Rasheda had not wanted Farid and his family to leave Dhaka before her. She had cried and insisted so much that finally her father and mother had to pack their things and leave.

It had been settled earlier that Shaokat would wait each day at Kamtapur station. He would take whoever had come from the other side of the border to a suitable place, and today he was escorting Farid's party.

Everyone was walking in silence when suddenly Rasheda's father, Ramzan, called out, "Shaokat-bhai –"

"Yes?" Shaokat answered without turning around.

"What's the situation at this place we're going to?"

"There's been no trouble yet, but –"

"But what?"

"It seems that the people in the area know that we have come."

Farid was coming along a little way back, the big box on his head, the bag over his shoulder, and Anwara on his arm. She was now weighing very heavily on him.

Farid's ears suddenly pricked up at Shaokat's words. Before Ramzan could answer, he said, "I heard that the place was an open field where nobody lives."

"That's quite right," said Shaokat.

"Then?"

Shaokat appreciated the implication in Farid's question. He said,

"You see, son, you'll not find anything more dangerous in all the world than human eyes and ears. Go to the jungle, or hide in the sea, someone or other will see you. And for every one who sees you, ten others will hear about it." He shortened a little the long steps he was taking, and went on, "The day before yesterday, Khaled went the four miles to the market at Barhauli to buy flour, dal, salt and chilis. When he got there, he heard the people talking about us – where we had come from, how we had suddenly taken over a field – all that. It was clear to him that someone or other must have seen us."

For a full three days they had not eaten or slept well. They had been continually on the move, on train, bus, cycle rickshaw, bullock dray, and now on foot. All the energy had drained out of them and they were immensely tired. Panting, stumbling along the rough, unmade road, they somehow managed to keep their bodies upright and go on walking. However, Shaokat's words had sent a chill up their spines. Ramzan asked the question everyone was thinking, "Will we be able to stay here, then, Shaokat-bhai?"

Emphatically Shaokat said, "We just have to try. Don't worry, Ramzan-bhai. I'm sure things will work out all right."

Following some twenty feet behind, Farid, appreciating what he had just heard, looked at Shaokat with immense respect. He had heard that in 1947 he had gone to East Pakistan with thousands of others from the Bihar countryside. At the outset Shaokat had played no small part in the settling of so many ordinary, poor Biharis in Dhaka. He had tried to offer the same opportunities to everyone, sympathising with all their requests. And again, forty years later, he was just as ardent in leading almost every day small groups of people who had crossed the border back to the homes of their forefathers. Shaokat never broke down, never let adversity get the better of him, and under no circumstances would he ever admit defeat. Farid revered this supremely optimistic man.

Ramzan had nothing more to say on the issue. He felt as though the last remnant of his vitality had been sapped away.

And so they went on, and on.

As he walked, Farid's mind became distracted. He had studied a little history at school and college. He could not talk much about the Hindu and Buddhist periods and had no idea at all about his ancestors during those times. He could only talk of the past two hundred years during which, for a few generations, they were Indian Muslims and citizens of British India. Then, with Partition, they had gone to Dhaka and become Pakistani. After that, they became Bangladeshis – at least in name. And right now he had no idea what their identity was as they walked on over Indian soil under this hazy dawn sky.

Like those stateless, anonymous adventurers of ancient times, they were travelling in quest of freedom and an assured identity. Who could say whether or not they would get it?

Just before the sun came up, Farid and his party reached the middle of a vast lowland some distance off the road. Here some thirty or forty shacks had been put up, made from bamboo, tiles, hessian, and old cast-off tin, and belonged to those folk who had set out earlier from Dhaka. None of them had woken up yet in this refugee colony that had sprung up virtually overnight in the middle of a desolate, silent field.

Shaokat announced, "We've arrived. You've had a really hard time of it for three days. Now you can have some rest."

They put down their luggage from their heads and shoulders and let their bodies relax and drop to the ground. Quickly Anwara was lain on her dirty shawl. After the strain of so much travel her chest rose and fell like a bellows.

Sitting to one side of them Farid eagerly looked all around. Shaokat had described it exactly. Wherever one looked, as far as one could see, there was not a sign of any human habitation. In one direction the ground seemed to be stony all the way to the horizon, while in the opposite direction much of the region was covered by marshland which was luxuriant with green, long-stemmed reeds. Alongside the marshes was extensive woodland with tall *simar* and *karaiya* trees, on the tops of which numerous heron sat silently, their wings wrapped around themselves.

Shaokat started to call loudly, "Hey, Osman-bhai, Rustam, Nababzan, Auntie Rahima! How much longer are you going to stay asleep! Come on now, get up, get up and come out here!"

At first one or two people, then, one by one, about a hundred came out of the shacks. Seeing the newcomers one of them said, "Oh, so you've just arrived?"

Feebly Ramzan said, "Yes. But it was almost the death of us."

Osman said, "Yes, you have to go such a long way on foot. It's a bone-breaking business. Did you strike any trouble on the way?"

"No."

"No suspicious Indians?"

"No."

"That's good. This is such a big country. Millions of people. Hard to keep anything to yourself here!"

Everything went all right then. Those who had already set up huts would share them with Farid and his group for three or four days, then they would go to the market at Barhauli and get some tiles and old tin with which to set up their own huts.

Farid seemed to be listening to everyone's conversation from a distance. In fact, three days back, he had experienced a kind of excitement within himself about crossing the border and coming over here. Now, having come to the middle of this vast field, that excitement had suddenly increased a few times over. He had heard that Manpatthal village was not very far from here, the village that his grandfather and his wife and children had left for East Pakistan forty years ago. An intense urgency to see the village of his ancestors pressed on him like a persistent demon squatting on his shoulders.

Suddenly Farid asked, "Uncle Shaokat, where is Manpatthal village?"

Shaokat, who was talking with the others, turned around to look at Farid. "Four miles from here is Barhauli market," he said. "Manpatthal is another two miles from there. Why do you want to know?"

"I want to go and see our village."

"Not yet, son," said Shaokat. "Wait a few more days and see if things are all right. The village isn't far. You can go if you like when the time's right. That's my village, too, but I haven't gone there yet, either."

All those who had come here from Dhaka had their origins in Manpatthal or one of its surrounding villages. They all joined with Shaokat in saying that they had not yet been to see their forefathers' land, nor had they been anywhere else, either. Afraid and apprehensive, they had kept to this stony place, although one or two of them had gone, with great caution, to get some supplies from the Barhauli market.

Farid could understand their attitude, and of course no one wanted to take any risks. While this had, indeed, been their country forty years ago, none of them belonged here any more. It would be too dangerous to go and see the land of their fathers – or of their birth – so no one had ventured out in that direction.

Farid said nothing more.

Shaokat had made arrangements for them for the time being. Until their shack was built, Habiba and Farid would stay with Osman and his folk. Rasheda and Anwara would stay with Nababzan and his family. Rustam and Gahar Sheikh would be responsible for Rasheda's two brothers and their parents.

After their midday meal Farid and the others sat down around Shaokat. No more people would come from Dhaka today, so Shaokat did not have to rush back to Kamtapur.

In the gleaming blue sky the sun was starting its decline towards the west. There was still a little heat in the sun but not enough to burn one's skin, and the wind gusted haphazardly over the open field. Usually everybody likes the sunshine and breezes of the month of Phalgun.

There was no talk about their future in India.

Farid said, "Uncle Shaokat, how long can we remain hidden here? On the way here you said that many people knew about us. They might find us out. Who knows whether or not they'll move us on? There's also something else I have to say."

"What?" asked Shaokat.

"We could bring only a very little money from Dhaka. If we don't get work, how will we get the money to survive? We'll have to move from here."

Everyone nodded his support of Farid's words, saying things like "True. That's right."

Shaokat had listened intently to what Farid had to say and observed the reaction of the others. Slowly he said, "I am mindful of all that you have said, son. But be patient. I've found out about someone from here who, I think, will relieve us of a lot of our hardship. You'll meet him in three or four days."

Along with all the others, Farid asked, "Who is he?"

Shaokat explained that he could not tell his name just yet, but he was the very powerful leader of a political party. In his name the tiger and the kid would drink at the same pond. Indeed, he was the only one who could ensure their survival, but it was no easy matter to arrange a meeting with him.

"Who told you about him?" Farid, and many of the others too, waited anxiously for the answer to his question.

Shaokat replied, "On either side of the border there are so many middlemen because of so much demand, you know? I found out about him from one of them."

Farid had his doubts. He said, "What if you can't get a meeting with him?"

"I'll get one. This is a matter of life and death."

There was a pause, after which Farid said, "May I ask one more thing, Uncle Shaokat?"

"Why only one?" said Shaokat. "Ask me ten, twenty, as many as you like. Go ahead."

"If we don't stay in this field, it would be good to go to our villages. Will those who have settled on our land give us some little space to live?"

Shaokat smiled at Farid's naivete. Although he was quite well educated, he had a child's mind on many matters. He probably believed that the world was swarming with saints and holy men and that one could have what he wanted simply by holding out one's hand. Shaokat could see as clear as a picture the likely consequences of people like him, who were not Indian nor Bangladeshi nor Pakistani, coming under cover into an independent country for refuge, making known their wish for some land. He laid a hand on Farid's shoulder and said gently, "Farid, son. No one is going to give you a square inch of land. What you have lost, you'll never get back. Do you understand that?"

Three days passed since Farid's group arrived, during which time some new people came from across the border.

On the fourth day, after a breakfast of leftover chapatis and molasses, Shaokat left for Kamtapur to bring some more people, and as the morning drew on, Farid decided that he would go to Manpatthal that day. It was as though some powerful force were drawing him to the home of his ancestors.

Some had made a neat and tidy space in front of their shacks and were sitting about casually, chatting; there was no question yet of the men looking for work. The women, of course, had lit a fire of wood and straw and were making chapatis; they, too, felt no urgency for anything. Having come such a long way on their daring expedition to the middle of this field to live under the shadow of uncertainty, they had nothing in particular to do for the time being, day or night, other than eat.

Farid walked off towards the marshland. He had learnt earlier from Osman how to get to Barhauli; once there, he could ask people exactly how to get to Manpatthal.

As Farid approached the marsh, he heard, "Hey, listen –"

He looked around and saw Rasheda. She was as slender as a reed, and her face and features were sharply defined. Her skin was the colour of ripened wheat, and her big eyes glowed with an amazing magic. She was nineteen or twenty. Rasheda was looking at him the way she used to when they lived in Dhaka, and he had no way of avoiding her eyes, or of moving one step from her.

Rasheda came close to him and asked, "Where are you going?"

Farid had thought that he would not tell anyone about going to Manpatthal. He said, "Nowhere in particular. Just wandering around for a bit."

"Nonsense."

"What do you mean?"

"You're going to Manpatthal."

Farid was taken aback. "No, no," he said. "What are you talking about?"

Rasheda continued to hold her gaze on him. She said, "Don't think you can throw dust in my eyes. Come on. I'll go with you."

Having been found out there was nothing he could do. Farid said, "It's a long way. About six miles. Then it's another six miles back. It'll be too much for you."

"Don't worry about that. I won't walk any further than you."

"No, no. Look. Be serious."

"I'm not listening to your excuses. I'm going. You know how determined Rasheda can be."

Farid had to bow to the inevitable.

Between the wood and the marsh ran a narrow, unmade road. Having taken that for about half a mile they came up onto the main road, which led straight to Barhauli. On either side were harvested, open fields. They walked along chatting and looking at the countless birds in the sky, and by the time they reached Barhauli it was well after midday.

Barhauli could be described as a small town, and was, in general, a busy place with many people. Electric light had come there, and the town was bustling with cycle rickshaws and bullock drays, and among them were also some auto-rickshaws and motor scooters. Most of the road was sealed, and on either side were many houses of both one and two storeys. There were, of course, houses with tin roofs as well as those with tiles. On one side was a flourishing market.

They were not sure whether or not they would get anything to eat in Manpatthal, so they bought a few things at a sweetshop in the market and asked the shopkeeper the way to Manpatthal. When they came out, they heard the shouts of a great crowd of people. Farid and Rasheda waited where they were.

At first none of the shouting could be understood until a little later when a huge demonstration, shouting slogans, came and circled around the crossroads. Now they could be clearly heard.

"In the coming election, give your vote to –"

"Ajiblal Singh! Ajiblal Singh!"

"Our society's hope is Ajiblal –"

"May he live forever! May he live forever!"

"Long live Ajiblal –"

"The pride of our nation!"

"Place your mark beside –"

"The symbol of the elephant! The symbol of the elephant!"

"Vote for Ajiblal –"

"Long live the symbol of the elephant!"

Farid placed his mouth close to Rasheda's ear and said quietly, "There's going to be an election."

They had seen elections and demonstrations and rallies and all in Dhaka, so all of this was not unfamiliar to them. Rasheda nodded slightly and said, "Yes."

By now the slogan-shouting demonstration was heading towards Farid and Rasheda, so they could no longer remain standing there;

they went off down a narrow street to their left. Then, after leaving Barhauli and its market behind them, Farid and Rasheda came up onto a sealed road. The sweetshop man had told them that this road ran beside Manpatthal. It also passed through open, harvested fields, and in the distance a peasants' village could be seen among the trees.

There were many tongas drawn by frail and skinny horses on the road, and there were long-distance buses, bullock and buffalo drays, and trucks. Farid and Rasheda kept to one side of the traffic. As they got closer and closer to Manpatthal, a storm of anxiety and excitement blew up inside Farid. It was not clear what Rasheda was thinking as she skipped along briskly like a bird beside him.

After walking two miles they approached Manpatthal. They learned from people they asked on the road that they should now leave the highway and take a turn to the right. A little way through the fields was Manpatthal village.

Farid had a strange sensation walking through those fields with Rasheda still skipping along beside him. Soon they came to Manpatthal. The sweetshop man had told them that Manpatthal was a dairy village, and all around them numerous cows and buffalo were grazing.

It was the middle of the day and the sun was directly overhead. The heat had increased greatly, but the breeze continued to blow strongly.

Although they had reached Manpatthal, Farid did not go straight into the village but just stood stock-still on the outskirts, keeping Rasheda from going any further, either. As Rasheda stood beside Farid, it seemed she had caught some of his anxiety and excitement.

After a long while Rasheda said, "What's the matter? Aren't you going in?"

With a start Farid said, "Yes. Let's go." As they walked, he lowered his voice considerably as he said, "Be careful. Don't tell anyone that we come from Dhaka. Remember that."

"I'll remember."

A little way into the village they came to a large pond. Farid said, "Let's sit beside the pond and have something to eat. Then we can look for where our ancestors' houses and land were."

Then, having eaten some bread and sweets, washed down with water from the pond, they set out in quest of their forefathers' lands.

Farid had been born in East Pakistan. He had never before been here. In Dhaka he had often heard his father and grandmother talk about Manpatthal, but he had never felt any kind of attraction to the place; nothing had ever swelled up inside him for an insignificant, unfamiliar tract of land in a village in far distant northern Bihar. His forefathers' land was just a word, no more than a vague idea, to him then. But having set foot on its soil, Farid felt that, although he had not been born here or seen the place before, the roots of his being were in Manpatthal.

An idea that preoccupied Farid was that with the Partition in 1947 his and Rasheda's grandfathers had lost everything in leaving this village and going to Dhaka. Now, exactly forty years later, their grandson and grand-daughter had come here in search of refuge and, perhaps, identity.

Like single-minded expeditionists, Farid and Rasheda set to looking around Manpatthal. But the younger villagers could not tell them whether or not there had ever been anyone here by the name of Farid's grandfather, Mudassar Ali, or Rasheda's grandfather, Samsuddin Hossain. However, they had heard that a long time ago some Muslims used to live in this village, but where they had gone, no one knew, and there were no Muslim families here now.

A little daunted, they nevertheless continued their search with undiminished enthusiasm, till at last the oldest man in Manpatthal told them that Mudassar Ali and Samsuddin Hossain had, in fact, lived in this village. He had even known them. A thrill ran through them like an electric shock. Farid asked, "Could you please tell us where they lived?" His voice was quaking with tension and excitement.

Slowly shaking his head the old man said, "There's nothing left, son. Then he pointed out a place in the distance where there was a bare cornfield and nothing else, no sign of a house anywhere. Farid and Rasheda went and stood there awhile, seemingly entranced. Then, somewhat benumbed, they went back.

Before the afternoon had advanced too far, they came back to the Barhauli market. This time, too, they saw another long demonstration, shouting slogans to each corner of the sky as it snaked along the roads.

"Long live –"

"Devout patriot, Rambanabas Chaube!"

"Who will be our representative?"

"Rambanabas Chaube!"

"Who will be a minister?"

"Rambanabas Chaube!"

"Who will give us perfect rule?"

"Rambanabas Chaube!"

"In the coming election give your vote to –"

"Rambanabas Chaube!"

"Who will work for us all?"

"Rambanabas Chaube!"

"As long as there is the sun and the moon there will be –"

"Rambanabas Chaube!"

"Long live –"

"Rambanabas Chaube!"

Rambanabas Chaube's election demonstration was a little bigger than Ajiblal's and a lot more spectacular. But Farid did not notice that aspect of it. He was thinking of their spacious home in Manpatthal with its paved floors, brick walls and, of course, its tin roof. But what had they seen just a little time ago? Now Farid felt besieged by disappointment.

Just before evening while there was still some daylight Farid and Rasheda reached their temporary refuge in the middle of that bare and stony tract of land.

About seven days went by.

In that time about a hundred more people arrived from the other side. Some eight or ten new shacks of bamboo, hessian, tiles and whatever were hastily put up and provision was made for the building of a few more. Altogether there were about two hundred and fifty people there now, and things were sufficient for accommodating that number for some time.

One morning after breakfast Shaokat said to Farid, "I want you to go somewhere with me, son."

Without any question Farid answered, "I will."

A little while later, they set off. They passed the marsh and crossed the unmade road, and when they came up onto the highway Shaokat said, "Do you know where we're going?"

Farid recognised where he was. A few days earlier he and Rasheda had taken this road to Barhauli and then on to Manpatthal. But Farid still did not know for sure where Shaokat was taking him – Barhauli or Manpatthal. Without answering he just looked inquisitively at Shaokat.

Shaokat answered his own question. "We're going to Barhauli town to meet that political leader. He's an important man – speaks English and all that. I need a literate man like him, so I've brought you along." Shaokat then went on without a break, saying, "I felt that we shouldn't wait any longer. It's best we meet him before we run into any trouble or maybe even get forced out. We'll straightaway fall at his feet."

Shaokat was very far-sighted, astute and intelligent. In his sixty years he had been a witness to national divisions and their countless accompanying riots, slaughter and other frenzies of violence. His vast experience of life had taught him to make correct decisions. He explained to Farid that if they were to stay in India political protection would be absolutely necessary. That was the purpose behind their excursion today.

Suddenly Farid asked, "Who are we going to see, Uncle? Ajiblal Singh or Rambanabas Chaube?" As he spoke he realised his blunder. It was now obvious that he had been to Barhauli, and therefore to Manpatthal as well.

Shaokat looked at Farid in considerable surprise. "How do you know those names?" he asked. "Have you been to Barhauli?"

Farid hung his head down.

Shaokat's eyes flared up. "You also went to Manpatthal, then?"

Barely audibly Farid answered, "Yes."

Shaokat said nothing for some time. Then he said, "All right, then. Later we'll hear about Manpatthal. First tell me how you heard of Ajiblal Singh and Rambanabas Chaube."

Farid then told him about the two demonstrations.

"Oh, I see," said Shaokat. "Well, we're now going to Rambanabas Chaube."

At one end of Barhauli town was the market, at the other was Chaturvedi House. In the middle of a vast compound was a huge, old-style home like a fort, at one end of which was a Ram-Sita temple. The compound was enclosed by a ten-foot high, three-foot thick wall. At the front was an enormous iron gate with leaf doors cut into it, at which was posted day and night a large sentry with a curled moustache, a rifle in his hand and a bandoleer around his neck.

When Shaokat and Farid reached Chaturvedi House, they told the sentry that they wished to see Rambanabas Chaube. The sentry, frowning, looked them up and down, and in a harsh voice he roared, "Clear off, you bastards!"

Shaokat and Farid stayed where they were, continuing to implore the sentry, who just as persistently refused them entry. The sentry's temper gradually got shorter as his voice got louder and, screaming, he warned them that if they did not go, he would open fire and blow their heads off.

Then came a deep and hoarse voice from inside saying, "Guard, let those men in."

On the other side of the gate was a big open space in which was parked an old-time, open-roofed car, two jeeps and a horse-drawn carriage. Two men were cleaning and polishing the car and the carriage.

Beyond, on the spacious marble veranda of the ground floor of the main house, Rambanabas lay back in a lounge chair, reading the post-edition of the newspaper. On a low table beside him were many other newspapers neatly arranged. There were also three or four urgent files, a pen and an expensive writing pad. Beneath the table a little smoke was rising from the bowl of a hookah.

Rambanabas was a robust sixty-five-year-old. Even at his age most of his hair had still not turned grey and he had all his own teeth, although he did, of course, wear glasses. He had a straight neck and a sharp-featured face, and his body had no excess flesh.

The veranda was about three feet above the ground, and Shaokat and Farid, apprehensive and almost holding their breath, approached Rambanabas and stood on the ground beneath him. Bowing and touching their hands to their foreheads they said, "Salaam, your honour."

Looking at them intently over his gold frames Rambanabas said, "What's the matter? Why all the hullabaloo?"

"We wanted to meet your honour, but the guard wouldn't let us in."

"Who are you? I've never seen you before."

Shaokat explained that they had come only recently but that he had been a resident of these parts forty years ago.

Rambanabas furrowed his brow. "What's your business?" he demanded.

Shaokat, looking anxious, gave a detailed account of how, after Partition, they had gone to East Pakistan; then, when Bangladesh had come into being, what their circumstances had been in Dhaka and how they had had no alternative but to return to India – and so on and so on.

Rambanabas reacted as though with an electric shock. He sat bolt upright and said, "You've come into India like thieves in the night! Infiltrators." And he emphasised it by saying it again in English. "Do you know what a serious offence this is?"

Shaokat and Farid were bent forward, their hands folded. With bated breath Shaokat said, "Your honour, you are our mother and our father, our saviour. There is no way we can go back. If we can't stay here, we'll be finished, along with our children. We are dependent on your mercy."

Rambanabas thought for quite some time, then he said, "How many of you are there?"

"About two hundred and fifty, your honour."

"Are there any more coming?"

"Yes."

"How many?"

"Quite a few. But to this place, not much more than seven or eight hundred."

There was a slight pause, and then Rambanabas asked, "Who told you about me?"

Shaokat did not name the touts. He simply said deferentially, "Who in all the world does not know your name? I heard of you when I came here, sir."

Rambanabas was quite happy with the flattery but he did not show it. "All right, then," he said, "You can go now."

Timidly Shaokat asked, "But what about us?"

"Give me a few days to think."

Although Rambanabas had told them to go, they still stood there. He became a little impatient and said, "What's the matter? What are you waiting for?"

Shaokat bowed his head a little further and said, "Your honour, many have come to know about us. What if they should cause some trouble?"

"You come to me in four days."

Shaokat was not brave enough to ask any more questions. "Yes, sir," he said, and, having offered their salaams a few more times, they left.

Rambanabas Chaube had not exactly reassured them. Of course, he had told them to come back in four days, although it was not clear that he would then tell them what he would do. Farid, in suspense, walked close to Shaokat. Shaokat had taken him to speak English but there had been no need for him at all. For the whole time at Rambanabas's mansion he had been merely a silent spectator. Now he asked all of a sudden, "Do you think it was wise to speak to Chaube-ji, Uncle?"

Shaokat was lost in thought as he walked and did not catch the point of Farid's question. "What do you mean?" he said.

"These political men. What if they make trouble?" In other words Farid had considerable doubt about the trustworthiness of politicians.

Shaokat said, "We have to get support from someone or other, and apart from political leaders there's no one who can protect us. Let's wait and see."

Farid said nothing more.

Then, after only two days, not four, a couple of short-necked, rowdy types came thumping their sticks and shouting, "Who are Shaokat Mian and Farid Ali?"

Panic spread instantly through the makeshift settlement in the middle of the field. Afraid, Shaokat and Farid said, "We are. Why?"

"Chaube-ji has told us to bring you to him."

Shaokat could not imagine why they had been summoned in two days and not four. Timidly he inquired, "Do you know why the master has sent for us?"

"No."

Shaokat asked no more questions. Giving some signal of encouragement to the alarmed people all around them, Shaokat went with Farid and the two men to Barhauli.

Two days earlier Rambanabas had been alone on the marble ground-floor veranda of Chaturvedi House. Today he was surrounded by four or five men seated on comfortable, cushioned chairs. It could be surmised from their looks and their dress that they were all prominent and respectable people. They were loudly and excitedly discussing something among themselves. They stopped when they saw Shaokat and Farid.

"These are the ones I told you about," said Rambanabas.

His companions looked intently at Shaokat and Farid. One of them said, "So these are the infiltrators! I'd heard about them before. They've taken over the lowland by the marsh and set up huts there."

A couple of others seconded him. "We've heard about them, too."

As they listened, Shaokat and Farid cringed and perspired in fear.

Rambanabas said to Shaokat, "I've called you here today on some urgent business. The other day you said that two hundred and fifty people had come from the other side."

In a shaky voice, Shaokat answered, "Yes, sir."

Rambanabas then turned to his companions and said, "You know that in the coming election Ajiblal will do well."

"Yes," they all said together.

"How many more sure votes do I need to win?"

"About six or seven hundred."

"Is that right?"

"Yes, it is."

Rambanabas turned back to Shaokat and Farid and said, "The

other day you said that another six or seven hundred are coming here from the other side. Have they come yet?"

"No, sir. I hear that they'll be here in a few days." Shaokat seemed to be holding his breath.

There was silence for a few moments, then Rambanabas said, "Do you know that we are having an election in eight months?"

Looking at Farid, Shaokat said, "I didn't know. But there were two election rallies in the Barhauli market. One for you, the other for Ajiblal Singh."

"Yes." Rambanabas sat swaying from side to side. He said, "For so long no one has cared much about elections. But Ajiblal has entered the hustings and we cannot remain sitting on our hands and feet. That son of a pig is throwing money about with both hands." His tone then became very grave as he said, "Be careful you don't fall in with him."

Shaokat looked frightened as he said, "No, master, no."

"And listen. Vote in the coming election. Vote for me. And the ones coming later must vote for me, too."

Farid now had gathered the courage to say, "But, master, we're illegals. How can we vote in this country?"

Rambanabas knew what he was thinking. Illegal immigrants certainly had no right to vote. He said, "All necessary arrangements will be made. But be warned, if you don't vote for me, you'll all be buried alive."

Shaokat spoke up frantically, "Yes, yes, master! We'll vote for you! That's no empty promise. But what about us? A few days ago Farid went to Manpatthal. They are now ploughing where our forefathers' homes had been. Where will we live? What will we do?"

"Nothing can be done there. But before you vote, you'll be as good as Indian. Then we can make arrangements."

Shaokat and Farid said nothing.

Rambanabas went on. "Don't tell anyone what we've talked about today. Keep your mouths absolutely shut."

"Yes, master."

Some more days passed, during which time a few hundred more people came from across the border.

On account of the election an atmosphere of tension gradually grew in the district. Then, one drowsy noon-time, two men came and registered all their names on the electoral roll. Three days later, on Rambanabas's instructions, they were given ration cards, so assuring their Indian identity.

Generally, the days passed uneventfully. There was still a lingering of worry, anxiety and fear, but so far no one had come and caused trouble. But after their electoral roll registration and provision of ration cards about three hundred of Ajiblal's men came one afternoon and created a disturbance.

"Down with –"

"Illegal immigrants!"

"Infiltrating foreigners –"

"Get out of India!"

They made a noise for a few hours, then left. Shaokat and Farid ran panting to Chaturvedi House where, out of breath and looking terrified, they related the whole episode to Rambanabas.

Rambanabas was not particularly moved. In a tone of unconcern he said, “Those bastards can only make a noise. Your names are on the electoral roll, and you have received your ration cards. Now you are Indian. No son of a pig has the power to lay a finger on you. Don’t worry. Just remember to vote for me.”

“Oh, yes! For the life of us we won’t forget!”

A few hours later, as he was returning with Shaokat to their makeshift home in the middle of all that stony land, ideas were whirling around inside Farid’s head. In the British period they had been Indian, then Pakistani, and after that, Bangladeshi. And now, forty years later, on account of the election they would have a new identity.

Farid walked along as though in a dream, offering in his mind a thousand salaams to the democratic process.

# THE DESTINATION

## *gantabya*

It was still night and not even the crows were awake when Janaklal Mishra set out by car from Biloniya through the pervasive fog. He had a long way to go – forty miles – to the insignificant little town of Naharpura and the house of Chaturanan, his daughter Parvati's father-in-law, whom he was to meet that day, an appointment he had arranged by letter. Parvati's future depended on this meeting. For her it was a matter of life and death.

Janaklal's younger brother-in-law, Maheshwar, also lived in Naharpura. After completing his important business with Chaturanan, Janaklal would stay the night with him and then go on to his own village about ten miles east of Naharpura the following morning.

The car in which Janaklal was travelling was probably one of the first ever made. It would be difficult to say what it had looked like originally. From the driver's seat forwards it was, perhaps, what it had been like at first, but apart from its huge steering wheel, an unreliable engine under a rusty and dented bonnet, two ungainly-looking headlights and battered mudguards, there was nothing much remaining of the original. Thick layers of hessian had been laid over the wooden decking beneath the driver's seat, and when the roof had been smashed, a tarpaulin cover was put over it, rather like the canopy of a bullock dray; the back of the vehicle was quite empty.

While running, the car trembled like an epileptic. The engine would give out a sound like hiccups and it would seem at that moment as though it would not hold together any longer. Indeed, it was not possible for this car to make the forty miles from Biloniya to Naharpura in one stretch. As the engine would give out after every three or four miles, it would then need a rest of at least half an hour, so travelling in this stop-start way would mean that Naharpura would not be reached before evening.

Sitting at the steering wheel was Musafir, a spirited young fellow with a dirty *gamchha* wrapped around his head like a turban. Behind him, under the canopy, sat Janaklal. He was about sixty, a corpulent, heavy looking man with a round face, bright skin, and big eyes. In the never-cut thick tuft at the back of his head a flower was pinned, on his forehead were three lines in white sandal paste, and there was a tip of sandal paste on the lobe of each ear. He was wearing a dhoti and a short-sleeve panjabi.

Janaklal was a staunch and devout high-caste brahman, strictly observant of the laws of touch and caste hierarchy and embracing wholeheartedly all the orthodoxy and traditions of his inherited superior status. He had never worked for a living; indeed, he was alarmed at the new laws that maintained conditions of equality in offices in independent India with the effect of indulging the people of the lower castes and the minority communities. To work side by side with such people and come into bodily contact with them was to him unthinkable. In his view there was a conspiracy at work throughout the whole country to minimise brahmans. But all was not lost, for even in these darkest of days many people still held at least some respect and devotion to God and to brahmans, so enabling Janaklal to support his own family by going from house to house officiating at ceremonies of worship, performing sacrifices and reading the scriptures.

About seven days back Janaklal had gone to Biloniya, a prominent market town on the bank of one of the various offshoots of the Ganges. The region had been devastated by a continual drought over the past three years; not a drop of rain had fallen during the monsoon seasons and everything all around had been scorched or reduced to ashes.

Should no rain fall this year either, the people would not survive. So to propitiate the angry god of the rains, the wholesale merchants of Biloniya, along with the shopkeepers and the villagers from all around, were making preparations for a sacrificial worship of Varuna, the god of the sky, and they had called in Janaklal to ensure that everything was done strictly in accordance with the scriptures.

The sacrifice had been completed the previous afternoon. Janaklal had spent the night there and left this morning. However, the people of Biloniya had raised strong objections to this, as the atmosphere along the route he would take to Naharpura had become very heated. There had been large-scale riots in that region a few months back, and injuries had been sustained and lives had been lost. Of course, order had been restored after the Central Reserve Police had arrived.

Seven days back, when Janaklal had come here from his village, he did not notice any renewed outbreak of unrest in the region as he passed Naharpura. Maybe the pronounced excitement surrounding the sacrifice had staved off any recurrence of riot. Time and again the people of Biloniya had made it clear that Janaklal should return home after three or four days, having given things a chance to settle down, but he did not listen to these warnings as he simply had to go to Naharpura today to save Parvati. He had not been able to give any of the promised dowry at the time of her wedding, and for that reason the situation at her in-laws' house had become terribly difficult. Clearly, the girl had not told him everything, but he could guess that they had started to beat her, so Janaklal had let it be known that today he would come and give some money to Parvati's father-in-law. There was nothing he could do if riots should break out again. Moreover, Janaklal also had some confidence in himself. He was a man learned in the scriptures, known and revered by almost everyone for fifty or sixty miles around. He could not conceive that anyone might harm him.

Janaklal had travelled quite a long way from Biloniya now, and the troublesome car was rattling and chugging along over the stony road.

Janaklal was leaning back under the canopy beside a great pile of goods. There were fifteen pairs of new dhotis and saris, a sewn-up sack of rice, one of dal and one of potatoes, a tin of pure buffalo ghee, a tin of ground mustard-seed oil, about forty coconuts, a basketful of betel nut, many new kitchen utensils, and all sorts of other odds and ends.

Janaklal had never been one to hold out his hand to anyone, taking only what he had justly earned from his religious offices, but bearing in mind his concern for Parvati he had demanded this time a little more than the sacrifice might have warranted. The people of Biloniya had not disappointed him; indeed, what they had given him was quite beyond his expectations. And as well as the foodstuffs and the clothing he had received about five thousand rupees. Who could think of getting so much for such a sacrifice? It was equivalent to almost six months' earnings.

In front Musafir sat up straight and kept a firm hand on the wheel but he could not keep the ungainly old car under control. It seemed to want to go its own way, almost running off the edge of the road, on either side of which was a dried up ditch about ten or twelve feet deep, so if the car should crash into it, it would not be seen and that would be the end of it and those on board. Musafir, his teeth clenched, was trying to steer the car along the middle of the road, while strange grunts and growls of anger kept coming from his mouth, along with such expressions as "You bastard of a car" and "You son of a pig, I'll kill you". Indeed, there was a steady stream of such language all the way.

Musafir had once been the driver of Janaklal's bullock dray for quite a few years. After that he had gone to Purnea and learned to drive a car, and now he drove for Janaklal. If Janaklal had to perform rituals and offer prayers anywhere nearby, he would go in his own bullock dray, but if he had to go some distance, he would send for Musafir who would take him and bring him home, just as he was doing today. If those on whose behalf he offered prayers should need to speak with him, they would pay Musafir his wages and the hire of the car, and give him food as well.

Janaklal could just make out Musafir's indistinct ranting. In fact, he was preoccupied with worry for Parvati and had no interest in anything else. Unwittingly he put his hand in the inside pocket of his panjabi, where he was keeping safe fifty crisp, new, one-hundred rupee notes, money which had brought him considerable peace of mind. Earlier he had got together two thousand rupees for Parvati's father-in-law's house, money he had brought with him from the village when he went to Biloniya and which was now in the right-hand pocket of his punjabi – altogether seven thousand rupees. If he took this money to Naharpura, his daughter could enjoy some peace, at least for some time. Then he would have to find another thirteen thousand – but that could wait for the time being.

Janaklal removed his hand from his pocket and looked out from under the canopy. It was now well into the morning and there was no longer any trace of the fringe of fog that earlier had hung everywhere. The sun had risen high in the sky and the Jyaistha morning had become very warm with a hot breeze blowing.

On either side of the road moribund trees hung over the dried up canals. Their dry leaves had long since fallen off, leaving only the thin, rough limbs reaching sadly up to the sky. Only three or four tiled or thatched houses could be seen, but no people anywhere. Wherever one looked, there was a dry, dusty haze as far as the eye could see. The fields all around were cracking up, the earth having broken up into dry clods not only on the surface but well below it. It seemed a very remote hope that one day this region would once again be covered with pleasant and green crop-bearing fields.

Somewhere a bird called, keeping some secret of its own, ringing through the stillness with a striking melancholy.

As he gazed out, Janaklal's eyes were suddenly drawn to the western sky where he saw a few stray, black clouds. The ritual had been completed only the day before, and this morning the first clouds of the year could be seen. His skin tingled to see such an immediate result of his sacrifice.

As a thrill of excitement ran through Janaklal, he heard Musafir's rough voice. "Pundit-ji." Everyone in the region called Janaklal by that name.

Janaklal turned around under the canopy and looked at Musafir. "What is it?"

Musafir said, "You've made a mistake."

Janaklal frowned. He asked irately, "What have I done wrong?"

"It would have been better to have stayed a few more days in Biloniya. The wholesalers and the shopkeepers all said so. But you wouldn't listen."

"Have you forgotten I have to be in Naharpura today?"

Musafir knew everything about Janaklal. He had been back from Purnea for about six months, but before that he had spent seven years in Janaklal's house. He knew that if Janaklal did not get to Naharpura today, Parvati's life would be at risk. He said, "Yes, yes. I know all about that. But –"

"You're worried about riots, aren't you?" said Janaklal.

"Of course!" said Musafir, raising his voice markedly.

Janaklal became impatient. Gesturing with both hands to the open fields on either side of them, he said, "Where is there a riot? Look! Can you see?"

Musafir turned to Janaklal. He said harshly, "Haven't you got ears, or are you totally deaf?"

No one spoke with Janaklal, the former master, in such a tone and in such a manner, but with Musafir it was a different matter. True, he was exceptionally headstrong, but more than that, he loved Janaklal with his life. Moreover, having lived in Janaklal's house for so many years Musafir had come to take liberties, like talking over the top of his master who, along with his wife, had indulged him for so long.

Janaklal suddenly became terribly angry and, raising his voice very loudly, he said, "You've got a big mouth! I won't have any more to do with you!"

Musafir did not look at all put out. So many times he had heard such empty threats. He said, "Don't get so angry. Keep a cool head and try to listen."

Although he had become a little curious, Janaklal nevertheless flared up in demanding, "And what am I going to hear?"

Musafir saw no point in answering. He just turned back and looked ahead.

Privately now Janaklal was a little embarrassed. Many times he had experienced evidence of Musafir's acute sight and hearing; the man was every bit as alert as a dog. He must certainly have heard something. So Janaklal pricked up his ears.

The car was now travelling very, very slowly, though it was quite likely that Musafir had wanted to reduce the speed.

Some minutes later, Janaklal thought that he could hear, coming from somewhere, the indistinct sound of some uproar. "What's that noise?" he asked.

With heavy sarcasm Musafir said, "Oh, you can hear something, then."

"Yes, yes, I can. Who is making that hullabaloo?"

"How would I know? Wherever you are, so am I. But it sounds like trouble."

Janaklal said nothing as he tried to discern the source and reason for the noise.

Musafir said, "What will I do, then? Turn around and go back to Biloniya?"

Janaklal now became quite heated. "Somewhere someone is creating an uproar and you want to turn back! You'll do nothing of the sort. What a coward!"

The car continued on.

After travelling some way the noise could no longer be heard. Janaklal discerned some misgiving on Musafir's face, and he asked in a very worried voice, "What is it? Can you hear something else?"

"No. But stay alert."

"Right."

The engine had become very hot and the bonnet had to be raised to let it cool down. After twenty minutes the car was on its way again.

The sun had now risen very high, and it was no longer possible to see directly overhead as the sky seemed veiled by the shimmering sunshine. The hot, dry wind was gusting and spreading the heat everywhere. Ever since his youth Janaklal had been a tireless traveller moving around from one side of Bihar to the other in any season of the year. Although the severe heat of Jyaistha bothered him, he was not greatly distressed by it.

However, his worries about Parvati returned to him as they drove on. After giving the seven thousand today, tomorrow he would have to find by hook or by crook the remaining thirteen thousand. Who could say how long it would take him to raise the money, or even if it could be raised at all before his death?

But before his thinking had advanced very far, he suddenly heard a tumultuous shouting and screaming coming from somewhere. Over Musafir's shoulder he could see in front and to the right for about a quarter of a mile a great number of tin-roofed houses, most of which were ablaze. About a hundred people of all ages were running and screaming like terrified beasts, crossing the highway to get to the large field on the other side, while another group of people wielding sticks, spears, axes and other deadly weapons were chasing after them. The assailants were screaming relentlessly, though what they were saying could not be determined from such a distance.

Musafir stopped the car. Turning around, he said, "Now what, Pundit-ji?" His face was white with fear.

Janaklal had listened to talk of riots for so long, but seeing one for the first time at such close quarters sent a chill down his spine. With a shaky voice he said, "Just sit there and say nothing."

By now the two groups had crossed the field on the left of the road and disappeared. In the distance to the right the village was burning; there was no one about and all seemed quite desolate. "Let's get away from here quickly," Janaklal said.

On account of having been running for three or four hours since early morning much of the power had gone out of the car. Although Janaklal had said 'quickly', the car could not get up much speed at all as it chugged along, but somehow they made some headway.

Once they had passed the village, a couple of other villages could be seen in the distance with coils of smoke spiralling up from them. Evidently the riots had spread. Janaklal and Musafir were not saying anything now and it seemed as though both of them had stopped breathing. Their one concern was how quickly they could get through this region.

Janaklal had no idea how long they had been travelling. But suddenly from the side of the road came someone's frightened, trembling voice, calling, "Pundit-ji!"

Janaklal was startled. Looking around he saw a large copse of old trees that had somehow managed to survive the intense three-year drought. Coming out of it were a young man and woman, probably a husband and wife. The young man was tall and thin, about twenty-three. He was wearing pajamas and a blue check shirt; he had a thin moustache, and bare feet. The woman was wearing a salwar-kameez of cheap cotton. She wore an ornament in her nose, earrings with floral ornaments set in stone, and coloured glass bangles. Both of them bore looks of terror on their faces.

In a choked voice Janaklal asked, "What? What is the matter?"

Musafir had not stopped the car. The young couple ran behind, and with hands folded called out anxiously to Janaklal, "Save us, Pundit-ji, please save us."

Janaklal knew what they wanted. He asked, "Why were you sitting in the wood over there?"

The young man told him that their village had been set on fire and that three or four people had been murdered. Who could say where all the others had fled to, pursued by the rioters?

"We too fled," said the young man. "But the situation – "He looked at his companion.

So far Janaklal had not taken much notice of the young woman, but now he observed her coarse hair, the dull look in her eyes, her hollow cheeks and sunken eyes and the dark shadows under them, and her skinny hands with the veins protruding. Her whole body seemed drained of blood and the bones could be seen under the skin of her scraggy neck – and yet she was so young!

Janaklal realised that the girl was suffering from some serious disease, so making it impossible for the young man to flee very far; in their fear they had hidden in the copse.

Anxiously the young man said, "Everyone in the world knows your goodness, Pundit-ji. Be gracious and save us."

Janaklal was embarrassed. He could not imagine what he could possibly do for this terrified young couple. He thought for a few moments, then said, "You should go to the police –"

"Where are the police? The station is about ten miles from here! We'll be killed before we get there!"

Musafir was not at all happy with Janaklal carrying on all this talk. In order to escape from the couple, he put his foot down on the accelerator a few times, but all that happened was that the car shook greatly and the engine gave off a strange rattling noise, gaining no speed at all.

Perplexed, Janaklal said, "Then what?"

"They've set up a camp at Chhattarpur. If you could get us there –"

Janaklal remembered that a few months back some of the villages of this region had been reduced to ashes by rioters and that a relief camp had been set up for them at Chhattarpur. No new houses had yet been built in those villages, and in that time the people had stayed in the camp under the protection of the Central Reserve Police. If they could just get to the camp, the young couple's fears would go. However, about ten miles from here there was an intersection at which Janaklal would turn to the north, while Chhattarpur was directly to the south. Moreover, there would be a major problem in taking the young couple in the car to Chhattarpur: the brahman's body cringed at the thought of physical contact with them under the vehicle's canopy.

Musafir looked over his shoulder in the front seat. Although in his faith there could be no objection to a high-caste brahman sitting beside this young man and woman on the way to Chhattarpur, he whispered a warning to Janaklal. "Don't let them into the car, Pundit-ji. Things are too hot around here and we don't want to get involved."

Janaklal was about to say something when suddenly a sound of frenzy came to him from his left. The slaughterers who a little earlier had chased away the group of terrified people were now coming back over the field by a roundabout path.

Catching a quick glance of the rioters the young man and woman fell into a panic. Their clothes had become soaked with sweat as they ran behind the car in the hot summer sun, and now their eyes radiated terror. Particularly the sick and frail girl could not go on. As she gathered together her last vestiges of energy, she could merely stagger on blindly.

In a cracked, harsh voice, the young man said, "Those men are coming back. They're going to kill us, Pundit-ji. Please do something–"

Janaklal could not decide what to do. If he took them into the car and the rioters saw them, his life and Musafir's would not be worth a penny. And then he was also very strongly bound to his brahman prejudices.

The young man went on mumbling, "Please do something, Pundit-ji, please do something," his Adam's apple rising and falling continually as he spoke.

The rioters were getting very close to them and suddenly Janaklal was alarmed and afraid. An intense storm seemed to have blown up inside him, and almost unwittingly he said, "Get in. Quickly."

This was what the young man had been so anxiously waiting for. As he ran, he picked up the girl in a flash, flung her into the moving car, and got in himself.

"You've made a mistake, Pundit-ji," said Musafir.

Maybe Janaklal did not hear him. He had noticed that the mob had seen the car and were running towards it. Janaklal had never been in such a dangerous situation before. At first he was confused. But in an instant he was possessed by the overwhelming realisation that, having accepted the young couple on board, he had to save their lives.

The car was lurching along slowly enough for the mob to catch up with them. The thought of what would happen to the young man and woman made Janaklal's blood run cold. To hide them from their murderers, he told them, "Lie down under these clothes." And he took out of a packet two new pieces of clothing which he threw over to them, saying, "Cover yourselves up completely." And the two young people lay down under the clothes, screened by the sacks of rice and dal.

However, the car could not go very far before the mob surrounded it, screaming at Musafir to stop. Many of them recognised Janaklal, and one of them said, "Oh, Pundit-ji. What are you doing here?"

Janaklal looked straight at them, unblinking. Everyone held a knife, a stick or a spear. The violent storm was raging in his heart. He told them where he was going and why.

The rioters were looking at the piles of clothes, the kitchen utensils, the tins of oil and ghee, and the other things under the canopy, and their eyes brightened. Someone said, "You've got a lot of goods there, Pundit-ji."

They could not see very well. Janaklal gulped and said, "Yes, the dues from my sacrifice."

"Tell us, will it rain this year, now that you have made the sacrifice?"

That was a good sign. It seemed that he, at least, would not be harmed. Janaklal said, "What can mortals do? Everything comes by the grace of God."

"That's right, indeed," one of them said. "Be on your way quickly. The situation's not good around here."

Janaklal did not say that it was because of them that the situation was not good. It was wise for him to keep his mouth shut for as long as possible.

When the men had surrounded the car, Musafir had turned off the engine. As he started it again, one of them said, pointing at the clothes and the dal and the rice and things, "Who's that?"

In spite of being so careful, the young man's hand was sticking out.

Janaklal froze for a moment, but then gathered himself again and said, "That's my nephew –"

"Then why is your nephew lying down like that?"

"He has a bad fever, so –"

One of them knew Janaklal well. He said, "But you don't have a brother, Pundit-ji, so how can you have a nephew?"

The breath seemed to have gone out of Janaklal, but somehow he managed to say, "He's the son of my cousin, not my brother."

The man seemed to have his doubts. "Let's see what sort of nephew he is," he said as he grabbed the young man's hand before Janaklal could stop him, and pulled him up. In the process, the cover also came off the girl, and the man sat her up too. Sarcastically, he said, "And so this Muslim bugger's your nephew and this is his lawfully wedded wife!"

Janaklal did not respond. His lips were trembling. This rash and incautious boy and girl had brought about their own undoing and had thrown him into great danger as well.

The reverence the mob had had for Janaklal just a few moments ago had now dissipated and their eyes flashed murder. Someone shouted out, "You bastard of a pundit, you tried to cover up this dog and his bitch with new clothes! You're no brahman! Now put them out – "But the others would not wait, and started to drag them out by the hands.

Janaklal begged fervently, "No, no, don't take them away."

"Shut up, you bastard!" one of them shouted violently.

Inexplicably, Janaklal had resolved to himself to save this terrified boy and girl. His voice shaking, he said, "What can I give you not to kill them?"

The mob were a little taken aback by this. They had a whispered discussion among themselves, after which they announced the price of the young couple's lives: two thousand rupees in cash, twenty coconuts, ten pairs of new dhotis and saris and a bag of rice.

Janaklal was stunned for a moment. It seemed that the whole world had been plunged into darkness before his eyes. Then he slowly took from his right pocket the two thousand rupees he had saved for the welfare of Parvati and handed it to the mob, and they took the coconuts and the rice and some of the clothes.

The car set off again.

They came across two more groups of rioters on the way, and they reckoned the remaining five thousand rupees and the rest of the goods paid as sacrificial dues as fair price for the lives of the young couple.

Having now lost everything Janaklal at first thought that someone had smashed each of his ribs with a hammer. But then his distress lessened. He decided that he could mortgage his land and take some money to Chaturanan-ji within fifteen days. During that time Parvati's welfare would be very uncertain, but what else could he do? He was bound by a promise to himself to save this young couple, and he had never reneged on a commitment in his life.

Just before evening they reached the crossroads.

So far Musafir had not said a word, but now, with intense bitterness, he said, "You've given away all your money. What a disaster for Parvati!"

Janaklal said, "It's not a disaster. She'll have to suffer a lot for a few days, that's all. Very soon I'll take some money to Chaturananji."

"But –"

"What?"

"Where will you get the money?"

Harshly Janaklal said, "That's none of your business."

Musafir was not brave enough to ask any more questions on the issue. He turned the car in the direction of Chhattarpura.

Janaklal said abruptly, "Hey! Not that way!"

"Parvati's father-in-law said to come as soon as you had the money," said Musafir. "Otherwise –"

"No. First we go to Chhattarpur."

"What are you saying! Parvati is your daughter –"

But Musafir had never seen the pundit looking like this. Frightened, he turned the car around. He could not understand why it was at all necessary to go to Chhattarpura.

# FOR A LITTLE WHILE

## *kichhukshan*

Beside a raised highway in northern Bihar on a low-lying, stony tract of land was the Madhopura Relief Camp, where countless tarpaulin tents had been set up. The camp was entirely surrounded by a sturdy barbed wire fence with a timber gate at the front, and it now held about a thousand people, including children.

Some fifteen days back there had been in the area a large-scale communal riot in the course of which five or six villages were burnt to the ground, seven or eight people were killed, and a great number were wounded, many of whom were taken to the district-town hospital. About a thousand frightened, confused and helpless people were taken from the ruins of their burnt villages and given shelter in the camp.

Only twenty yards from the gate were seven or eight tents of the Central Reserve Police Force. In front of them a few of the armed police, wearing either lungis or baggy short pants, were relaxing on charpoys, their rifles with bayonets fixed lying beside them. Parked close by were two jeeps and an imposing looking black van.

Even fifteen days after the riot the atmosphere round was still very tense and various rumours continued to float around. Although the fervour had subsided, it would still take time for everything to be restored to normal; hence, it was necessary to keep a guard over the camp day and night. A total detachment of eighteen police had charge of the lives of a thousand people. There was no way anyone could throw dust in their eyes and enter the relief camp – not even a fly.

It was the end of the month of Kartik when it was quite cool at night, but the days were lovely and comfortable, neither cold nor hot. It was now midday and there was not a scrap of cloud in the clear, sparkling blue sky, rent for the moment by a flock of wild parrots in their flight from north to south. A light dry breeze blew gently all about.

Rafique was sitting lost in thought, leaning against the relief camp's barbed wire fence. Beside him was his wife, Farida, nursing in her lap their four-month-old baby. Only some twenty-five or thirty yards from where they were sitting were a number of leafy trees, their branches closely intertwined, and beyond them there was a drainage trench. On the other side of the trench was the raised highway which ran to Patna in one direction and to Purnea in the other.

A convoy of lorries passed along the highway disturbing the noon-time with their raucous noise. There were also long-distance buses crammed full with passengers and cargo, there were cycle rickshaws and auto-rickshaws, there were small trucks, buffalo and bullock drays and a stream of people on foot.

Rafique was watching the people and the traffic on the highway. He was about twenty seven, wearing a lungi and a slightly grubby singlet with short sleeves. He was a healthy man of strong build and it was clear that he was well fed. From a good look at his face it could also be discerned that Rafique was a very straightforward, decent sort of young man with not a semblance of deceit.

Rafique's wife was very much like him. The dark-skinned girl had a very gentle face; her fine nose was adorned by a stud set with a green stone and her ears with silver rings. She had silver bangles on her wrists and was wearing a green striped sari. Like her husband, she too was watching the highway.

"How much longer must we stay shut up in here?" Farida asked, a question she asked several times a day. She no longer liked spending her time in a tent, confined by barbed wire, like a prisoner. There were many other young men and women in the camp, and a liberal attitude towards privacy prevailed.

The question was on Rafique's mind too but he did not know the answer. Staying in the camp had become stifling. At the beginning it had not been permitted to set foot outside the confines, but in the last few days they had been allowed to go as far as the highway. However, if anyone should start to cross the road, a deep, strong voice would come from the C.R.P. tents, warning,"Stop there!"

Rafique held out his hands to his wife in dejection. "Who knows?" he said.

Just as Farida was about to say something, she noticed a party of twenty or thirty people who had come down from the highway, crossed the culvert over the trench, and collapsed with all their bags and bundles under the trees in front of the camp. They looked poor and hungry, their faces bearing the obvious marks of hardship and exhaustion, and it seemed that they had been walking for some days over a long distance.

In the party there was a very sick baby who cried continually in the lap of his sick and emaciated mother. Everyone else, however, was quiet; they most likely had no energy left for talk.

Something of a commotion suddenly erupted over at the C.R.P. tents. Now that the tension of the riots had lessened somewhat, the armed guards had been giving little more than the occasional cursory look about. In the middle of the day, some of them even took a nap while on watch. And it was then that the unforeseen happened – a group of poor, pitiable people unexpectedly turned up in front of the camp, but no order had come from above to let anybody come close to it.

The armed guards' orderly sleep that comes of indolence and an excellent lunch had been disturbed. Still yawning they got to their feet with their rifles in hand and ran over to the destitute newcomers. Brandishing their rifles above their heads they shouted, "Piss off, you sons of pigs! Get out of here."

All the newcomers instantly shrank in fear. Even the continual screaming of the sick baby, who might well have burst its lungs, had now completely stopped.

One of the party, a young man of about thirty called Ganua, stood up with his hands folded. He said, "Sir, we've been walking for seven days. There is no strength left in our bodies. Let us stay here just for the middle of the day, and we will leave before the sun sets. Please grant us this favour, just for four hours."

Ganua's entreaty seemed to have some effect. The armed guards looked over the group one by one, making the women with children particularly apprehensive.

The C.R.P. men had one major worry. The atmosphere had not yet calmed down sufficiently to make it unlikely that outside rioters might make a raid on the camp. However, none of these weak and hungry and inoffensive people had the strength even to scratch anyone. So with almost a touch of gentleness in his voice, one of the armed guards said, "You're not going to make any trouble, are you?"

"No, sir!" Ganua said, leaning forward.

Pointing towards the relief camp the guard warned, "Take one step towards them over there and I'll put a bullet right through your head – okay? Just remember that."

They would not have to get up from under the trees and leave just yet; that was some small blessing, and they were all very grateful for the compassion of the police. Ganua's head was bowed almost to the ground as he said, "We'll remember, sir. We'll surely remember."

After issuing a few more warnings the armed guards went straight back to their charpoys to make good the afternoon snooze that had just been interrupted.

The baby who had been crying penetratingly a little while ago probably had an eye on the future. Right at birth he must have been told that to survive in the world one must fear the police, for only after the armed guards had gone did he launch again into a deafening wail.

Ganua, who had been talking with the guards, now came and sat beside his wife and baby. "The little jackal's howling is giving me a headache. You must stop him, Lachhima."

Lachhima was the baby's mother and Ganua's wife. She had no flesh on her body to speak of. Her breasts were flat, her hair was rough and tangled, and her eyes were yellowish. She said, "How can I stop him? He's hungry. You know that all he's eaten for three days is flour blended in water. And today there's not even any flour." She pushed a dry nipple into the baby's mouth; he tried once or twice to suck it but then started crying again. There was not a drop of milk in his mother's breasts.

Ganua put his hands over his ears and shouted, "Then choke this son of a crow and put an end to it. I can't stand his screaming any longer."

"I won't need to choke him," said Lachhima. "He'll die today anyway if you can't find something for him."

Ganua looked at Lachhima and the baby with intense unease, then turned away from them. After some more crying the baby became weak and stopped.

The others in the group were opening their bags and bundles and starting to eat whatever morsels they had been able to save, such as some wild grains or boiled maize. Ganua and Lachhima's food had run out the night before, so they had eaten nothing all day. Until they could find something to eat, they would have to depend entirely on water.

About ten yards from Ganua and Lachhima, on the other side of the barbed wire fence, Rafique and his wife were still sitting, taking in everything about the group who had come from the north. Rafique was a very sociable, amiable sort of man. Suddenly he called out, "Hey, brother – "Ganua turned around straightaway and, as their eyes met, Rafique smiled. "Where are you coming from?" he asked.

Pointing his finger in a vaguely northerly direction, Ganua said, "A village up there. Jankipura. Have you heard of it?"

Rafique thought for a moment then said, "No. Is it very far?"

"Yes."

"How far?"

Ganua considered, and said, "About sixty, sixty-five miles."

Rafique looked at him in amazement, then said, "So many of you have left your village. Where are you going?"

"Town."

"Why?"

Ganua went on to explain that there had been a vast flood that year in the Jankipura region and that for one and a half months all the fields had been under some four feet of water. Consequently, there had been no cultivation. Ganua's people were landless labourers; if there was no work, they got no wages, and without wages where would they get something to put in their stomachs? In none of the homes of people like them was there ever anything extra put away that might get them through the bad times, be it flood or drought. In their village there was no work other than farming; therefore, simply for the sake of survival, Ganua and the others left the village to look for work in Purnea or in Katihar. They believed that if they went to the city they would find something. How much longer could they go without food?

Rafique could readily sympathise with the hardship of these deprived and miserable people of Jankipura. Hesitantly, he asked, "Will you actually find work?"

"Who can say?" Ganua replied. "It's all in the hands of God."

Neither man spoke for a little while. Then Ganua said, "Can I ask you something?"

"Yes, yes," said Rafique. "Of, course."

"Which village are you from?"

"Naoserganj."

"Is that very far?"

"No, it's quite close. Maybe a mile, mile and a half away."

Ganua stared for some time in astonishment at the sign, MADHOPURA RELIEF CAMP. Then he said, "But your village is so close! Why have you left your home to come and live in a tent?"

Rafique did not answer straightaway. His brow furrowed and his mouth hardened. He said, "You don't know about it?"

"No, brother."

"You heard nothing?"

Ganua thought for a moment, then said, "Oh, we heard there was a bit of trouble somewhere. A lot of people died, homes were burned –"

Before Rafique could reply a few of the others started calling out at once, "They didn't die, they were killed. Eight or ten villages were burned right to the ground. They were our villages, our people –"

Rafique and Ganua looked around. They had not noticed that a few men from the middle of the camp had come and stood behind Rafique and were looking exceptionally rancorous. Their faces blazed intensely with hatred and malice. They were now looking at Rafique and gesticulating threateningly as they spoke. "What are you doing talking with that fellow? Stop your chattering, get up and come away from there!"

"Now, now, brothers, what is his fault?" Rafique tried to placate them. "He's just a poor, wretched fellow who's been walking sixty or sixty-five miles from his village. For many days –"

Rafique was interrupted by a young man shouting out, "Maybe he has no fault, but it was men of his community who burned our village and killed our people."

"Save your anger for those who are guilty, not for him! You're being unjust."

The young man raised his voice a little more. "Shut up, bastard!"

The uproar that ensued brought a few other men running from the middle of the camp. An old man with spotlessly white hair and beard, his back bent with age and looking worried, asked, "What's going on?"

The young man, now greatly agitated, was on the verge of speaking just as Rafique got up and went and stood in front of the old man. "Uncle Anwar," he said, "hear my side of it first."

It was clear from the respect they all showed him that the old man was a leader of the asylum seekers in the relief camp. "All right," he said. "Go ahead."

But the young man stepped forward arrogantly and, waving his hands about, said, "No! I'll speak first."

The old man was cool headed. He looked at Rafique, then at the young man, then slowly said to Rafique, "Say your piece, son."

Rafique calmly gave an account of the whole affair. Having heard him out, the old man said, "All right, then." Looking at Ganua and his group, he said for the young man's benefit, "Those people have nothing to answer for. You want to cut one man's throat for another man's crime. What sense is there in that? Go away from here and don't make trouble."

The old man had not raised his voice at all, nor was there any anger or impatience in his tone. Yet he bore such firm authority that none of the residents of the relief camp had the strength or the courage to disobey him. The young man and others of like-minded aggressiveness went quite some way off, mumbling among themselves.

The armed guards had heard all the uproar and for the second time had had their afternoon nap interrupted. They sat up, and one of them called out, "Hey, what's going on? What's all the fuss about, eh? Can't we get some sleep?"

The old man raised his hands reassuringly to the armed guards and said, "There's nothing the matter, officers. You go back to sleep."

"Very good, then. You see to it that there's no trouble, Uncle."

"I will, sir," said the old man, flashing a gentle smile amid the jungle of his beard and moustache.

The armed guards appreciated that the old man was greatly revered and carried a lot of influence. Tendering him the temporary responsibility for the relief camp, they lay down again on their charpoys and went straight back to sleep.

The old man went over to Ganua and his group to express his regrets for the hostile behaviour of the hot-headed young man. "Don't take offence or bear any grudge, son. People were killed in the riots and villages were burned. So now we're all living in tents guarded by police and some of us have become a little irrational. But it's not right to blame any of you for this."

The old man was really like a father or uncle. Ganua was deeply touched by his compassionate and affectionate demeanour. He said, "No, no. We're just humble people. We won't take offence or bear grudges." He also made it known that when the heat had gone out of the sun they would leave this place and forget all about the incident.

"All right. You have some rest. I'm going." And the old man slowly went towards the middle of the camp.

This was all that had been needed to ease the tension considerably and now things were quiet for a while. After the old man had gone, Rafique went and sat down again in the same place beside the barbed wire fence. Farida and the baby were sitting there as before.

Some awkward moments passed before Rafique called hesitantly, "Hey, brother –"

It was most likely that Ganua had his ear tuned for this call. He looked up quickly and said, "Yes? What is it?"

"What a to-do, eh? You're not really angry, then?"

"Oh, no, no. Like I told old Uncle." Ganua thought for a few moments, then said, "Can I ask you something, brother?"

"Yes. What is it?"

"Who started the riots here?"

Rafique was quite taken aback by the question. Then he turned up his hands and, with a melancholy look on his face, said, "Who knows! Let's forget it. What happened happened. I feel really bad just thinking about it."

Ganua nodded. Just as he was about to say something, the baby in Lachhima's lap started to howl again. He had been dozing all the while, but now he started to cry once more with renewed strength.

Ganua looked angrily at his sickly wife of mere skin and bones and shouted, "The son of a pig's started his racket again! Stop him, will you!" And he turned to Rafique and asked, "Do you have any family?"

Rafique looked at Farida and their baby boy and said, "That's my wife and son."

"You have just one son?"

"Yes."

Lachhima was utterly exhausted with the baby. The child had nothing on his body, only the loose, dirty skin covering the thin and frail bones. Yet even in this condition he still seemed to have the strength of ten powerful horses, and he bit and kicked at Lachhima with such ferocity that she was quite worn out. Along with that came a continual sharp, piercing cry like that of a hawk.

Ganua angrily turned to face Lachhima. He said, "Give him to me. Give me that animal's kid. I'll throttle him and finish him off."

Ganua got up to go and seize the baby from his mother's lap but Rafique, looking worried, cried out, "Hey, brother. Sit down, sit down. What's wrong with your baby that makes you so angry?"

Ganua suddenly covered his face with his hands and sank to the ground. In a very heavy tone, he said, "It's hunger, brother, hunger. For so many days we've eaten only flour mixed with water. And now that's run out, too. You can see the condition of his mother. She hasn't got a drop of milk in her breasts. What can we do? If the baby can't eat, he'll die." Ganua wept helplessly.

All the while Farida had said nothing, but had looked on at everything in silence. Now she went over to Rafique and whispered something to him. Rafique looked at his wife in speechless amazement for a few seconds, his face beaming. Then he ran to the barbed wire fence and said, "Brother, give us your little boy for a while."

The words were so sudden and unexpected that Ganua just stood there stupidly for a few moments.

Rafique hurried him. "Come on, give him to me. Don't worry, we're not going to snatch him away. Give him to me, now. He's been crying so much, any more and he'll burst."

As though in some strange sort of trance, Ganua took the baby from Lachhima and handed him over the barbed wire fence to Rafique. Then Farida gave their own little boy to Rafique and took Ganua's child some way away to the privacy of a thick clump of bushes. A little while later, when she brought him back, he was no longer crying. Now that his stomach was full, he moved his hands and feet playfully, and he was handed back to his mother.

Ganua and Lachhima, their hands folded in gratitude, said admiringly, "Sister, you have saved our little boy's life. May good fortune ever go with you."

Farida said nothing, but Rafique said, "It's nothing. Could we ever let a baby die before our eyes?"

Once the afternoon sun had started to fall towards the west, Ganua and his group got their bags and bundles together and got up. Ganua went over to the barbed wire fence and said to Rafique and Farida, "Brother, sister, we'll always remember you. We'll never forget your kindness." And then Ganua and Lachhima went up to the highway, and as they walked they kept looking back at Rafique and Farida who were standing absolutely still by the barbed wire fence of the relief camp, watching them go.

# WHERE THERE IS NO FRONTIER

## *jekhane simanta nei*

When, after fifty one years, Abdur got down apprehensively from the second class compartment of the train at Azimabad station, the winter sun was starting to decline in the western sky. The sunlight had lost its shine and was now the colour of faded turmeric, and the north wind gusted all about like a mad, unbridled horse.

His full name was Abdur Hussein. He was sixty, of medium height and slender build. There were heavy shadows under his eyes and he had prominent jawbones. His eyesight was no longer strong and he wore heavy-framed glasses. His whole body bore the marks of age, with his skin rough and wrinkled and his hair and beard mostly grey.

Abdur was wearing an extremely crumpled pajama and a sherwani, over which he also wore a long-sleeve woollen pullover. Even that was not enough to stop the indomitable cold of north India, so over the pullover he had a thick woollen shawl wrapped around himself. On his feet he wore heavy sandals. Abdur carried a large leather suitcase in his right hand and, in the other, a holdall containing his pillow, a thin mattress, a pair of blankets, a bed-cover, and sundry odds and ends.

Two years after Partition, when he was nine, Abdur and his family left Azimabad for West Pakistan and had settled in Karachi, where they lived in the very crowded part of the old city, a locality that became a colony for Mohajirs, the Urdu-speaking Muslim refugees from India.

He had two reasons for coming back to India after fifty one years. One was to go to Ajmer Sharif; the other was to come to Azimabad and visit his elder sister, Fatima, who had remained behind when the rest of the family went to Pakistan after Partition. Many people had told them that they would have no security in India and that their future would be bleak, so it did not make sense for them to risk staying here under those conditions. However, Fatima's father-in-law, Sheik Badruddin, was a very dogged character who said simply that he and his family would not be leaving his own country, the land of his birth, for anywhere. Let happen what may.

Before Partition and for some time after there had been quite a few riots between Hindus and Muslims which had culminated in arson, bloodshed and murder. No one of either community would trust anyone of the other; there prevailed only mutual hatred, malice and suspicion. Once the terror had reached a height for the Muslims and groups of them started leaving for West Pakistan, Badruddin still did not succumb to mistrust of others, believing that not all men had become inhuman.

It was not possible for an ordinary man like Abdur to come from Pakistan into India at the drop of a hat. After days of running around and experiencing all sorts of harassment, when he had almost given up hope he was given a fifteen-day visa. Having gone from Karachi by plane he had to travel by train from Delhi to Ajmer Sharif, from where he had come to visit Fatima in Azimabad; then he would have to go back to Delhi and take the plane to Karachi, returning the same way he had come.

Abdur had landed in India some seven days back. When he was leaving, the people of his locality had warned him again and again that in India Muslims, especially Pakistanis, were unsafe. In the seven days since arriving in India he had done a lot of travelling by train, bus and taxi, but so far he had had no reason to believe that there was any threat to him at all. This was a huge country with millions of people and no one had even looked at him twice. However, for the few days that he would be here he would have to be careful as he went about. He would not neglect the warnings of his neighbours in Karachi.

Abdur got down from the train and waited, looking all around with immense wistfulness in his eyes. He was not alone, as many other passengers had got down from the train too, and there were a good many people all over the platform waiting with their luggage to go to various destinations. The whole station concourse was bustling.

When they had gone to Karachi, Abdur had been terribly nostalgic for Azimabad, but after a few years he no longer felt that way. Thousands of other Muslim families had left India and crossed the border with them, and with a new country, new friends, school and study, the insignificant town of Azimabad in some corner of Uttar Pradesh started to become as vague as a remote star. But at the end of this winter's day, all his memories started to come back to him one after the other.

Abdur recalled the one-storey red building of the station of fifty one years earlier and its platform spread with brick-dust. Since then there had been some additions. The platform in those days had been bare, but now at one end of it there was an imposing shelter, set up to offer passengers protection from the rain and the intensity of the sun. Abdur also noticed a big stall close to the ticket counter, where tea was available and there were many types of sweets on display in a glass showcase; above the showcase were big glass jars with a variety of biscuits and savoury items; and beside the jars was a stack of loaves of bread. The tea stall, too, had not been there before.

Fifty one years back Azimabad had been a very insignificant station with only a couple of up trains and a couple of down trains running through in a whole day. There would be a bit of activity when the trains came in, but for the rest of the time the entire station concourse would remain quiet and still, as though sunk in a profound sleep. Both up and down trains used to run along a single line, but now another pair of tracks had been laid out, and on the other side of the line a new platform, also with a shelter, had been set up.

As he stood at the station it seemed to Abdur that since Partition there had been a great increase here in the number of people and their hustle and bustle and constant come and go. He was reminded of Karachi and how many people were there when they arrived after Partition. In fifty one years there had been a population explosion there, with dense crowds everywhere all the time. Indeed, all over the world people were gradually increasing like insects, so why should Azimabad be any exception?

Abdur brought himself out of his reminiscing. He looked at the passengers on the platform for a few moments but did not recognise any familiar face, though it soon occurred to him that the people he knew in Azimabad when they went to Karachi would have changed so much that he would not be able to recognise them anyway. Moreover, how could he say how many of the people he knew then were still alive? And even if they were, there was no reason to think that they would have come all together to the station right then. And if anyone should remember him, was there any resemblance at all between his boyhood appearance and the way he looked now? Surely no one in Azimabad would know him.

Abdur waited no longer but moved with the throng towards the gate.

When he had arrived in India some seven days back, he bought a postcard from a post office in Delhi and wrote a note to his elder sister, Fatima, telling her that he would very soon be visiting her, but he was not able to say with certainty on what day he would come. She would probably send one of her sons to the station. But would he be able to recognise Abdur? Fatima's eldest son had been only one when they had left for Pakistan. Who could say what that one-year-old little boy looked like now? Anyhow, if no one came to pick Abdur up from the station, he would have no trouble finding Fatima's house in the northern part of the town. And now as he set foot in Azimabad the old picture of its streets and its various localities started to appear before his eyes.

The ticket collector, wearing a black coat, was standing at the gate. After giving him his ticket Abdur walked a few yards away to the flight of stone steps, and although they had all been damaged by the constant tread of feet, they were still much as they had been at the time of Partition. On his way down Abdur remembered that there had been altogether twenty-five steps; he counted them, and the number was still the same. Memory, with its secret storehouses, is a strange thing.

When he reached the bottom of the steps, Abdur was struck by how busy it all was. At the time of Partition there had been a narrow brick-dust road here, on one side of which there were three or four shops with tarpaulin awnings and cracked tin roofs selling tea, or paan and biris. On the other side a few tongas used to stand waiting for passengers. The tonga drivers and their horses would doze for almost the whole day, as though they had been weighed down by the deep and unending indolence of this remote place. But now its appearance had totally changed. The old brick-dust road had been sealed and was ten times wider, and on both sides there were rows of shops as far as the eye could see, with four or five feet of the road having been taken over by the shopkeepers for the display of their wares, while inside crowds of people buzzed around like flies. The scene was exactly the same as that of the station area in any mofussil town in Pakistan, and in this regard there was no difference between the two countries.

Abdur noticed a line of tongas waiting under some luxuriant pipal trees. At the time of Partition there would not have been more than three or four tongas; now there were at least ten. There were also a lot of autorickshaws under some trees on the opposite side. Who could say when they had come on the scene, for there had been no autorickshaws when Abdur's family had left India. Old Karachi swarmed with autorickshaws, but Abdur did not really like to travel in them, and so he went to the tonga stand under the pipal trees. He hired one and got up with his suitcase and his holdall, and the middle-aged driver set off.

The road was a confusing turmoil of hordes of pedestrians, bullock drays, autorickshaws, tongas, vans, hand-carts and so on. Brandishing his whip that hissed in the breeze the tonga driver kept on shouting at the top of his voice, "Come on, get a move on! Get out of the way!" And it was not only him, but other drivers of tongas, autorickshaws and vans all called out in the same manner as they forced their way through the traffic. It took fifteen or twenty minutes to get clear of the station precinct, and then the road was a lot less busy.

Azimabad town was quite a way from the station. Abdur recalled clearly a brick-dust road joining the station with the town; they were now travelling along it, but it was no longer like what it used to be. Fifty one years ago there had been vast stretches of stony land with bushes and jungle on either side. Now the jungle had been cleared and in its place there were countless big houses and an occasional temple.

The sun had now sunk in the west and was obscured by the taller houses. The dim reddish glow that lingered in the sky would last only a few more minutes and then the winter evening would suddenly come down – the arrangements were almost complete, for the day was no sooner coming to its end than the dew was falling subtly all about and the north wind had become like the blade of a knife cutting at any exposed parts of the body.

However, Abdur had not noticed the decline of the winter's day in this mofussil town of Uttar Pradesh. Suddenly he called to the tonga driver, "Hey, brother!"

The driver, wrapped in a grey blanket, looked over his shoulder and said, "Yes?"

"The town has changed quite a lot, hasn't it?" Abdur said.

"Oh, yes."

Gesturing to both sides of the road Abdur said, "Once all that was open land."

The tonga driver was a very courteous man who knew how to be respectful to his passengers. Looking in front of him, he answered, "Yes. Now you won't find a hand's breadth of open space in this town. Just houses and houses." He paused for a moment, then went on, "To my mind the town's become too big!" He was very likely an uneducated man, given his pronunciation of 'town' as 'tone'.

"As the population grows, so does the town," said Abdur.

"True."

Around the neck of the spirited horse drawing the tonga was a string of brass bells which, with the rhythm of its movement, made a sweet, melodious sound. Sitting there on a thick piece of sackcloth over the hard and cold seat on the timber decking, Abdur felt that he was being taken in this ancient carriage back to a previous existence now fifty one years past. It was a strange thing that, having come such a long way from distant Karachi to see Fatima, the faces of Ramu, Lachhman and Dhanua were now starting to appear before his eyes. He thought of so many others, too, whose names he had forgotten. All of them had been his friends and playmates in the same class at the Azimabad primary school.

As Abdur thought of Dhanua, his face suddenly appeared clearly to him. He remembered long back how his father Lajpat Singh and his mates had started a riot in Azimabad just before the Partition. Despite the friendship of the sons Abdur's family was not spared when those men tried to burn their house down. Who knew if Lajpat Singh was still alive? If he were, how would he react to Abdur's sudden arrival from Pakistan? Deep down, Abdur felt very ill at ease.

Having set foot after a long time in the land of his birth all kinds of thoughts had kept on indiscriminately invading his mind, and no sooner had one gone than another came. His anxiety over Lajpat Singh did not last very long, however, as he recalled the memory of two tonga wallahs, Fakira and Hanif. Fakira was a truly fine fellow. Sometimes, if he did not have any passengers, he would let Abdur and his friends get up onto the tonga and take them on a round of the streets of Azimabad. Hanif, though, was terribly quick-tempered and peevish, as though every few minutes the blood was rushing to his head. He would not let Abdur and his friends even come close to his tonga, and if they did, he would let out a stream of abuse. However, Abdur and his friends were very persistent, and while Hanif was looking ahead, perhaps driving the tonga, they would quietly go behind and swing from the decking. But Hanif had ten pairs of eyes and could sense all that was going on, and without even turning around he would brandish his whip at the back while the tonga kept going.

"Brother!" Abdur called.

"Yes?" the tonga wallah answered immediately.

"Do you know Fakira and Hanif? They must be very old. Are they still alive?"

"Who are they?"

"A long time ago they drove tongas in this town."

The driver thought for a few moments and suddenly, as though he had just remembered, said, "Oh, yes, I remember. Uncle Hanif and Uncle Fakira stayed in the old quarter of the town. But they both died ten or twelve years ago."

Hearing of the death of two men familiar to his childhood made Abdur feel a little sad. When his family went to Pakistan, Hanif and Fakira would not yet have been forty. If they had died ten or twelve years ago, they would have been at least seventy-four or seventy-five – not a short span of life. Most people do not live as long. Nevertheless, he still felt heavy-hearted for the two tonga wallahs of those times.

A little river called the Motiya flowed through the middle of the town of Azimabad. When they came to it, Abdur was dumbfounded. In his boyhood days there had been a sturdy timber bridge over it joining the two parts of the town. Pedestrians, tongas, cycle rickshaws, bullock and buffalo drays and a few motor cars all used it to go from one side to the other. But not a splinter of that old timber bridge remained. In its place there was a concrete bridge, three times as wide, with footpaths and a row of lamp posts on either side.

As they crossed the bridge, Abdur said, "I say, brother, when did this bridge replace the old one?"

"About thirty, thirty-five years ago," said the driver.

Abdur asked no more questions as he looked wistfully at the bridge. It seemed that very little remained of the Azimabad of his childhood.

The driver turned around and said, "Can I ask you something?"

Abdur was a little surprised. "Yes, yes. Go ahead."

"Listening to you speak, it seems that you're returning to this town after a very long time."

"I am."

"Did you live here?"

"Yes."

"Where do you live now?"

The tonga wallah's curiosity was innocent and there was nothing suspicious in the questions he was asking, but in a flash Abdur was reminded of his neighbours' repeated warnings when he had left Karachi not to let anyone know, as far as was possible, that he was a Pakistani.

Abdur retreated for a moment. He had lived in India until he was nine years old, and in that time he had never set foot outside of Azimabad except for a visit once to Agra and Delhi. After going to Karachi what little connection he had had with India faded in time so that he now knew almost nothing of the country. Of course, he had heard the names of a few big cities, and on arrival from Karachi he had landed in Delhi, where he had once gone in his childhood. As well as Delhi he knew only such names as Calcutta, Bombay, Madras, Cuttack and Bangalore. Almost in a panic, then, Abdur said, "I live in Calcutta." He tried for the life of him to sound natural, lest the driver should be in any way suspicious.

"Calcutta's not all that far away," said the tonga wallah, "yet you're coming here after so long a time!" He sounded quite surprised.

It suddenly seemed to Abdur that the man was becoming nosy, cross-examining him like a lawyer. What if he should carelessly answer some question and so create difficulties for himself? He would have to stop the man. Casually Abdur said, "There are so many problems with my business – "He did not go on any further.

Cordially the tonga wallah asked, "Do you have any family here – father, mother, any relatives?"

To have answered the tonga wallah truthfully would have invited many other questions, some of which might have made Abdur quite uncomfortable. Quietly and indistinctly he muttered something incomprehensible. The driver guessed that he was not going to get an answer to his question, and he said nothing more.

The tonga had crossed the bridge and come over onto the other side. Here the road ran through the most privileged quarter of Azimabad. Inside the large compounds were grand mansions of a bygone age in front of which were flower gardens, lawns and pebbled driveways. Fifty one years ago each home had a carriage pulled by a healthy horse with a shiny coat; in only a few was there a motor car. The upper-class neighbourhood was much the same as it had been before, except that it had grown many times bigger.

Apart from just one Jankinath, he could not remember after all this time the people to whom these houses once belonged. He remembered the name of Jankinath because two years before Partition the English District Magistrate had come to his house from the district town. Abdur had heard from his father that the white saheb was a high-ranking officer and that such an important man had never before been to Azimabad.

There had been great excitement in the quiet, insignificant little town. Jankinath-ji, dressed in an expensive coat and trousers and wearing on his head a turban of five yards of cloth, had gone direct to the station along with the other important people of Azimabad. In order to prevent the dust of the town from getting onto the shoes of the District Magistrate, a red jute carpet had been spread over the entire platform and the steps leading down to the road, and to impress such an historical event on the memories of the people of Azimabad forever, Jankinath-ji had brought four musical bands from Allahabad. Abdur's father had also told him that as well as the bands a Muslim chef had been brought from a famous hotel there.

Abdur remembered how Jankinath-ji had taken the DM to his own house in an open carriage drawn by six horses. An attendant dressed in splendid uniform stood on a platform at the back of the carriage, all the while holding a coloured silk umbrella over the DM. Abdur could still remember the scene, for in those times the visit of an English DM was a truly grand event in such a small town, and in order to see him in person the people of Azimabad had crowded along both sides of the road. Abdur's father had taken him along too.

In front of the procession were two of the bands, then came Jankinath-ji's carriage as the guide, followed by the DM's carriage in the middle, after which had come a number of the distinguished citizens of Azimabad. Bringing up the rear of this splendid cavalcade were the other two bands.

Within three months of the DM's visit Jankinath was awarded the title of Rai Bahadur. One night on returning home Abdur's father had broken the news in a voice full of pride and excitement, for there could never have been a Rai Bahadur in Azimabad up until now. In those childhood days Abdur was not able to appreciate how much honour there was attached to the title and to the one who had received it, but it had seemed to be something quite momentous.

Abdur wondered if Jankinath was still alive. He stopped himself from asking the tonga wallah lest his curiosity should provoke an unwelcome question in return. He now noticed that evening had started to fall. Lights were on in the houses, the rows of streetlights were lit, and the cold was becoming more intense.

They reached the locality at the far northern end of Azimabad with its very many houses; one part of it was a Muslim quarter, the other Hindu. The locality was much the same as it had been fifty one years ago and Abdur had no trouble recognising it. He got down from the tonga with his suitcase and holdall, paid the fare and had a good look around at the maze of unprepossessing houses of the old locality, the Muslim quarter much duller than the Hindu one. Even on this winter evening there were many people on the streets. Abdur remembered that Fatima's father-in-law's house was very close, about a five-minute walk from the main road, and that a little further in was Abdur's old family home.

There were many narrow lanes leading into the Muslim quarter, but Abdur quickly realised that after all these years he had no idea which one he should take to get to Fatima's house. Fatima's husband's name had been Sheikh Ziaul. If he mentioned his name, surely someone or other would be able to point out their house to him. He was just about to ask someone on the street when two men came out from an alley on his left. One of them was his age, heavy looking and of medium height, with a bushy moustache and wearing a dhoti and a full shirt over which was a warm shawl and, on his head, a woollen cap. He was evidently a Hindu. His companion was in his mid-thirties, thin and frail looking, with a longish face, big eyes, sharp nose and a tidy, well-trimmed beard. He wore a pajama and long kurta over which was a thick woollen sweater, and a round cap on his head. It could be assumed that he was a Muslim.

The two men walked straight up to Abdur. The elder, heavy man – the Hindu – looked at Abdur and kept his eyes on him for a few moments. Then he asked, "Are you Abdur Hussein?"

Abdur was taken aback. He said, "Yes, I am. But I do not recognise you."

Immediately the man cried out, "You old owl! You ass! I'm Dhanno – Dhanua!"

In their childhood Dhanua had been rather skinny and frail. Who would ever have thought that fifty one years later he would have put on so much weight! There was not the slightest resemblance between the boy of those days and the Dhanua of today. However, one thing had remained the same – the intensity of his expression of emotion. He was always loud, for he could not speak without shouting.

Abdur could not have imagined meeting his boyhood friend in this way. Yet he was very much taken by Dhanua's heartiness which momentarily took him back to their childhood. Abdur embraced him, saying, "After so many years we are meeting, Dhanno!"

"So many years!" Dhanua – or Dhanpat – said, "We've now

grown old. Who would have thought that I would ever meet you again in this life!"

There was a pause. Then Dhanpat, indicating the young man beside him, said, "Of course, you don't recognise him. He's Latif, sister Fatima's younger son, your youngest nephew."

When Abdur and his family had left for Pakistan, Latif had not yet been born and now, when the long journey of Abdur's life was drawing towards a close, he had come to India without any knowledge of this nephew.

Latif bent to touch his uncle's feet and Abdur raised him up and held him close. He said, "My boy, may you live for a hundred years."

A few moments later Latif took up Abdur's suitcase and Dhanpat took the holdall. Abdur objected but Dhanpat exclaimed, "Hey, you old owl, you're a guest in India. Please let us make you welcome. Come on."

They went into the alley opposite, Latif first, followed by Abdur and Dhanpat walking side by side.

Dhanpat said, "Since sister Fatima got your letter, Latif and I have been going to the station two or three times every day. But there are seven or eight trains a day coming here from Allahabad, and we didn't know which one you'd be coming on. We were both going again just now when we saw you getting down from the tonga. But if you had sent a letter letting us know, then –"

"I didn't know how long I would be at Ajmer Sharif, so how could I tell you on what day I would leave there for Azimabad?"

"Oh, I see," said Dhanpat, slowly nodding his head.

Abdur asked, "My appearance has changed utterly, like yours, so how did you recognise me after all these years?"

"I didn't. I just guessed." Dhanpat hurriedly explained that he knew everyone in Azimabad, and that Abdur was expected to arrive at any time, any day. When he saw a man of his age getting down from a tonga it occurred to Dhanpat that there was an eighty percent chance it would be Abdur.

Abdur smiled.

Then Dhanpat said, "Now tell us all about yourself. What work do you do in Pakistan? How many children have you got? Your wife –"

Abdur interrupted his friend. "You can hear all about me later. But first tell me about yourself."

Dhanpat gave a rapid two-minute account not only of himself but of various things about the town of Azimabad. After Abdur and his family had gone, Dhanpat had not gone very far with his education and had left school after twice failing eighth class. After spending a few years as an unemployed layabout aimlessly wandering around here and there, he eventually trained as a motor mechanic at his father's insistence and then opened a garage. He had made good money. He had a son and a daughter. The boy had passed B.A. and worked in a government position, living in Lucknow. The girl was married and lived with her in-laws in Allahabad. There were no real problems in his family, although the health of his wife and father were a worry, as they both suffered from this disease or that.

Abdur was so overwhelmed with emotion at seeing his old friend after so many years and by his affectionate generosity that he had momentarily forgotten Dhanpat's father, the Rajput kshatriya Lajpat Singh and those other men who, at the time of the riot just before Partition, had set fire to their house. So many people in Azimabad like Lajpat had been the reason for their going to Pakistan, people who nurtured immense anger and hatred for Muslims. Their murderous and violent looks at the time of the riot were indelible in Abdur's memory. It had seemed then that they would rip him and his family to shreds, but somehow, by the mercy of Allah, they had survived. However, his fear had lingered for a long time after going to Karachi.

In fact, Abdur was stung by the news that Lajpat Singh was still alive, and a strange pang of fear erupted inside him.

Dhanpat went on talking, not looking at Abdur, telling how none of the prominent citizens of those times was still alive. Rai Bahadur Jankinath, the big businessman Mahavirprasad Shrivastav, and the government lawyer Baburam Gupta and all their ilk were now dead, but all of Abdur's close boyhood friends were still alive. Ramu had made millions as a contractor and lived in the grand mansion he had had built in Lucknow, coming to Azimabad for a few days once in every year or two. Lachhman had got his degree in science and taken up a position in Delhi with a noted pharmaceutical company. Baiju, of course, was still in Azimabad and had a number of warehouses beside the Motiya river stocking rice, paddy, wheat, sesame, linseed and mustard seeds. It was a family business that Baiju now supervised.

Dhanpat also remarked that the old times had completely changed.

Apart from that riot Azimabad had gone a long time without any disturbance. It had been a very peaceful town, free of agitation, through which the stream of life flowed very slowly. However, after a few years bloodshed, highway robbery and bank holdups increased remarkably, and for this the political leaders who came after Independence were very much to blame. They gave refuge to ruffians and gun-wielding thugs who helped them hold on to power. At election time these scoundrels cast fake votes, the genuine voters not going near the voting booths for fear of their pistols and bombs. Those who created the parliamentarians would get away with murder and robbery and the leaders would not lift a finger. Should the police arrest any of these hired thugs, a phone call to the station would ensure his immediate release. The leaders had given them a licence to do as they pleased.

Dhanpat was still talking when they reached the house of Fatima's father-in-law, an old-style, two-storey home. Through the main door there was a paved courtyard, on one side of which were a bathroom and a kitchen. Facing three sides on both storeys were many other rooms.

The house had been hazy in Abdur's memory, but now it was all starting to come back to him. Fatima's father-in-law had had it built just before her marriage. The new house had been painted crimson, with the doors and window-frames in green, and it had had a sparkling appearance. How he used to enjoy coming here from time to time after his big sister's wedding! But the house was no longer what it once had been. The plaster was coming off various parts of the walls and exposing the brickwork, the cornices were broken, and in one place the head of a banyan sapling was poking through. And there were so many cracks in the courtyard! The house had gone a long time without proper maintenance and its days seemed numbered – with luck, maybe ten or twelve years.

Lights were burning in all the rooms as they crossed the courtyard and entered the main part of the house. There was an amazing stillness all around them, yet once there had been so many people in that house with all the time the noise of children running about resounding from the ground floor to the roof. Now there seemed to be no one but the three of them, although the sound of sizzling coming from the kitchen meant that someone was cooking.

Inside there was a wide passage on the left of which were three rooms, and on the right was the staircase leading to the upper floor. Many of the steps had become damaged and uneven. Going up the broken staircase behind Latif a sudden anxiety welled up inside Abdur – he had come to see Fatima for the first time since he had left for Pakistan as a nine-year-old boy, a long fifty one years ago.

Latif took him and Dhanpat into a huge room which Abdur recognised as the bedroom of Fatima and her husband, Sheikh Ziaul. Electric lights were burning from the tops of the walls on two sides. As far as Abdur could remember, the decor of the room had not noticeably changed at all. As before there were some three or four bulky almirahs, an old-fashioned dressing table, a few cushions, a couple of chairs and the like. Right in the middle was an immense crafted bed, beside which were three or four small, low tables. A little way away was a television set on a high stand.

The furniture was dark and dull under a thick layer of dirt. Evidently it had not been polished for quite a long time.

The grubby bed was made up on a mattress a foot thick; an elderly lady was lying on it with a blanket over her. She had a thin, emaciated face, pure white hair, a broad brow and a dull look in her eyes. Seeing the three men she turned aside and groped beside the pillow for her glasses, put them on, and said in a weak voice, "Oh, Dhanno and Lati, you have come!" Apparently Lati was the pet-name of Latif.

"Yes, Mother," said Latif.

Now wearing her glasses the lady – Fatima – said, "There's someone with you. Who is it?"

In a gently jocular tone Dhanpat said, "Oh, sister, you ask 'who?' Can't you recognise him?"

Fatima slowly raised herself up and fixed her gaze intently on Abdur's face for some moments, as though searching. She then took a breath and said, "Is it you, Munna, come from Pakistan?"

How many years had it been since Abdur had heard his own pet-name! After the deaths of his mother and father no one had called him by it and he had quite forgotten about it. But Fatima had not forgotten it.

Abdur looked straight at Fatima. When they had left India, there was an album amongst their chattels. It contained photos of the time of Fatima's wedding, of the wondrous fairy princess his sister had seemed to him then. And now before him was this aged, bed-ridden, frail lady, like a heap of ruins. The blood of the same parents ran through the veins of both of them, yet how remote was the woman. He was Pakistani, she Indian; between them was not only a fifty-one-year estrangement, but also a virtually impenetrable frontier.

As he looked at this ageing and frail old woman his heart ached terribly, and from its depths their emanated something like a howl that seemed to gather into a lump and stick in his throat and his breathing was stifled, as though by some weird and mystic force he had crossed the frontiers of time and of lands and was now returning to his childhood.

Nevertheless, he tried to speak, but at first his throat seemed choked. He almost ran and sat beside Fatima, and then with great difficulty gave voice to his words. "Yes, sister, I am indeed your Munna."

Embracing Abdur's head with her two frail and trembling hands, Fatima burst into sobs. Through her tears she said, "You remembered me after all this time! I've grown very old. It won't be long before I'll be no more. I'll be under the ground." Her body writhed in a cascade of sobbing.

Abdur was infected by Fatima's emotion. He had, indeed, passed through much tumult in the last fifty one years. The riots, murder, arson, Partition, leaving India and going to Pakistan – it had all been a continual struggle for survival, one that had hardened him. He did not cry easily, but at that moment Abdur felt that his eyes were bursting with tears. His voice choking, he said, "Don't cry, sister. Don't cry."

But Fatima's crying did not stop; rather, her tears welled up even more.

After a little while Fatima settled down a little and took her hands from around her brother's neck. Under the strain of her sobbing, her breathing had become heavy. Abdur said, "You are getting distressed, sister. Lie down now."

But Fatima remained sitting up. Catching her breath she said, "After all these years I am seeing you again. How can I lie down?"

"I'll stay beside you. You can talk lying down." With great affection Abdur supported his elder sister by the shoulder and helped her to lie down. Taking her frail hand in his own he asked, "How did you get like this?"

It was Latif who answered the question, explaining that Fatima had had a stroke three years back. On top of that she had developed a liver complaint and shortness of breath. Indeed, he couldn't reckon the number of ailments that had come to occupy his mother's weak body.

Alongside Latif Dhanpat spoke up. "Look at this," he said, pointing to a table beside the bed on which there were bottles of various kinds of medicines and countless packets of capsules and tablets. "Your elder sister survives by the doctor and his medicines."

Abdur nodded slowly and sadly. He said nothing.

"Abdur," Dhanpat said, "I can't stay any longer. I have to get back to the garage. I'll come again early tomorrow morning." To Fatima he said, "Goodbye, sister. After all these years you now have your brother, so don't cry any more. You'll only make yourself sick."

Once Dhanpat had gone, Abdur asked, "Does Dhanpat come here every day?"

"Not every day," said Latif. "Usually twice a week, to see how we are getting on. He looks after us."

Fatima said, "That time when I was so sick he took me to the hospital. I was unconscious for three days and he stayed there with me day and night. He also set Latif up in business. I can't tell you how much he has helped us. We rely on Dhanno so much. There's no one like him."

Abdur was dumbfounded. The son of that Lajpat Singh who had started the riot in Azimabad and tried to burn down their house was now the stalwart of Fatima's home! Before Abdur could say anything, Fatima said, "You have come such a long way on the train, you must surely be tired. No more talk now, while you go and wash your face and hands and change your grubby shirt. Then come back and have some tea with me." She asked Latif, "Has the bed been made up in Uncle's room?"

Latif inclined his head. "Yes," he said.

"Tell Bano to put some hot water in the bathroom and then to make tea and *puris* and bring them up here. Tell her to bring some sweets too."

Abdur did not know Bano, but he did not ask about her. Having come to the house he would surely meet her sooner or later.

Latif left the room and came back in a few minutes. Fatima said to her son, "Take Uncle to his room now. Give him some fresh soap and a towel and show him the bathroom."

Taking up Abdur's suitcase and holdall Latif took him to a room on the right. He put the luggage on the floor and switched on the light. It was a very big room, though not as big as Fatima's, and was exceptionally clean and tidy. Apart from a sturdy and freshly made up bed on one side there was also an almirah, some wicker stools and cushions, a wall mirror, a table and a chair.

Latif said, "This is your room."

Abdur guessed that the room had been spruced up especially for him. He sat on the chair, took off his shoes and socks and put them to one side. He opened his suitcase and, as he was taking out a shirt and pajama to wear about the house, it occurred to him again how extraordinarily still the whole place was. So far he had not seen anyone here other than Latif and Fatima, though there was someone called Bano, as yet unknown to Abdur.

For some time after Partition there had been some correspondence with Fatima's family, which then had become irregular and eventually died out. Through it, however, it had been learned that Fatima had had two sons and two daughters. Of course, the first son, Niyaz, had been born while Abdur's family was still in India; the other three had been born after they had left. They had also got a letter telling them of the death of Fatima's father-in-law, Sheikh Badruddin, but Abdur could not remember any news of the death of her husband, Ziaul, reaching Karachi. He had no knowledge of who were his nephews and nieces, how they were and what they were doing.

Abdur told Latif to sit down and asked him, "Is there anyone other than you and your mother staying in this house?"

"No," said Latif. He told him that his elder brother, Niyaz, had gone to live in Munger after his marriage. He was heartless and selfish and did not visit the house in Azimabad. The two sisters were married; the elder one, Nurbanu, lived in Rae Bareilly, and the younger, Mumtaz, lived in Saharanpur. However, the two daughters were so busy that they could hardly ever visit.

There was a brief pause, then Abdur asked, "How far did you get with your education?"

"I passed matriculation," Latif replied.

"What work do you do – service or business?"

"I have a small business. I get stainless steel utensils from a big merchant in Allahabad and sell them here at five percent commission." Latif considered for a moment, then said, "It was Uncle Dhanno who took me to meet the merchant. He stood surety for me and provided the capital so that the business could get established. All my savings had been spent on my sisters' weddings, so I had to borrow. Of course, I've paid him back."

In Fatima's father-in-law's house – as in Abdur's family home – there had never been any strict observance of purdah, and in their younger days Abdur would often take Dhanpat there. Everyone from Sheikh Badruddin down had liked him very much. Even after his friend had gone to Pakistan, Dhanpat's coming and going alone to the house had in no way been restricted; later, during hard times, he had always been by Fatima's side and had put Latif on his feet, even though there was no blood connection between him and Fatima's family. Even their religions were different. Abdur's heart was full of gratitude to Dhanpat.

"You've not married?" Abdur asked Latif.

"I did, but –"

"But what?"

Looking downcast Latif said, "The marriage didn't last."

"Why not?" Abdur was a little surprised.

Latif told him that he had married a girl from a wealthy home, one used to luxury. She wanted this, she wanted that, and Latif found it impossible to satisfy his wife's cupidity. The biggest problem was her unwillingness to live with her mother-in-law, an aversion encouraged by her own family. However, Latif could not even think of leaving his mother, and consequently there developed unrest, petty squabbling and acrimony until eventually the relationship broke down.

After a pause Abdur said, "You are still young. You have a long life ahead of you. Find a nice girl from a good family and get married again."

Latif explained that there was no certainty that marrying again would fill the family with joy or bring a smile to his mother's face. Who could say that the same kind of troubles would not start up once more? Better the way he was than that.

Abdur could see that the experience of the first marriage had made Latif wary and unwilling to tread that path again. Abdur would have liked to see his nephew happily married, but what could he do about it? He had come to this country for just a few days; once he had returned to Karachi the memories of this place would grow dim and the concern he had shown for Latif probably would fade too.

The sound of a woman's voice came up from the ground floor. "Latif-bhai! I've put the hot water in the bathroom."

Although he could not see her, Abdur guessed that the woman must be Bano, to whom Fatima had sent Latif a little earlier to tell about the hot water.

Latif opened an almirah on his right and took out some soap and a fresh towel. "Come on, Uncle," he said.

Having washed his face and hands and changed his clothes, Abdur went back with Latif to Fatima's room. As before, his sister was sitting up on one side of the bed. Almost immediately a big stainless steel tray bearing *puris,* halwa and *gulab jamuns* was set down by Bano on a fresh white towel laid out on the bed beside Abdur.

Bano had a strong, hard appearance, and must have been a little over forty. She was wearing a thick shawl over a cheap chintz salwar-kameez. Her skin was of a copper colour, and there were smallpox scars on her fleshy face.

Fatima was sitting up. Pointing to Abdur, she said to Bano, "This is Uncle who has come from Pakistan." Then she said to Abdur, "She is like a daughter to me. Four years she's been here now, looking after all the bother of the house. We couldn't survive a day without her."

So Bano was the housemaid, a courteous woman of gentle nature. She bowed and greeted Abdur with *"Adab,"* and said, "I've heard all about you from Latif-bhai and Auntie. We've all been looking forward to your arrival."

Abdur smiled.

Fatima said to Bano, "What are you giving Uncle for dinner tonight?"

"There's some meat, fish, vegetables," Bano replied.

"Prepare it well. Oh, and make some *kheer*. But before you put it all on the oven, give Uncle some tea." Fatima paused. Sadly she said almost to herself, "I see my brother after all these years and I can't even cook for him –" and her voice broke off.

Bano had gone.

After a little while of eating in silence, Abdur said, "I've heard everything from Latif. It's very sad, sister. I can understand your daughters not being able to come and see you. Girls don't have that freedom any more after they get married. But why hasn't Niyaz come to Azimabad since his marriage?"

Fatima remained quiet for a while. Then, tapping her forehead with her finger, she said sadly, "I don't blame him. It's all my fate."

Abdur sensed that Fatima would make no complaint about her eldest son. After a few moments he said, "And Latif's marriage broke down. He needs a family."

"I've said so many times. But he doesn't agree. What can I do, then?"

"How will he get by when you have gone?"

"There's nothing I can do about that. What must be will be."

In other words, Fatima had committed everything to fate. This was very likely part of her becoming old, sick and frail. All Fatima's will, all her spirit, had been spent.

Again Abdur was about to say something but Fatima went on.

"You've heard all about us. Yet even though we were born of the one mother, I know virtually nothing about you. I heard the news of father's and mother's deaths, but tell me about Asma and Nazzu." Asma and Nazzu – or Nazim – were their sister and brother, who also had gone with their parents to Pakistan.

Abdur told her about them as he went on eating. After Partition, they went with countless others across the border and straight to Karachi. Their father, Nabab Hussein, and hundreds of thousands of Indian Muslims like him, had the idea that if they could reach the land of their dreams, Pakistan, they could hold the moon in the palm of their hands. Their joy knew no bounds as they looked forward to the big mansions that were being made ready for their accommodation. But as soon as they set foot in Karachi, they were sent to a refugee camp and their dreams were shattered.

However, Nabab Hussein was not one to be kept down. He was an exceptionally honest, enterprising and hard-working man. While staying in the refugee camp he set about working to start his life again in his new country. With the aid of a government loan he opened a small cloth shop in the market of old Karachi. He was not willing to remain in the refugee camp, so as soon as he had arranged the finance, he took two rented rooms in an old barrack-type house and moved in with his wife and children. The children were enrolled in school.

Within a few years the business had grown quite big and its income had increased so Nabab Hussein left the small shop and opened a big one. He had saved some money and bought a house. However, as soon as he had got his family established, Nabab Hussein died after a few days of fever. Abdur had just completed his matriculation, Asma was in Class Nine and Nazim in Class Seven. They were all thrown into uncertainty.

Abdur had been a very good student. He had thought that he might go as far as M.A., but his wish was not to be fulfilled. After mourning his father's death he took over the shop in order to support his family. His business grew from one shop to acquiring another two. He then had Asma married once she had completed her matriculation. Nazim passed his B.A., took a job in government service, then got married and lived in the government quarters. Of course, Abdur got married himself after Asma's marriage, but not long before his wedding another tragedy struck with the death of his mother. Abdur had one son and a daughter. The boy was doing a master's degree in science, while this year the girl would present for her B.A. final examinations, after which her marriage would be arranged.

Although Fatima had got the news of her parents' deaths, she had known none of all this about her brothers and sister. She said nothing for a long time, then she asked, "Nazzu and Asma are in Karachi, then?"

Abdur nodded slowly. "Yes," he said.

"Do you see them?"

"Oh, yes. They visit on holidays. I visit them, too."

"They're all well?"

"Yes."

"I really long to see them. But it won't be in this life. Will you tell them to come here if they can?"

"Of course I will."

Somewhat distractedly, Fatima said, "There are often reports in the newspapers of unrest in Karachi."

Abdur explained that Karachi was a big port city and that it had its experience of bloodshed and gunshots. There was, of course, the Sunni-Shia rivalry, but there was also the unwillingness of the original residents to accept on fair terms the Urdu-speaking refugees who had come from India. Although such a long time had passed since the birth of Pakistan, they still would not break bread with those who had settled there after fleeing India. As a result there was on-going mutual mistrust and unrest as well as political turmoil, strikes, mass arrests, police shootings, agitation.

Fatima looked anxious. "None of you have been attacked, though?"

"Don't worry, sister," said Abdur. "We had to learn to live with all of this as soon as we got there."

Again there was silence. Then Abdur went on, "In Karachi we often hear of serious attacks on Muslims in India. It seems that anyone could be killed at any time. You have no fear of that, then?"

Latif was sitting on a chair beside them. He told Abdur that the turbulence created by the destruction of the Babri Masjid had spread to Azimabad where, after the bomb blasts in Bombay, the situation had become somewhat inflammatory and riots had broken out. The Muslim locality had been targeted. However, Dhanpat and many men like him had put a stop to that. There were also several political parties that had taken out peace marches. At that time Dhanpat and others spent many days defending the Muslim quarter.

"But –" Latif said.

"But what?" asked Abdur.

"Though they don't actually say it, there are many people who don't want us to stay in India. Pakistan was established as a separate state for Muslims – they say we should go there."

Abdur suddenly felt very concerned for Latif and his people. He said to Fatima, "Sister, I haven't seen you in such a long time. I wasn't aware of all this. If you say so, when I return to Karachi I will try to bring you and Latif to us there." He did not know what was the necessary procedure or even of the possibility of taking two Indians across the border, but what he said carried with it his fear and anxiety.

Fatima said, "But just a little while ago you said that they don't like Indian Muslims. You've been there a long time, it's all right for you. But if we suddenly turned up, would they be happy about that?"

Abdur was a little embarrassed. He could not think of anything to say.

"There's no need to worry," said Fatima. "Just as there are bad men here, there are also good and honest ones – much more so. I trust in them." She paused for a moment, then said, "After Independence my father-in-law and my husband wouldn't let any of us leave the country. As long as I live, I'll stay in Azimabad."

There was a resolve in Fatima's tone that was not to be resisted. It was as though she had taken on the doggedness of her father-in-law and husband. She would not leave her country to go anywhere.

A thought suddenly occurred to Abdur, and he said, "Not just Niyaz, I won't have met any of my other nephews and nieces before leaving. I made some guesses and brought salwar-kameez-dopattas, Pathan kurtas, and some cloth for trousers and shirts. I'll give them to you tomorrow. You can pass them on."

Abdur had heeded the warnings of his neighbours in Karachi and had kept quiet about visiting Ajmer Sharif and of returning to Pakistan after visiting his elder sister. But when he awoke the next morning he felt an overwhelming emotion and restlessness. He had been born in this town and had spent the first nine years of his life here – not only he, but his father and his grandfather and his grandfather's grandfather – five generations – had been born, grew up, were educated and worked in Azimabad. Having come back here after so long, who could say if there were any chance that he would ever come again? So he decided that he would look around the town. He would also visit the house that they had left.

Abdur washed himself, had some tea and breakfast, and asked Latif, "Do you have any pressing work today?"

"Why do you ask?"

"I'd like you to come to our old house with me."

"Certainly. You're here for just a few days, I'll come with you."

"It won't be any disturbance to your work?"

"No. I have someone to look after things. From time to time I'll drop in to check up."

But just as they were about to leave a great number of people from the Muslim quarter, ranging from young boys to old men, suddenly appeared, all of them with boundless curiosity on their faces. Somehow the word had got around that Nabab Hussain's son had come from Pakistan. Latif brought the older ones inside and offered them seats, while the younger ones stood crowding around outside the door and children peeped through the windows.

One very frail looking old man who must have been eighty or even eighty-five said, "My name is Jan Mohammed. Nabab Hussein was my friend. I heard that your father and your mother had both died. I was very sad to hear it. He paused for a moment, then went on, "Son, I knew you in your childhood so long ago. Your appearance has changed completely."

Abdur was unable to recognise Jan Mohammed at all, but he could hardly say so directly. He smiled and said, "Uncle, I have now turned sixty. I couldn't look like a boy forever."

"True –" The old man slowly nodded his head.

Another old man asked, "How are you all getting on in Pakistan?"

"We manage," said Abdur.

The other men all put to him question after question concerning the state of things in Pakistan, what the people who had gone there from Azimabad were now doing, who was doing what work, and so on. Abdur told them what he had told Fatima about Pakistan the night before. He also mentioned that the majority of those who had gone from Azimabad had settled in Karachi and were working either in business or in service professions. A few families had gone to Lahore, but Abdur had no connection with them and could not say how they were.

In the midst of all the hubbub of their conversation Dhanpat arrived. He pushed through the crowd into the room and said to the men of the Muslim locality, "What's all this? You've already got news of Abdur?"

They all answered as one, "Yes," and said that they had been hearing about things in Pakistan.

Dhanpat could see, from the way in which Abdur was hemmed in by them all, that he would not be able to easily get away. Yet he had decided to take him around the town and, if they had the time, to take him to his own house and his garage.

Trying not to offend anybody, Dhanpat said very respectfully, "Uncles, please don't be angry. Abdur will be here for a few days and will go to all your houses. But now please be so kind as to let him take leave of you."

At Dhanpat's words the old men insisted that Abdur visit them all and also share a humble meal with them. Were they not able to entertain the son of Nabab Hussein, their regrets would know no bounds. Abdur mentally calculated that if he accepted the invitations of so many men he would have to stay in Azimabad for at least twenty days, and there was no possibility of that. However, as a means of getting away he promised to eat at all their houses.

After the men had gone, Abdur raised his eyebrows in a look of amusement and asked, "And what was your purpose in driving them all away?"

Dhanpat replied, "I was rescuing you. Otherwise who knows how long you would have remained captive!" He paused for a moment, then said, "Are you going to stay sitting here in the house? Come. Let me show you the old town."

"I've already asked Latif to do just that. I had no idea that you would come so early. Just as we were thinking of going out, they all arrived. But I want to go and see our old house first."

"All right. Let's go, then."

The three of them left after telling Fatima they were going.

In Abdur's boyhood most of the roads in the Muslim quarter were unmade; only on one or two was there any asphalt. Now all the roads were sealed. On both sides the houses were so close together that they were touching each other.

Many of those who had come to meet Abdur a little while ago had not returned to their own homes but were grouped about chatting on the road. Seeing him again they immediately pursued him like jackals. Women of various ages were looking curiously through the windows of every house, and those people who were sitting on the front veranda or courtyard getting some of the winter sun called out a few words, having guessed that the companion of Dhanpat and Latif was the son of Nabab Hussein, who come from Pakistan.

It was about a fifteen-minute walk through narrow winding lanes from Fatima's house to Abdur's old family home. The house was not exactly as it had been before. When Abdur's family had left for Pakistan there had been two storeys, but now an extra floor had been built on top. The whole place had recently been painted, and the smell of fresh paint still hung around the doors and window-frames. The front courtyard was still much the same. There, with a quilt wrapped around his body, an old man was half lying on a charpoy, while five or six little children were raising a hubbub all around him. From the outside it could be guessed that a good many people lived in the house.

Dhanpat took Latif and Abdur up to the old man and called to him. "Uncle Akbar –"

The old man quickly sat up, supporting himself on his hands. He was over eighty but his movement was by no means impaired, and his eyesight too was, on the whole, quite good. Seeing the three of them he said, "Oh, Dhanno, Lati. I see you have brought someone with you."

"Yes. This is Abdur, the son of Nabab Hussein," said Dhanpat.

"Which Nabab Hussein?"

"The one who was the owner of your house."

"You mean the one who took his wife and children to Pakistan after Independence?"

"Yes."

Akbar was quite taken aback. He looked straight at Abdur and asked, "You've come from Pakistan?"

"Yes, I have," answered Abdur.

Suspiciously, Akbar asked, "You've suddenly come to India?"

Abdur could guess roughly at the cause of the old man's suspicion. Before leaving for Pakistan he had heard that one Akbar Ali had given some cash to his father to live in their house. It must, indeed, have seemed very suspicious that the son of Nabab Hussein should suddenly turn up here so many years later.

Before Abdur could answer him, Akbar Ali again asked, "Have you all come back to India?"

In other words the old man was worried that he had come back to India to settle in this house. Abdur smiled to himself and said, "No, Uncle. There is no possibility of our returning here." He then explained the reasons that had brought him to India.

While Akbar Ali's worries dispersed it suddenly occurred to him that he was not being exactly hospitable to the son of Nabab Hussein. In a fluster he said, "Why are you standing up? Sit down, sit down!"

They sat down very close to one another on the charpoy. The children had become quiet and stood at a distance looking attentively at the unfamiliar Abdur.

Akbar Ali said to the children, "Go and tell your parents to come here to me right now."

The children ran off. Then Akbar's three sons and their wives, accompanied by the children, came out of the house and stood near the charpoy.

Akbar Ali introduced Abdur to them all and said, "This house once belonged to his family. Now, fifty one years later, he has come from Pakistan to visit the home of his forefathers." He paused, then said, "But first give him tea and sweets. Then I will show him the house myself."

Although he had eaten breakfast not long before, he could not avoid eating again. The wives of Akbar Ali's sons brought *balushai,* laddus and spiced hot tea. He had to have it all.

Then, when Abdur had finished his tea and sweets, Akbar took him to show him around the house. He could remember very clearly which room had been his, which had been his brother Nazim's, which had been his sister Asma's, and which had been his parents'. As he looked at it all a tremendous wave of nostalgia welled up in his breast.

Latif and Dhanpat did not accompany them but remained sitting on the charpoy in the courtyard. A little later, when Abdur came back and was about to take his leave, Akbar Ali suddenly remembered something. He called Abdur over to another corner of the courtyard and said to him in a low voice, "It is good that you have come from Pakistan, son. There is a rather urgent matter –"

Abdur was taken aback. "What matter?"

Akbar Ali told him that before going to Pakistan Nabab Hussein had given him the right to the house for about ten thousand rupees, but he had not had the property registered by the court as he had been in such a hurry to get away with his wife and children. Afterwards, of course, Akbar Ali, through bribes and stratagems, had had the house put in his name. However, there remained a hitch in his mind - what if the the title deed was with Nabab Ali and one day his sons should return and want their house back? Then there would really be a problem.

Abdur said, "Father never told me any of this. The deed to this house is not with us either. You don't have to be concerned about that, Uncle. If I ever return to India, I won't want the house back." He paused, then said, "Apart from that, we are foreigners. Why would an Indian court pay any heed to us?"

"I believe what you say," said Akbar Ali, "but your brother and sister –"

Abdur interrupted him. "They won't want it either."

"But I have one request to put to you."

"What request?"

Akbar Ali told him that if he should write on a stamped affidavit that he and his brother and sister would never claim title to the house, then he could die free from worry.

"I will do as you ask," said Abdur. He had heard that many Hindus did not want those who had left India to return there. Now he could see that there were also some Muslims who were not likely to welcome them back, either.

They came out from the old house onto the main road and took a tonga. Indicating Abdur, Dhanpat said to the tonga wallah, "My friend here has come back to Azimabad after a very long time. We want to show him the town."

"Right," said the tonga wallah.

As it had seemed to Abdur when he had come from the station the day before, Azimabad had grown tremendously. He had no idea of how many new neighbourhoods there now were. He noticed two big parks, a girls' college, a big hospital, a couple of fine nursing homes, even a sports stadium, none of which was there fifty one years ago.

And so the noontime passed in sightseeing around the town.

Looking up at the sky Dhanpat said, "We should stop now. I'll drop you two home, and in the afternoon I'll come and take you to my garage."

Dhanpat let Latif and Abdur get down at the main road in front of the Muslim quarter and went on his way. Three hours later he came back to take them to his garage in the Chowk Bazar in the middle of the town.

In Abdur's boyhood days the Chowk Bazar was very small, with little shops on either side of it. Under a high roof the vegetable sellers, fishmongers and butchers were all spread out, and on each side were several old, one – or two-storey tin buildings. But now the place was barely recognisable. The old buildings had been pulled down and new ones put up. There was also a rather grand supermarket, as well as a line of so many shops, banks, a post office, private telephone booths, a Xerox office – more than Abdur could take in. To one side was a vast courtyard for car-parking where about a hundred scooters, jeeps and private cars were standing.

Dhanpat's garage was on one side of the Chowk Bazar. Inside a tall shed there was a workshop for cars, autorickshaws and scooters and, next to it, a well-appointed office with a desk, chairs and telephone. Dhanpat took Abdur and Latif to the office, where they sat down. He told one of the men working in the shed to bring tea and biscuits and then called to the neighbouring shopkeepers to come and meet Abdur. Some of the people who had brought their cars for repair also wanted to be introduced.

There was a tremendous curiosity about Pakistan. Abdur answered their various questions as he had those of Latif and of Jan Mohammed of the Muslim quarter. However, there were a few discordant voices among them.

"What do you want in coming back to India, Mian?" and "We have a billion people in India. Don't try to burden us with any more."

As he listened to all this Abdur's face became pale. But Dhanpat burst out angrily, "What are you all saying! He's not come here to put any burdens on anyone. His sister is in India, as are his nieces and nephews and other relations. He has come to see them. After a few days he'll be going back."

"It's best that he does," said a few of them.

Having shut up the garage at eight at night Dhanpat was taking Abdur and Latif home. He said, "Don't worry about what they said. They're just a pack of ignorant pigs."

Abdur was not affected by it. He shook his head slowly and said, "There are also such people in Pakistan. Let anyone from India go there, he too will be unwelcome."

It was about twenty minutes by tonga from the Chowk Bazar. On their way Dhanpat suddenly remembered something. He said, "Oh, I forgot to tell you."

"What was that?" asked Abdur.

"I was telling my father about you. He asked me to bring you to our house. When will you come?"

This startled Abdur, and he saw once again the picture of Lajpat Singh setting fire to their house fifty one years ago; he felt beset by a strange sense of panic. Why should the man be inviting him? No, he would not meet that man at all, though he did not tell that to Dhanpat directly. Abdur remained silent for a little while, then he said, "I am in Azimabad for only a few days. I'll go and see Uncle before going back to Karachi."

"But you must eat with us when you come."

"All right."

Dhanpat went once a day to Fatima's house to try to get Abdur to go with him to his house; in an endeavour to avoid this Abdur was taking up the invitations of the old men of the Muslim locality, although he had originally thought not to take up anyone's invitation.

Dhanpat was greatly put out. Becoming angry, he said, "What is it with you? I've told you how my father sends me every day to bring you to our place. Why do you have some objection to coming to our house?"

With an embarrassed look Abdur said, "Don't be angry, Dhanno. The old men of the locality keep at me so much, I can't say no to them."

"I have been asking you too."

Abdur did not respond except to take the hand of his old friend in his.

Then in no time at all came the time for his return to Karachi. His visa would expire in just a few more days and he would have to be on the plane to Pakistan.

Abdur had decided to catch the local afternoon train that day at three o'clock to Allahabad and then take the Delhi Mail. He would arrive in Delhi the following evening. He would spend the night at some hotel and the next day do some shopping. He would have to spend that night too in Delhi, and the next day fly to Karachi.

Abdur had already announced the time of his departure, and since morning the atmosphere in the house had been extremely glum. Now and then Fatima would break into a feeble sobbing. Taking her two hands, Abdur said, "Don't cry, sister. I'll come again." But as he spoke his voice ran dry and he felt a strange discomfort welling up inside him. Latif was a manly man and did not cry like his mother did. Nevertheless, his face was marked by a profound melancholy.

Dhanpat had said the day before that he would come at around one thirty, and he and Latif would take Abdur to the station and put him on the train to Allahabad.

Abdur was still uncomfortable with Dhanpat. Dhanpat no more insisted on his going to his house, though it was clear that he was terribly disappointed. However, Abdur still had not told him why he would not go.

Later in the morning Fatima brought out from the almirah a jewel box and took out of it an old necklace, an emerald, a few rings and some earrings, and said, "Take these and give them to your family."

Abdur was taken aback. "No, no, don't give these to me."

"Can't I give something to my own brothers' and sister's children if I like?"

Abdur explained that he was a foreigner and unable to take away any gold or jewellery or anything of value. He would have to surrender it at the airport.

With a sorrowful look Fatima said, "They're my things. Why can't I give them to my own family?" And covering her face with her hands she began to cry again.

Abdur had great trouble consoling his elder sister. He explained that it was the law and he could not thwart it. It would be especially dangerous for him to take out gold and jewellery.

Dhanpat arrived just before one o'clock. By then Abdur had packed his suitcase and holdall and had had his lunch.

"All ready?" asked Dhanpat.

Abdur nodded. "Yes."

"Come down with me for a moment."

"Why?"

"I need you to."

Dhanpat went out with Abdur to the alley in front of the house. An old man was sitting in an autorickshaw there. He would have been in his mid-eighties and it was obvious that he was very frail.

Indicating Abdur, Dhanpat said to the old man, "Father, here is Abdur."

Abdur had not thought that Lajpat Singh would come himself. His heart started to thump.

Lajpat got out of the auto and, taking Abdur's hand in both of his, said, "I sent word through Dhanno time and again, but I know why you never came. Son, a long time has passed since Independence. We were not in our right minds then. I treated your family appallingly. I used to think then that if the Muslims left it would be for the good of India. Later, with a cool head, I came to see the injustice of that. I wanted you to come so that I could say this. You didn't come, so I had to come to you."

Abdur just looked at him, stunned. Was this the same Lajpat Singh who one day had set fire to their house?

Lajpat went on. "After you had all gone, I told Dhanno to look after whoever had remained in the Muslim quarter, especially your sister and her children."

Abdur tried to speak but the words would not come out.

Lajpat kept on. "My son, you have all suffered so much on my account. Now, more than fifty years later, no one can do anything about it. Forgive me." Catching his breath he said, "Next time you come to India, be sure to come to my house."

Abdur mumbled, "Of course I'll come, Uncle."

Because of his continuous talk, Lajpat was quite out of breath and could not remain standing there any longer. He added, "Son, I have grown very old. My body is very weak. I have suffered from fever for the last fifteen years and it now troubles me greatly. I must go home and lie down. Goodbye –"

Abdur went on standing there for a while after Lajpat Singh's autorickshaw had gone around the bend in the lane and out of sight. He felt that he would have to come again to India, not just for Fatima and her family, but for this man, too.

# FATHER

## *janak*

In the middle of any winter's day, when the sun had risen directly overhead, Shobhana would be carefully arranging the couple of Bengali newspapers, the copies of *Ramayana, Mahabharata* and *Chandi* and the spectacle case beside the bed on the red carpet on the long first floor balcony facing west. In the meantime her father-in-law, Shekharnath, would have finished his midday meal. Having rinsed his mouth and wiped his face with a towel, he would drag his unsteady, eighty-year-old body onto the balcony.

Reading his religious books and newspapers in the middle of the day had been Shekharnath's cherished habit for a long time, but in recent years he had become severely racked by arthritis. From time to time he had excruciating pain in his shoulders and hips that felt as though someone had thrust a burning hot blade into those parts of his body. Physiotherapy and strong doses of medicine had had little effect. Nowadays, once his lunch had settled in his stomach his eyelids would get heavy and any more reading of his books or newspapers would send him off to sleep.

When he came onto the first floor balcony, the rays of the midday sun shone steadily across his legs, but as the sun tended towards the west its warmth gradually spread over his entire body, providing a tonic that he so badly needed. Today, as on other days, Shekharnath fell asleep almost as soon as he had lain down, and when he woke up it was well into the afternoon and the sun had gradually become screened from him by the tall buildings and trees to the west.

Shekharnath continued to lie there, awake. He took his round bifocal glasses from their velvet case and put them on. His whole body was bathed in the balm of the dim golden sunshine of the late afternoon. He knew that Shobhana would soon come with a cup of saccharine-sweetened tea and that no sooner had he finished it than the last of the day's light would start to fade. The winter evening would fall softly and the temperature would suddenly drop a few degrees. Then Shobhana would not let her father-in-law stay a moment longer on the open balcony but would hurriedly take him inside. Shekharnath was waiting for that.

It was Sunday.

At the other end of the balcony a group of yellow-beaked blackbirds scampered about, now and then bursting suddenly into a joyous chirping, while from the ground floor came a tremendous racket, which meant that Sandip, Shobhana, Raja and Ruku were engaged in a lively game of table tennis or carom.

Sandip, an executive of a leading multinational company, was Shekharnath's one and only son and Raja and Ruku were his grandchildren. Raja was studying first year English honours at St. Xavier's and Ruku was in Class Eleven at Calcutta Girls'. Sandip and Shobhana were like friends to their children, spending their spare time with them in conversation, watching good videos or playing games such as carom. At this time there was no sound coming from anywhere other than the frenzy of the blackbirds and the frivolity from downstairs.

In front of the house was the thirty-foot wide Abhay Haldar Road which ran straight to the tramline, on the other side of which was a middling-size park. In Shekharnath's neighbourhood, most of the houses were of one or two storeys, though there were several of three storeys, while on the other side of the park there was a stretch of high-rise buildings.

There was hardly anyone on Abhay Haldar Road, and on the main road only one or two trams and a truck or a minibus were running, seemingly in no hurry and with no destination. Further on, in the park, countless children wearing various coloured clothes ran all about, and groups of mothers or nurses watched over them. It was like a scene in a silent movie in Eastman colour.

Shekharnath was sitting up and looking out at the road. The blanket around him had come loose, and as he was slowly readjusting it he noticed a taxi pull up opposite the tramline and a middle-aged lady get out of it. She asked something of someone in the street – apparently inquiring about an address – then started walking towards Shekharnath's house, but the taxi remained at the junction. Shekharnath's dull, eighty-year-old eyes could barely make out that there was someone as well as the driver in the taxi.

The lady was about fifty and she had a handsome, dignified appearance. A little excess flesh had accumulated on her cheeks and around her neck and waist, but the last vestiges of beauty had not yet disappeared from her face. She was wearing an expensive sari, and her eyes were featured by a fashionable pair of glasses; on her right shoulder she carried a very fine lady's bag, and, in her left hand, was a large suitcase.

Shekharnath watched without curiosity, but was surprised when the lady, looking at the numbers of the houses, stopped in front of his house, 'Shanti Niwas'. Although she had become a little portly, there were still remnants of one who, thirty years ago, might have been a slender and vivacious young woman: her innocent, oval mouth, her sparkling eyes with their thick lashes, the dimple in her chin and her smooth, unlined cheeks. Shekharnath muttered to himself, "My God, let it not be her!"

The front door was directly under the first floor balcony, and when she came to it she could no longer be seen from above. When she pressed the doorbell, its musical sound rang throughout the house, and a few moments later Shekharnath could hear the door being opened. He guessed that Sandip and the others would be eager to see who the caller was.

Shekharnath remained seated, his nerves on edge. Then he could just make out the lady saying, "Is this the home of Shekharnath Bandyopadhyay?"

He recognised the voice. Although it had become a little rough after all that time, it still sounded like the vibrant, resonating hum of the sitar.

Sandip said, "Yes. Who do you want?"

"I – I have come from Dhaka. Can we sit down and talk?"

"Yes, yes. Of course. Come in." Shekharnath heard the door being shut.

The visitor said she had come from Dhaka. Then it had to be her. Despite the abundance of fresh air on this winter afternoon it seemed as though his breath had stopped and that his lungs would crack.

The excited racket had stopped and everything downstairs had become quite still. At first Shekharnath could not decide what he would do. But after looking for a few moments down at the street in the dying rays of the sun, he made up his mind. In a few minutes Sandip or Shobhana, or both of them, would run up to the first floor, but he would not look at the face of the one who had come from

Dhaka. After all this time she had died in his mind. Yet no, she was still alive, though Shekharnath had tried to forget her, praying for her death year after year. Now would her coming to Calcutta after thirty years once again open up that old wound buried deep in his breast?

Shekharnath hoisted up his worn old body and a current of pain shot from his waist down to the soles of his feet. On another occasion he might have uttered a sound of grief, but he no longer had the feeling for it.

His own room was on the left of the balcony. There were two doors to it: one led into the house, the other out onto the balcony. His heart thumping, Shekharnath went into his room and shut both doors.

There was very little furniture in the room. A freshly laundered bed was made up on a thick mattress on an old-style bedstead against one wall. On the other side there was a small stand with figures of gods and goddesses ranging from Kali to Ganesh. There was also a clothes rack, a wardrobe and a couple of antiquated steel trunks. On one wall there was a Bengali calendar with a picture of Lakshmi, the goddess of wealth, and above that was a framed photograph of a woman in her mid-forties. The smiling and beautiful lady was Hemlata, Shekharnath's wife. The photograph had been taken in 1963, the year in which she was burned to death in Mirpur. It was the last picture ever taken of Hemlata.

Shekharnath bolted both doors against whoever might come and got up onto the bed. In a strange reverie he sat and looked at his wife's photograph.

So many times Shekharnath had resolved not to look back, for in the passing of those thirty years he had been buffeted both inside and out. Who could say how much heart-ache he had suffered? Sandip had been only a fifteen-year-old boy then. As he looked at her face, Shekharnath tried to forget the grief, the sorrow, the distress.

Time's magic hand had healed so much of the pain, and Shekharnath sometimes felt that it had all been forgotten, but the dark side of memory had preserved intact all that he thought had been dispelled – the terror, the panic, the nightmare. He remembered how Hemlata had been so terribly frightened when, in the time after Partition, waves of refugees were rolling out of East Pakistan into West Bengal, Tripura and Assam. She had said to Shekharnath, "Come. Let's go and find a place to live in Calcutta." At that time in East Pakistan it was not such a problem to sell property.

Shekharnath, then thirty-five or thirty-six, was a junior administrative officer in MacKenzie Brothers' jute-mill, which was situated beside the Dhaleshwari river at Mirpur, about forty miles from Dhaka. Shekharnath's family had lived in this town for a hundred and fifty years, and his was the seventh generation. In all that time no one had ever thought of moving anywhere else. For generation after generation, the roots of the Bandyopadhyay family had been set deep in the soil of this old town. It would not have been at all easy to pull them up.

Shekharnath had retorted, "Why should we go to Calcutta? Have we done anything wrong? This is my home, and here I'll stay."

"But don't you see? Everyday so many people are leaving –"

"Let them. We are not going."

Hemlata looked worried as she said, "I know in my heart that we won't be able to keep on staying here."

On the one hand, Shekharnath was staunchly orthodox, assiduously observing all the rituals and practices integral to the life of a brahman; on the other, he was infinitely trusting of his non-Hindu neighbours. He said emphatically, "We know everyone in this town. None of them would ever so much as scratch us."

Hemlata said nothing.

Shekharnath went on, "There have been not a few riots in Mirpur, but have we been hurt? Haven't people run to us in time of danger?"

Their neighbours were magnanimous and compassionate and had always stood by them in any time of trouble. At the time of the 1946 riots, when blood flowed throughout undivided India, they allowed no one to lay a finger on Shekharnath. But be that as it may, Hemlata did not have the same faith in people that her husband had – he had maintained a foundation of trust even after Partition – though she did not, of course, openly express whatever suspicions she may have had about anyone in the town. She asked apprehensively, "But what about Khuku? What will be her future?" Khuku was the pet name of their only child at that time, but to the world she was known as Manika, and she would later earn her living in education. Khuku then was five.

Shekharnath had no trouble discerning the clear implication in Hemlata's question. She was the daughter of a traditional Barishal brahman family, like his, who had come to her father-in-law's house saturated with all the old values and conservatism of her father's house, so the orthodoxy of the Bandyopadhyays was a part of her too. Hemlata's thoughts and ideas, her worries and concerns, were all enclosed by a strong iron frame beyond which it was impossible for her ever to stray.

Secretly Shekharnath felt a little amused. He had said, "You must be mad to be worrying now about the future of a little five-year-old girl!"

"I wouldn't be worrying if the country had remained as it was. Anyhow, Khuku won't be five forever."

"Do you think that everyone around here has become inhuman?"

"Perhaps not. But Khuku's –"

"You want to talk about her marriage?"

Hemlata had said nothing but looked straight at her husband.

Shekharnath had said, "The country may be divided, but not everyone is going to shut up their homes and go across the border. From among those who stay, you will certainly find the boy of your choice for Khuku." ...

... Suddenly, there was a gentle tapping on the closed inside door and, along with it, Shobhana's quiet voice could be heard. "Father – father –"

Shekharnath was woken from his memories, but he refrained from giving any answer. He knew why Shobhana had come.

After calling for a little longer, Shobhana went away. A little later there came the familiar sound of another pair of footsteps running impatiently up the stairs and stopping in front of the door. This time it was Sandip.

"Father, open the door!" he called, urgently. He sounded agitated and excited.

Shekharnath sat there, silent, as though struck dumb.

Sandip went on, "Open the door, open the door! Didi has come from Dhaka."

Shekharnath's heart seemed to stop, then started to beat with such force that he could almost hear it. It was as though a thousand drums were being beaten wildly inside his chest.

Sandip was calling anxiously, "Father, won't you come and see Didi?"

Shekharnath remained seated. Crestfallen, confused and embarrassed, Sandip stopped calling and went back downstairs.

Instantly Shekharnath was again lost in his memories of those days beside the Dhaleshwari. . . .

. . . Soon after the talk with Hemlata about Khuku, the atmosphere at Mirpur quickly changed. Like the flood of refugees who had gone to India, countless people were now migrating to East Pakistan, having been uprooted from their homes in the states of Bihar and Uttar Pradesh. After the big cities of Dhaka, Chittagong and Khulna had been filled, many of them went to Mirpur. Like the East Pakistani refugees, these people from India felt angry and resentful for all they had lost and were singularly bent on revenge. The jaws of Mirpur's new arrivals took on a ruthless set and their eyes blazed with fire.

The poison of the profound hatred and mistrust that were integral to the two-nation theory in no way abated after Partition; indeed, it gradually increased. Relations between India and Pakistan were so complex and sensitive that for the flimsiest of reasons a violent commotion might be ignited on either side of the border. Malice had set its gunpowder to the winds; all it wanted was a spark.

In the meantime Mirpur too became heated, and from time to time petty riots broke out. However, as before, Shekharnath's neighbours kept him and his family safe.

A number of years passed in what seemed to be no time at all, during which the British directors of MacKenzie Brothers made the jute-mill over to a Dhaka industrialist and left the country. The environment at the mill was no longer the same as it had been before and Shekharnath could see that now he was unwanted. He talked about this a lot with Hemlata. By now Khuku had grown, and they also had another two children, the boys Sandip and Sanjay.

It was not only the atmosphere at the factory but the looks and actions of their neighbours in whom they had placed their hope and trust also began to change. The boundless faith in people that Shekharnath had maintained even after Partition was starting to crack. One minute he would think of going to Calcutta, the next he would decide to hold out a little longer. Actually, Calcutta was totally unknown to him; he could not imagine where they would live nor how his wife and children would survive should they go there.

Eventually another spontaneous riot broke out in Mirpur, but before their formerly well-disposed neighbours could run to their aid, their house was set alight, Hemlata was burnt to death, and Khuku was abducted. Shekharnath, who was at the mill, and the boys, who were in school, survived it all.

Now Shekharnath was no longer resolved to stay in this country. Sympathisers advised him, "Go to Calcutta. It's no longer good to stay here." And so they arranged for the sale of the house, realising no more than an eighth of its true value.

After they got to Calcutta, relations who had gone there straight after Partition bought them the house on Abhay Haldar Road. Sandip and Sanjay were enrolled in a good school, and Shekharnath got a minor position in a mercantile firm. But Sanjay did not last very long, dying of a wrongly diagnosed disease a few years after coming to Calcutta.

After losing almost everything, Shekharnath hung on close to Sandip, in whom his life was now bound up. Sandip was a very peaceable and amenable boy and he was also an exceptionally talented student. He took a master's degree in commerce with first class honours and, after graduating, was appointed to a company secretaryship in a multinational firm. Then Shekharnath arranged for his marriage.

Shekharnath had come to Calcutta with two gaping wounds in his heart – Hemlata and Khuku. Hemlata had been murdered, but Khuku? Everyday he prayed to God that Khuku too might be dead. But God had not heard his prayer.

Shekharnath was not aware that evening had fallen until he noticed the small circles of fog that had formed in the cold winter dark under the street lights outside.

Shekharnath did not want to get down from the bed and turn on the light in his room, and he was quite oblivious to the cold north wind coming in through the open window. He remained sitting there, unaware, unfeeling. For some time he thought of nothing, then he noticed the sound of four pairs of footsteps on the stairs. This time Sandip and Shobhana had come together, and Raja and Ruku had come with them.

Again there was a knock at the door and they all started calling together, "Father – Father – Grandfather – Grandfather –"

And, as before, Shekharnath sat there inert and unresponsive through it all.

Then Sandip's voice came over all the others'. He said, "Don't worry, Didi has gone. You won't have to see her. Now open the door." There was a mixture of pain and sorrow and worry in his voice.

How amazing! Now that he heard she had gone, Shekharnath felt a strange sense of anxiety for the one he had not wanted to see, the one whom he had wanted to be dead for the last thirty years. He dragged himself down from the bed, switched on the light and opened the door.

For a few moments they all fixed their eyes on him, then they all came into the room together.

Shekharnath was wearing nothing other than a dhoti and a short-sleeve, homespun shirt. The cold wind continued to blow through the open window onto the street and he was shivering with the cold, though he did not realise it. Shobhana ran to a corner of the room and took a shawl from the clothes rack, wrapped it tight around her father-in-law, and helped him up onto the bed.

Sandip, Raja and Ruku came close to Shekharnath but they did not sit down. Sandip said, "What's the matter, Father? Didi has been trying to find us for so many years. At last she got this address from the Indian High Commission in Dhaka and rushed straight here, but you sat in your room with the door locked and didn't call for her at all! She left in tears. She won't come back again." He paused for a moment, then went on, "What do you imagine Harun-da thinks?"

"Who is Harun-da?" Shekharnath choked on the words.

"Didi's husband."

No sooner had Sandip uttered the word than the look on Shekharnath's face changed altogether. He looked extremely distressed, even as though he had stopped breathing. Immediately he heard the Muslim name Harun, he was thrown completely off balance by all his old brahmanical prejudices. In a broken and indistinct voice he mumbled, "Husband – Khuku's husband –"

Sandip noted his father's reaction. He had been all the while calm, unperturbed and forbearing, but now he became a little agitated. "You know, Harun-da has done so much for Didi! If he had not reached out to her, who knows where she might be today!" He then went on to explain that at the time of the riot in Mirpur in 1963 when some of the rabble abducted Khuku, Harun was a sub-divisional officer in that region. Some months later he rescued Khuku and took her into his own house. Then he tried to find Shekharnath and his family in order to return her to them but by then they had gone to

Calcutta. After a few years of trying and getting no news of Shekharnath he married the rejected girl for the sake of her respectability. There was no objection of any kind from his parents; rather, they accepted Khuku with open hearts. Harun, the young officer of those days, was now a joint secretary in the Ministry of Education. They had one son, a doctor, and two daughters, who were studying in college.

"Perhaps you will say," said Sandip, "that it would have been right for Didi to have committed suicide. But I say that it was right that she married Harun. There was nothing more honourable she could have done."

Shekharnath was nonplussed. What was Sandip saying, the son of an orthodox, conservative brahman family? Shekharnath just stared at him, utterly stunned.

It seemed that something had come over Sandip. Speaking his mind he said, "Could you have found such a boy for Didi in our community? Never." To underline his feeling, he said in English, "They are happy. Extremely happy."

Shekharnath wanted to say something, but he could not articulate the words.

Sandip went on, "It is terribly wrong, Father, that Didi will never come back here to us."

Shekharnath said nothing, and Sandip continued, "Harun-da had come too. He wanted to see how the daughter was received in her father's house, then he would come in himself. But that was the end of it."

There was an element of irony in what the son had said, but Shekharnath was not aware of it. Breathing heavily, he said, "He came too?"

"Yes. He waited in the taxi opposite the tramline."

Shekharnath remembered that he had seen someone sitting in the taxi when Khuku had left it that afternoon. That must have been Harun!

A few moments later Sandip and the others left. Shobhana brought dinner for Shekharnath at half past eight – two wholemeal chapatis, some potato and cauliflower curry, a bowl of milk and a sweet. Having served her father-in-law his meal, she made up his bed, helped him into it, tucked the mosquito net in all around him, and left the room.

On any other night, Shekharnath's eyes would have shut as soon as he had lain down, but tonight he could not get to sleep. Time and again Khuku's face came before his eyes. After lying there for a long time he drew aside the mosquito net, got down from the bed, and walked somewhat unsteadily around the room. He felt that his heart was continually cracking, quite beyond his control.

Towards daybreak, having not slept all night, Shekharnath had made up his mind. He went into the bathroom attached to his room, washed his face, then went to the other end of the first floor and stood outside Raja's room. He called a few times, and Raja woke up. He was surprised when he opened the door. "Grandfather," he said, "it's you! What's the matter?"

"Nothing," said Shekharnath. "Where is your aunt putting up in Calcutta?"

"At some hotel in Park Street."

"Can you take me there right now?"

Raja could hardly believe his ears. Astonished, he said, "You want to go there?"

Shekharnath nodded his head slowly. "Yes," he said.

"But you won't see her if you do."

"Why not?"

"They're going to Dhaka today on the early morning flight. They'll have left the hotel by the time we get there."

Shekharnath thought for a moment, then said, "In that case, have a quick wash and get ready. We'll go to the airport. There's no need to say anything about this to anyone now."

Shekharnath returned to his own room and quickly changed his clothes. Beside him was a small iron trunk; he opened it and took out a small leather bag, then closed the trunk.

When Shekharnath left the house silently with Raja a few minutes later, none of the others had woken up.

On this winter morning the houses all around, the tramline and the distant park were all clouded in fog. No one had turned off the street lights yet, which were lustreless like the eyes of dead fish. The sun was still very late in rising.

When Shekharnath and Raja reached the airport by taxi, they saw that Khuku and Harun had got there before them. Khuku – or Manika – caught sight of Shekharnath from a distance. She and Harun stopped in their tracks, as did Raja and Shekharnath. Shekharnath's heart started to thump, and he noticed that Khuku's lips were trembling. On her face were sorrow and joy and pride and accusation – so much was reflected there!

Without realising it the father had, step by step, come up to his daughter. Suddenly the fifty-year-old Khuku began to sob like a child. Then, with an extraordinary passion, she threw herself at her father's feet, but did not touch him. With both his hands Shekharnath raised his daughter up and held her to his chest for a long time. He felt his chest being bathed in tears.

Harun was standing a little away from them. He had an exceptionally handsome, intelligent and vivacious face. Shekharnath called him. He came and touched Shekharnath's feet and Shekharnath held him, too, to his chest.

The announcement came over the public address system that passengers for Dhaka should board the aircraft, which was now ready for take-off.

Very slowly Shekharnath released Khuku and Harun and took from the leather bag a gold necklace, a pair of gold bangles and a diamond ring. Giving his daughter the necklace and the bangles, he said, "I've not given you anything. Your mother had these made for your wedding." Giving the diamond ring to Harun, he said, "Put this on. I don't know if it will fit you. If not, take it to a goldsmith and have it altered."

Nothing was said for a while.

After another announcement from the public address system, Harun said, "We have to go now."

Shekharnath slowly nodded his head.

Harun said, "Do come to Dhaka some time. I will arrange it all for you."

"But before that, bring the children," said Shekharnath.

"We will."

Harun and his wife walked towards the security enclosure. As he watched after them, Shekharnath thought to himself, "What a fine boy!" And at that moment he was not at all aware of all the age-old tradition running in his blood.

# THE FOREIGNER

## *bideshi*

It had been Altaf Hossain's time-honoured habit to wake at daybreak, and so today he had got up at five and was sitting on the hotel balcony.

It was the middle of November and fogs had started to fall in Calcutta. The sun had not come up yet, and the biting north wind, blowing strongly and spreading its chill over the city, indicated the early arrival of winter this year.

Over his pajama and warm panjabi Altaf Hossain was wearing a thick woollen shawl, which he had wrapped closely around himself. He was quite comfortable in this early morning cold. From where he was sitting everything was dim as far as he could see. In the fog the high-rise buildings all around looked like a vague pencil sketch. The broad asphalt road sixty feet below was quite deserted, and it was only the grating sounds of a few milk trucks and newspaper vans that shattered the dawn silence.

Ten days ago Altaf had gone from Dhaka to Ajmer Sharif via Delhi, and on his way back from there had come to spend a few days in Calcutta. He was now seventy six. He had last come to this city forty five years earlier, before the country was partitioned. He had a particular reason for coming here this time.

Even at seventy six Altaf's health was, on the whole, very good. He could still come and go on his own. Still, there was no saying how long he would live. He had now come to India wanting to meet once again his boyhood friends. Maybe he would not get that opportunity again.

However, he was not at all sure of what he would see. He knew nothing of his old friends from the small country town in East Bengal before the Partition how many of them were still living or where they had drifted to and what their addresses were. It would be impossible to trace four or five men in this vast metropolis of ten million people.

The Calcutta he had come to previously, forty five years ago, bore no particular similarity at all with the city of today. Countless high-rise buildings, hundreds of thousands of products of a population explosion, an endless stream of traffic on the roads, and a city that spread out in so many ways in so many directions he could not imagine that he had ever been to such a place. Who could have thought that the city of his memory could have changed so much! There was only a slight resemblance to the Calcutta before the Partition, apart from which everything was unfamiliar, unimaginable and even startling. One could wander the streets here for five years and never find one's friends. But on consideration, he had one lead. When he had arrived in Calcutta three days back and had checked his luggage into the hotel, he got hold of the addresses of three newspapers, one English and two Bengali, and had gone to each of their offices and lodged a letter with the letters page department:

I was born in the small town of Bajitpur in Dhaka district, in the house of four generations of my family. The first thirty years of my life were spent in this town. After the country became East Pakistan in 1947, I went to the capital, Dhaka. I have been a permanent resident of Dhaka for the past forty five years.

While I was in Bajitpur I had a few close friends from boyhood days: Paritosh Goswami, Manimohan Ghosh, Ambika Chakladar, Bhupatinath Basak and Nripati Sarkar. For generations their families, too, lived in the same town, but after Partition they left for India. Of these, Manimohan was a freedom fighter, and was jailed under the British Defence of India Act for his part in the movement of August,

1942. It is important to mention this about Manimohan, for many people in India may know him.

I do not know where my friends are. In these last years of my life I am very eager to meet them once again.

At present I am at the Dreamland Intercontinental Hotel in Circular Road. I will stay here another five days. If my friends read this letter, I hope they would contact me. If, unfortunately, they are not still alive, their sons or daughters would bring great joy to their fathers' friend if they should come to this hotel.

Altaf Hossain.

He entreated the department editor to publish his letter as soon as possible but until yesterday it had still not come out, perhaps for want of space. Consequently, Altaf started to become very anxious.

He was unaware of how long he had been sitting on the balcony, but all of a sudden he noticed that the fog seemed to lift as the sun started to come up. There were now many people out on Circular Road or further away on Camac Street or Chowringhee, and everywhere there was a steady flow of buses, minibuses and private cars. With the breaking of the dawn the city almost immediately became bustling and noisy and full of life.

He got up slowly and went to the bathroom. Soon after he came out, the room boy came to clean his room and the bathroom and change the sheets and make up the bed. Then a waiter brought a tray on which were arranged breakfast, tea and three newspapers. He had told the waiter to bring each morning a copy of each of the papers to which he had submitted his letter.

The waiter set the tray down on the table and left, whereupon Altaf skimmed through the papers. Today his letter was published in all three. He thought of thanking the department editors as he poured tea and milk into his cup and stirred in a sugar cube, hoping that his friends would see the letter that morning. If they were still alive, the phone would surely ring after two or three hours. But straightaway a sudden doubt struck him. He had assumed that his friends would be living in Calcutta or nearby, but what if they were not? As he sipped his tea uncertainly, he wondered if they might all be outside of Calcutta. If they were, the newspapers might not cover the distance to them until midday or even afternoon or evening. He hoped that they would contact him, then, if not today, tomorrow or the day after, or even the day after that.

His grandchildren and his daughters-in-law had told him to bring from Calcutta some *Baluchari* silk saris, Indian cosmetics and good material for shirts and trousers. But what if one of his friends should ring when he was out shopping? Altaf decided that today, tomorrow and the day after he would not go out of the hotel. If his friends did not reply to him within those three days, then there was nothing more he could do.

After breakfast, Altaf lay down with the newspapers. There was a telephone on a small table beside the bed. Although his eyes were on the paper, his whole attention was directed to the phone.

At eleven twenty-five Altaf decided to have his bath, but just as he was getting down from the bed the phone rang. Eagerly he picked it up and said "Hallo?" From the other end came a deep voice, "I am

Manimohan Ghosh. Am I speaking with Altaf Hossain?"

His plan had worked. Of all his friends Manimohan had been Altaf's favourite, and he held him in exceptionally high esteem for his role as an unflagging warrior in the freedom struggle.

The sound of Manimohan's voice set off a profound commotion in Manimohan's heart. "Yes," he said, "this is Altaf. It's been so long since I heard your voice." He spoke with an east Bengali accent.

"I can't tell you how happy I was when I read your letter in this morning's paper. I had more or less forgotten Bajitpur, and now this, out of the blue! It's almost as though your letter has taken me back to a previous life."

"But I didn't know your address. I had no means of finding you other than the letter to the paper."

"It was a good reconnaissance strategy."

They both laughed heartily at this. Then Altaf said, "I want to know all your news. But first, tell me, how are the others? Where are they?"

Manimohan told him that after the Partition they and their families had all gone directly to Calcutta, except for Paritosh who had gone with his family to Assam; Manimohan had not heard any news of him. Nripati and Bhupati had died. Nripati's wife was no longer alive, either, and their two daughters had gone abroad after marrying. Bhupati had not lived long after arriving in Calcutta; his wife had gone to live with their son-in-law's family in Jamshedpur. She was still alive about four years back, but as for now Manimohan could not say.

Ambika was not only still alive but he was still exceptionally active. When he came to Calcutta after Partition, he went into business, setting up a factory, and made a great deal of money. He now lived in a huge house like a palace in New Alipore. His sons were all well-educated and accomplished and managed the seven or eight factories of their father's vast business. But ruling over all of them was Ambika, their bulwark. At his direction so many establishments ran smoothly. None of his sons had the temerity to disobey such a strong character as Ambika Chakladar.

Altaf said, "It's good to hear that about Ambika. It couldn't have been easy coming to this country as a refugee and rise so high. I just hope that he sees my letter and calls me. But if you could give me his address and phone number –"

Manimohan gave him that information, then said, "Now tell me about you, Altaf."

"I'll tell you everything, but first let me hear about you."

"You'll hear everything. Come today and have dinner with us, and you will see everything for yourself."

Overjoyed, Altaf said, "I certainly will. Oh, how much I used to enjoy your mother's cooking in Bajitpur. It was all so mouth-watering. Now tell me your address and how to get there."

Manimohan lived in a narrow street near the Tollygunge tram depot. He gave Altaf the address and told him to take a taxi and come towards evening.

"All right," said Altaf, "I'll be there."

"But what about you, Altaf?" pressed Manimohan. "How many

children do you have? What do they do?"

Altaf replied, "Even though you're keeping me in suspense, I won't do the same to you. I'll tell you." And he then gave a brief history of his family over the past forty five years. After Pakistan had come into existence, he had gone with his wife and eldest son to Dhaka where he started up a clothing business and a printing works. Straightaway he was blessed with good fortune as the money seemed to flow in. He invested most of the money in new enterprises which also turned out to be profitable. He now had two garment factories near Tongi where, with foreign collaboration, jeans and shirts were made, eighty percent of which were exported to Australia and the Middle East. He had started his printing works with six treadle machines, and now the place had twelve five-colour offset machines and twenty-two DTPs.

At Bajitpur he had had only one son, but after going to Dhaka he had another two sons and two daughters. All had higher education. The first and second sons managed the garment factory, while Altaf and the youngest son ran the printing works. One of the girls was an architect and the other was a doctor. Both had married well and had houses in Dhanmandi and four or five cars. He had everything he had ever wanted in life, and no worries.

After hearing all this Manimohan said most sincerely, "My goodness, what a great success story. I'm so glad to hear it." He paused for a moment, then said, "But you are coming this evening. I should fetch you from the hotel and bring you here, but this afternoon –"

"Don't even think about it," Altaf interrupted him. "I know Tollygunge reasonably well. I'll be right on time."

After his conversation with Manimohan, Altaf took his bath, had some lunch, and lay down. It had always been his habit to have a couple of hours sleep in the afternoon. A nap refreshed him. He thought that as he had Ambika's address and phone number, he would call him later on if Ambika had not contacted him first.

But sleep was to be denied him, for as soon as he had shut his eyes, the phone rang. When he put the phone to his ear, he heard an unfamiliar voice, "I would like to speak with Altaf Hossain."

He had told his wife and children in Dhaka where he would be putting up in Calcutta and they would call him each evening, so he guessed that this would Ambika's voice. He had finished his chat with Manimohan an hour and a half ago, so who other than Ambika would be calling him in this city? "This is Altaf speaking," he said. "You must be Ambika."

From the other end he heard, "How can you tell?" Ambika sounded quite amazed. "We're seventy five, seventy six years old. In all these years we have developed such intuition?"

"Of course!"

The two friends then returned to their dream-days in Bajitpur forty five years earlier. After being absorbed in their old memories for some time, they got on to such questions as "What is so-and-so doing?" and "How many children does he have?" Both of them were fascinated and pleased by each other's history of remarkable and on-going successes after the Partition. Of course, Altaf had already heard all about Ambika from Manimohan.

Ambika then said, "I'll send a car for you in the evening. You must come. We'll have dinner together. My sons, their wives, my wife, you, me – we'll all have a great chat together."

"But I won't be able to today, brother," said Altaf.

"Why not?"

"Manimohan has invited me to eat with him. I have to go to his place."

"You've met Manimohan, have you?"

"No. He saw my letter in the paper and called me a little while ago."

"Oh, I see."

There was a pause. Then Altaf asked, "What is Mani doing now?"

Ambika avoided the question, asking, "Why, he's just been talking with you on the phone and he hasn't told you anything?"

"No. But I'm sure to find out everything when I go to his house."

Ambika said nothing.

Altaf went on, "Mani should be made a minister for the sacrifices he made for the country. If he can't be a minister, he should certainly be an M.P."

"I'll say nothing about what he could have been and what he has become. But in all my life I have never met a more unpractical man, one so lacking in worldly wisdom, than Manimohan. There isn't any room in his nature for adjustment."

Altaf asked no more questions.

The November evening had fallen over Calcutta when, about four hours later, Altaf got out of the taxi in front of Manimohan's mossy and water-stained one-storey house in Nabin Haldar Road, near the Tollygunge tram depot.

Manimohan was waiting there for him. Hearing the taxi, he had come outside.

The appearance of the young Manimohan and that of the young Altaf Hossain of forty five years ago had both completely changed. If their meeting here now had not been arranged, neither would have recognised the other.

They just looked at each other for a few moments. Altaf was in very fine condition for his age, but as he looked at Manimohan, he felt very sad.

At last Manimohan said, "Altaf?"

Altaf Hossain slowly nodded his head and said, "Yes."

"Come." Taking his boyhood friend by the hand and leading him inside Manimohan said, "How long is it since I saw you? I wouldn't have thought that you'd have remembered us."

Altaf said, "What a thing to say! We spent thirty years of our lives together. Now, of course, we are citizens of two different countries. But does that mean the friendship is to be forgotten? But –"

"What?"

"How did you get to look so run down, Manimohan?"

Manimohan gave a little laugh but did not answer.

The front door opened onto the street and they went first into a brick courtyard, on the left side of which was a washing area and a kitchen. In front of them was a row of three bedrooms behind a broad veranda with a tiled roof.

As they entered the house Manimohan raised his voice and called, "Hey, Sona, your Uncle Altaf has come."

Lights were burning in all the bedrooms and the kitchen. An exceptionally beautiful woman in her late twenties came out of the kitchen. She greeted Altaf with *pranam* and said to Manimohan, "Take Uncle to your room, Father. Go on, Uncle, I'll be along in a moment."

To Altaf the house looked as decrepit on the inside as it had appeared on the outside. The plaster was falling off the walls, a number of the window shutters were broken, and the doors were not entirely in one piece as their days had been numbered by the unseen work of woodworm. It also seemed to him that the house was extraordinarily quiet. Apart from Manimohan and Sona there was no one else to be seen. Was she Manimohan's one and only child? And where was his wife, Mamata? Was she no longer alive? Having come to see them after all this time, surely she would have come running and fussing over Altaf if she were still alive. But –

Before his thinking was complete, Manimohan took him into the last room on the right. There was a bed on one side, spread tightly with a freshly laundered bed cover. On the other side were two old glass-door book-cases filled with books. In the middle of the room were four cushioned cane chairs and a centre table. From the look of the cushion covers on the chair and the clean cloth on the centre table, Altaf suspected that they had been changed just for today. The same seemed true of the bed cover. Because Altaf was coming, everything had probably been made as neat and tidy as possible.

Manimohan said, "Sit down, brother."

The two of them sat down facing one another.

Altaf asked very hesitantly, "Is there no one in the house but you and Sona?"

"I have an older son, but he doesn't live here."

"Why not?"

"So much urgency! Just sit for a while. You'll find out everything."

"But I've not seen Mamata."

Manimohan smiled sadly. He said, "No. I see you are just like you were before. Impatient." After a brief pause, he said, "Mamata has cancer. She's been in hospital for four months. She'll have an operation next month. Whether or not she comes home at all, who knows?"

Altaf was shocked. "This is awful!"

"Now I've upset you," said Manimohan. "If you hear the whole story of my family, I don't know what you'll do. It's best we leave it, Altaf. You've come to Calcutta for just a few days. What's the point in bothering your mind? Let's talk about something else."

His voice a little choked, Altaf said, "No. You go on. I'm listening."

Just then Sona came in with tea, biscuits and savouries. She said,"Uncle, it's getting very cold. Drink your tea now. I'll have finished cooking in another half an hour. When would you like to eat dinner?"

Altaf realised that after Mamata had become unwell, all the responsibility of the house had fallen on Sona. He thought comparatively of his own daughters. Apart from studying they had never done any work in the house. Then they had got married, and both their fathers-in-law were extraordinarily wealthy. Moreover, they got ample income from their own professions. In fact, in the house they had never moved a piece of straw. The life of this sweet-natured daughter of Manimohan too could have been as happy and comfortable.

Altaf smiled sadly. He said, "You've gone to so much trouble on my behalf."

A soft smile came over Sona's face as she said, "You mean cooking?"

"Yes, I mean –"

"My goodness, must I not cook for us? Now, you haven't told me when you would like to eat."

"I will eat whenever you serve it."

"All right." Sona went out.

Manimohan then began his story. After the Partition of the country he sold his house and land in Bajitpur and, with the proceeds, bought this place in Tollygunge. Because he had done time in jail for his service to the country, a lot of opportunities and advantages were available to him, such as the freedom fighters' monthly stipend and, later, the award of a copper plaque. But he did not want to accept money for his patriotism. In fact, had he put his mind to it, he could have stood as an election candidate, but he was dismayed by the nature of politics after Independence. There was a group of leaders who came to the fore, stepping over all those people who, under

British rule, had sacrificed everything for their country, spent year after year in dark jails, and unflinchingly bore all the savage oppression of their colonial masters. This new generation of leaders had not spent even one day in jail, had not sacrificed one penny. Their only aims were to grab power over independent India and accumulate wealth. Manimohan realised that he could never respect these post-Independence patriots. Gradually he distanced himself from politics. However, most amazing and most painful was the fact that many Independence fighters like himself adjusted and compromised themselves to these artful, power-hungry, new servants of the nation.

One of those in power at the time had offered Manimohan a job, but he lasted in it no more than three or four years due to the rampant bribery in that office. He made known his objection and resigned from the job. He worked in three or four other places after that, but everywhere it was the same thing: this uncompromising man of integrity could not adjust to anyone, anywhere.

People like Manimohan had once dreamed, sitting in the jails of colonial India, that after Independence the citizens of this country would be honest and decent and free from greed. They built up such a splendid ideal of an India that would bedazzle the whole world. But what he actually experienced led Manimohan to withdraw, disappointed and defeated. Yet something, at least, had to be done, and so he started to teach children. Twice a day, two batches of students would come to his house and study under him. This had provided his livelihood for a few years.

Of course, Mamata had had a government job, but in a department where there was no opportunity for bribery; otherwise, the wife of Manimohan would have had to resign. She had retired about five years back, and now her family depended greatly on her pension.

Mamata and Manimohan had three children. After their two sons their only daughter, Sona, was born. The elder boy, Pranab, was an exceptional student who had done remarkably well in the school final and higher secondary examination, but while studying for his degree in science he had got caught up in the extremist agitation of the seventies. In an encounter with the police he had been shot in both legs. He lost his legs, spent a few months in hospital, then served a short jail sentence after which he came home for a time. He was quite unable to move about.

The younger son, Rajib, was generally a good student, but a very selfish careerist. After completing a master's degree in applied physics he took up a scholarship in Canada and studied for his doctorate at a university there. He had married a colleague, a girl from Brazil, and they had both taken out Canadian citizenship. There was no chance of his ever returning home and he no longer kept up any connection with his family.

Sona was the youngest. About four years back she had completed a master's degree in modern history with a high second class honour. From time to time she taught at various colleges, filling leave vacancies for others, but still she had not got a permanent position. When she would, or even if she would, who could say? After Mamata contracted cancer, she took over the running of the house.

Altaf was disturbed at hearing all this, but at the same time his respect for his utterly honest, unselfish and idealistic friend grew even greater.

Manimohan said, "Do you know what my greatest problem is, brother? My daughter is now twenty-eight, and I can't arrange for her marriage."

Altaf was completely taken aback. He asked, "But Sona is so well educated, so beautiful! What is preventing her from being married?"

"Money." Sadly Manimohan said, "If I want to get her married into a good home, I have no way of meeting the expense of that."

Altaf's astonishment increased. He said, "What are you saying, Mani! You made such sacrifices for the country, it should be an honour for someone to take your daughter."

Manimohan gave a tired smile and said nothing.

Altaf was thinking: Manimohan had grown quite old, his wife was bed-ridden with cancer, his elder son had lost both his legs in political agitation and his younger son had no relations with him any more. Given all this, it was just not right that his twenty-eight-year-old daughter should have to remain in her father's house. It was imperative that Sona be married while her charm still lasted. He, himself, was a successful and wealthy man and could afford to pay for ten daughters' weddings, let alone one. He was about to say, "You arrange for Sona's marriage. Let me worry about the money – but he stopped himself. This was the man who had refused the copper plaque, who had rejected the freedom fighters' pension, who had resigned from one job after the other on account of corruption. Would he be likely to accept help or favours from another?

Altaf finally decided against pursuing the matter. After dinner, having said "Yes, I'll come again" and "I'll go with you to the hospital to visit Mamata" and other such things, he returned quite late to the hotel. He was overcome by melancholy from thinking about Manimohan and his family. A selfless fighter for national independence should not end up like that.

The next evening Ambika sent an expensive foreign limousine to bring Altaf to his house in New Alipore.

Ambika's house was like those of the new rich in Dhaka after the Partition. The architecture was very impressive; there was a lawn like a green carpet, a flower garden, and six or seven cars, Indian and foreign.

Ambika was sitting waiting for him on a huge balcony on the first floor. He came down as Altaf was getting out of the limousine. He embraced his boyhood friend and took him up to a vast drawing room, summoning everyone who was there.

After a short time, Altaf was the centre of quite a sizable gathering. There was, of course, Ambika, his wife Nirupama, his two daughters-in-law Sujata and Bipasha, his three sons Sandip, Dipak and Rajesh, all sitting around him.

Ambika introduced first his sons and their wives to Altaf. They were all quite accomplished. However, the youngest son Rajesh still had not married. The two daughters-in-law were exceptionally beautiful, smart, jovial and well educated, and they deported themselves with considerable charm.

At various gaps in the conversation two liveried waiters offered tea and coffee, cashew-nut snacks and fish fingers. The whole time was given over to reminiscence, along with stories about Calcutta and Dhaka. In the midst of it all Sujata and Bipasha said, "Uncle, you must bring all your family to our house one day."

"Certainly," said Altaf. "And you must all come to Dhaka."

"Oh, we will!"

The conversation went well, but Altaf's eyes kept returning to Rajesh. This youngest son of Ambika was truly a handsome young man. He was about six feet tall and had a long face, sharp nose, sparkling eyes, thick eyebrows and a strong chin – all in all an exceptionally intelligent appearance. Altaf's mind became diverted from time to time while looking at him.

The gathering in the drawing room broke up at ten o'clock and dinner began in an immense dining hall on one side of the first floor. Everyone in the house sat down to eat with Altaf. Ambika's wife Nirupama gestured with her eyes with machine-like efficiency to the two waiters to serve the food.

As in the gathering in the drawing room dinner also gave rise to happy anecdotes and snippets of pleasantries. And here again Altaf's eyes were drawn to the face of Rajesh.

Once dinner was eventually finished, Altaf did not stay any longer. It had got very late. Right now he had to return to the hotel and go to bed. He was a very orderly and disciplined man who never stayed up too late at night for any reason. If he did, his body suffered.

Altaf said to Ambika, "I must go now. But –"

Ambika looked at his friend curiously. "But what?"

"I have an urgent matter to raise with you."

"Good. Go ahead."

"Not now. Can you come to my hotel for a while tomorrow morning?"

"When?"

"I don't have any business here. I'm free the whole time. What time would suit you?"

Ambika thought for a moment and said, "Early, around nine. On my way to the factory I'll call at your hotel."

"Please do," said Altaf.

Ambika arrived right on nine the next morning.

After a bit of a chat about this and that, Altaf said, "Let's get down to business."

"I'm ready," said Ambika, smiling.

"The day before yesterday I went to Mani's house."

"I know that."

Altaf paused for a moment, then said, "I'm sure you know all about their situation."

Ambika slowly nodded.

Altaf went on. "As a friend, there's something you should do for him."

"I have thought about this so many times," said Ambika. "But you too are his boyhood friend. You know him very well. He won't accept anyone's help."

"I'm not talking about financial help."

"What then?"

Altaf said nothing for a moment as he looked directly into Ambika's eyes. Then he asked, "Will you keep a promise for me?"

Inwardly Ambika was somewhat taken aback. Slowly he said, "I'm listening. What is the promise?"

"Mani's daughter is wonderful. She has an M.A. in modern history. She's good-looking. She would suit beautifully your youngest son. My wish is that they marry each other."

Ambika's face became very serious. In a strong voice without emotion he said, "That cannot be, Altaf."

This was not the answer that had been hoped for. Altaf was surprised. "Why not?"

"Mani's and my family's status are not the same. This marriage would not be a happy one."

"What are you saying! Mani sacrificed so much for this country. People honour him. Is he not respectable despite having no money?"

"Everything Mani has ever done has been done out of emotion. No one today is swayed any more by all that Freedom Movement sentiment."

Now Altaf took both Ambika's hands and pleaded with him. "Please, Ambika, let Mani's daughter be your son's wife."

Slowly freeing his hands Ambika said, "Don't put pressure on me, brother. You are a foreigner, come to India for just a few days. Enjoy your chats, but keep out of this sort of thing."

Altaf sat there numb for a few moments. Then, in a harsh voice, he said, "I am now a foreigner! Someone who has unwittingly gone beyond the bounds. Someone who doesn't understand how far it is proper to go."

Ambika did not answer. Suddenly and impatiently he got up and said, "It's getting late. I have to be at the factory. I must go now –"

## ROOTS

*shikar*

Rajmohan was sitting stretched out in his own easy chair beside the window, drinking tea. He had retired twelve years back and since then drinking tea and relaxing like this had become his favourite habit.

From his first-storey window he could see a very long way to the east and to the south. An eighty-foot-wide road ran directly to the east and to the south there was a park, so there was no chance of the view ever being blocked out in those directions. In fact, this part of Park Circus was still very quiet, peaceful and well preserved and its luxuriance was enjoyed by a great many birds, although it could not be said with confidence how much longer the trees and the birds would be seen there for the construction companies had their eyes on this part of Calcutta as they had had on so many others. Their agents would invade a place with attache cases full of bundles of crisp new notes and then set spinning the heads of those who had vacant land or small houses. To the northwest a lot of high-rise apartment buildings were now starting to go up where smaller houses had once stood. How much longer would this go on? In six or seven years this kind of box architecture would have spread throughout the locality.

A big developer had come to Rajmohan a number of times. He wanted to demolish Rajmohan's two-storey house in the middle of a quarter-acre plot and erect an eight-storey apartment building. He had offered Rajmohan an entire floor and so much cash that, should it be placed in a fixed deposit bank account, would enable his succeeding five generations to spend their lives crossing their legs and twiddling their thumbs.

On the first occasion Rajmohan had said no, but the man was remarkably persistent and had come back again three or four times until at last Rajmohan had rudely sent him on his way. He would not be putting up any high-rise here.

Rajmohan's decision did not please his only son, Manish, who tried to explain that a small house amid such spaciousness did not make sense. Moreover, given the huge monetary return promised, it would not be far-sighted but foolhardy to say no. Rajmohan did not feel the need to answer any of his son's arguments, yet he knew that barely two months after his death Manish would call in the construction companies himself. Manish had no sentiment for such things as gardens and birds and solitude.

In 1947, within a month after the Partition of India, Rajmohan had exchanged their house in Dhaka for this one. He was twenty-nine then, Manish was three, and his parents and his wife Manimala were still alive. Forty one years had passed since he had come to this house.

Of course, this house bore no comparison with the one they had left in Dhaka. There they had had a medium-size three-storey house in a fashionable part of the city covering about half an acre. There was a big garden at the front and at the back there was a large pond. Rajmohan was born in that house in Dhaka and there his roots were struck. But then forty one years is not a short time. After coming to this house in Park Circus his father died; some four years later his mother died; and Manimala had left them only the year before. Manish, now forty-four and into middle age, was an executive of a big multinational company. His wife Parama was teaching at a college in what was at present a temporary position but which would soon become permanent. They had a son and a daughter, Raja and Buna. Raja was eighteen and doing first year honours in economics at St. Xavier's; Buna was sixteen and in her final year at school.

Rajmohan felt that over forty one years he had put down a second set of roots in this house in Park Circus.

The November afternoon was gradually spreading its sunlight, the colour of faded turmeric.

As he sipped his tea and gazed out over the park, Rajmohan was lost in his thoughts. He looked at the same picture that greeted his eyes every day: some elderly men sitting on a bench, a few people strolling casually along the track around a green field, and many young boys with bat and ball come to set at least ten test matches underway throughout the park.

As on any other day Rajmohan's mind was full of fragments of various thoughts. Lately memories of the house in Dhaka had been on his mind, but like old photos in an album those memories had greatly faded. Still, he dearly wished to go back to Dhaka one day. Last year he had turned seventy, so if he did not go soon he would never be able to go.

Suddenly he heard the sound of the door bell – probably it was Raja or Buna returning from college or school. As he went on looking out of the window, he sensed Parama going down the stairs on the other side of the house. A little later she came into his room and stood in the doorway. "Father," she called.

Rajmohan looked around.

"A gentleman has come from Dhaka," she said. "He says his name is Abdul Karim. A boy and a girl have come with him. He wants to meet you."

This was uncanny. Just a few moments ago Rajmohan had been

thinking about Dhaka and now Parama had come with word of Abdul Karim! Forty one years ago this house in Park Circus had been his.

Rajmohan felt a surge of excitement within himself. He got up eagerly from his easy chair and asked, "Where are they?"

"I've shown them into the drawing room downstairs."

"Come on."

As she went downstairs with her father-in-law, Parama suddenly remembered something. "Didn't you exchange houses with him when you came to Calcutta?"

"Yes," said Rajmohan, "I told you that. Don't you remember?"

Parama smiled and said nothing.

Karim Saheb was sitting in the drawing room. He was about seventy five. He was almost six feet tall, with a straight nose and brilliant white hair and beard. He was wearing pajama and panjabi. For his age he seemed to be in excellent health. Of course, he was a little stooped, his skin was no longer as taut as it used to be, and his hair had completely changed colour, but still he looked much the same as he had forty one years ago.

On Karim Saheb's right sat a bright looking girl of about twenty or a little more and on his left was a sixteen-year-old boy. Both were wearing jeans; the girl had on a loose-fitting shirt and the boy wore a sporty T-shirt – all obviously foreign clothes, made in America, probably, or Canada.

As soon as Rajmohan came into the room, Karim Saheb got up and embraced him with great emotion. In a deep voice he said, "You are well, then?"

"I don't get any younger," Rajmohan replied. "But tell me about yourself."

Karim Saheb unburdened himself to Rajmohan. "You can say the same about me. But I have had a heart attack, there is arthritis in my left shoulder, and two years ago I had cataracts. Now I'm as well as can be expected. I am happy." He smiled.

He certainly bore no bitterness or disappointment in nearing the end of his life. He could take the sweet with the sour and showed a stoical acceptance of the realities of his life.

Smiling, Rajmohan said, "Sit down, now. Sit down."

The two of them sat facing one another. Rajmohan looked at the girl and boy and said, "These must be your grandchildren?"

Karim Saheb nodded, and explained that the girl, Tahamina, was the daughter of his elder son. His younger son was the father of the boy, whose name was Shamim. Tahamina was studying third year medicine and Shamim was coming up to his matriculation examination.

"It's very nice that you've brought them with you," said Rajmohan. Then he introduced Karim Saheb to Parama.

Parama greeted him with *namaskar* and said, "I've heard so much about you from Father. Now while you're all chatting, I'll get some tea."

When Parama had gone, Karim Saheb gleaned all he could about Rajmohan's family and also spoke of his own. He had two sons and a daughter. The elder son was an important officer in the Bangladesh government and the younger son was a doctor. The daughter had married after graduating in economics and now she and her husband were doing research in Toronto; they had no children.

Along with the tea, Parama brought a lot of cake, sweets and savoury snacks. Karim Saheb took only one sweet, saying, "I am totally forbidden sweets. But I'll have just one of these *sandesh.* I have not seen this kind for so long a time and I can't control my weakness for them." He went on talking as he ate. "You certainly looked surprised to see us!"

Rajmohan smiled as he said, "I was indeed. So suddenly, without any warning –" and he broke off.

Karim Saheb understood what Rajmohan was thinking. He said, "I thought I would give you a surprise. But after we'd boarded the plane at Dhaka, I was worried that I would not recognise the house. Maybe it had been pulled down and a bigger one put up in its place, or perhaps you had sold it and moved somewhere else." He paused for a moment. "Then once the plane had taken off, I thought that I would go there once and have a look. Had I not met up with you, or if a new house had been put up in place of the old one, I would have gone straight back to Dhaka."

Rajmohan said nothing.

Karim Saheb went on. "But I'm lucky. The house is still the same. You know, Rajmohan-bhai, for a long time I have wanted to come back here once more. Three generations of us lived in this house. I was born here. My marriage also took place in this house. And my two sons were born here. What memories!" His voice trembled with emotion. "Now I am reaching the end of my days when I will go under the earth. I thought that it would be wrong not to come and see for the last time the house of my father and grandfather. The pull of the blood, you understand."

Karim Saheb's emotion spread to Rajmohan. He nodded slowly.

Karim Saheb went on. "I also insisted on bringing my grandchildren. Everyone should know where their roots are struck. It must be terrible not to know where in the world your origins are. If it hadn't been for Partition, they would have been born here and grown up here."

"That's right," Rajmohan said, "but –"

"What?"

"Where is your luggage?"

"I checked in at midday to a hotel in Park Street. I've left the suitcases and things there."

Somewhat put out, Rajmohan said, "What a thing to do! This house is as much yours as it is ours. We've been here forty one years, but your family lived here for generations. My grandchildren will be home soon and they can go with Tahamina and Shamim and bring your luggage here. You must spend your time in Calcutta with us." He then said to Parama, "Will you make arrangements for their stay?"

"Right away, Father," said Parama.

In the meantime Raja and Buna had come back. Buna was wearing her school dress and Raja was wearing jeans and a shirt. When they were introduced to Karim Saheb, they bowed and said *"Namaskar."* But they greeted Tahamina and Shamim with "Hi!"

All the while Tahamina and Shamim had been quietly listening to the chatter of the two old men, looking as though they had been dragged out of their own environment and brought to somewhere where they did not feel at all comfortable. But seeing Raja and Buna the looks on their faces changed completely. Gesturing with their hands, they both replied, "Hi!"

Karim Saheb said happily, "Here too this 'Hi!' word is said?"

Raja smiled and said, "And why not? It's part of the international language of youth."

The other three young ones nodded their heads in agreement.

Rajmohan said, "We don't understand you, young man."

"Generation and communication gap."

"All right, all right. Now you and Buna must do something for me."

"What's that?"

"Get the car out of the garage and take Tahamina and Shamim to their hotel. Pick up Karim Saheb's luggage and bring it here."

"Fine."

"And remember –"

"What's that?"

"Go and come. And don't speed."

Jokingly Raja said, "Grandad, you are travelling in reverse gear. Let us travel in forward gear."

"That's just like my grandchildren," Karim Saheb said. "Here the young people are just the same."

Rajmohan said to Raja, "Remember what I told you, nevertheless."

He looked and sounded serious.

Raja flashed a glance at Rajmohan and said with a smile, "By order of the Chief of Army Staff. Very good, sir, we will come back soon, and I will not drive rashly. Don't worry." He turned to Parama and said, "Mother, I'm terribly hungry. Can I have something to eat?"

"Me too, Mother," said Buna. "I'm just going up to change out of my school dress." And so saying she left the room. When she came back down five minutes later, she was wearing jeans and a shirt.

Rajmohan looked at his own grandchildren and then at Karim Saheb's. No, as far as this generation's clothes were concerned, there seemed to be no difference between Dhaka and Calcutta.

Raja and Buna wolfed down the last of their snack and the four young people went out together.

Karim Saheb said, "This modern generation of young people are the same in Calcutta as they are in Dhaka. They're all cast in the same mould. It's lucky that Shamim and Tahamina have met Raja and Buna, or else they would have nagged me to return to Dhaka.

Rajmohan smiled fondly. "Come," he said, "let's go upstairs."

As they went up the stairs, Karim looked about with profound curiosity. The iron-grill railing of the staircase had a wood-crafted banister, over which he ran his hand with obvious affection. "My grandfather's father was a man of very refined taste," he said. "He didn't mould the railing in cement but had a Chinese carpenter set it in Burmese teak. All the doors and window-frames are also in Burmese teak."

As he came into his own room, Rajmohan offered Karim Saheb an antique chair, and as he settled into his own easy chair he said to his daughter-in-law, who had come in with them, "Fix up my room for Karim Saheb. Do we have any single beds in the house?"

"We do," said Parama.

"Then get Haru to bring one into this room and make it up."

"Very well."

Then Rajmohan said to Karim Saheb, "Shall we have another cup of tea, then?"

"I won't have any more now," said Karim Saheb. "If I drink too much tea I can't sleep at night."

"All right, then."

Evening was starting to fall. At this time in the middle of November a light fog starts to come down and by now the distant park and the road at the front were clouded by it. Of course, the street lights had been turned on, but nothing outside was clearly visible.

Parama switched on the fluorescent light and said, "I'm going now. I'll send for Haru. If you need anything, just call."

"All right," said Rajmohan.

Parama went out and Karim Saheb said hesitantly, "I'm afraid I've put you to some inconvenience, turning up suddenly like this. At the hotel –"

Rajmohan interrupted him. "Please don't ever mention it again."

Laughing, Karim Saheb said, "All right, I surrender."

For a time, the two of them became lost in their old memories, bringing to life in their minds the Partition, the riots and the refugees who were uprooted from the homes of their forefathers. As though it were on an invisible television screen they could see clearly the picture of the exchange of houses and the going from this side to that and from that side to this, and the atmosphere in the room became heavy with melancholy.

Rajmohan said, "Come, Karim Saheb, I'll show you around the house. After every two years we have it painted but we don't change anything else. We've kept everything as it was – beds, wardrobes, tables, chairs."

When this house was exchanged, Karim Saheb took nothing with him, leaving all the goods and chattels and going away empty-handed, nor did Rajmohan and his family take a stick of furniture from their house in Dhaka.

Karim Saheb said, "Forget about today. We'll look around tomorrow with the grandchildren."

Neither said anything for awhile. Then Rajmohan said, "There's something I really want to know."

Looking inquisitive, Karim Saheb asked, "What?"

"Is our house in Dhaka still the same? I've heard that Dhaka has changed quite a lot."

"That's true. But we have kept your house in Dhaka as it was before. But I don't know how much longer we'll be able to."

"What do you mean?"

"Your house stands on almost half an acre. The men from the construction companies keep coming and pestering me everyday. They want to build a multi-storey building there. They're offering a big flat to each one of the family, along with a few hundred thousand in cash. My sons are putting pressure on me to agree."

It was the same story. Rajmohan told Karim how the promoters, and Manish, were pressing him in the interests of a high-rise building. Then, looking sad, he said, "Times have changed so much. The young people of today have no feelings for their forebears any more."

Karim Saheb's story was just as sad. He agreed, saying, "That is so true, Rajmohan-bhai. When I went to Dhaka in 'forty seven, my elder son was ten and the younger was six. My daughter was born over there. Yet they have no affection at all for the house in which they have spent so many years. When I die, not even a month will pass before my sons put it in the hands of the developers."

Rajmohan slowly nodded his head.

Karim Saheb then said, "You must bring everyone to Dhaka for a few days. If you don't do it soon, you may not get another chance to see the legacy of your forefathers."

Taking Karim Saheb's hand in his own, Rajmohan said, "For so long I have been thinking of that. I will go. I will go again to Dhaka very soon. Before I do, I'll write to you and let you know."

In Rajmohan's room on the first floor Parama was making up the small bed that had been brought in for Karim Saheb. A passage ran past this room, at the far end of which were three rooms side by side: one was Raja's, one was Buna's, and the third was Manish and Parama's. It was decided that Tahamina would stay with Buna in her room and Shamim would stay with Raja in his.

It was half-past nine. Rajmohan and Karim Saheb were still talking.

Although the four young people had gone off to the hotel some time back, they had still not returned. Suddenly Rajmohan became aware of this. He said, "From here to Park Street takes not even twenty minutes. Half an hour at the most. They left at six. They've been gone three and a half hours!"

Karim Saheb smiled. He said, "They're sure to have gone out somewhere after picking up the luggage from the hotel."

Half an hour later, when it was just past ten, they returned very noisily.

"What is this?" Rajmohan demanded. "I told you to go and then come. What has taken you so long?"

Raja said, "Oh, but this is the first time that Shamim and Tahamina have come to Calcutta. We've been showing them around our city."

"You weren't speeding?"

"You've got this fixation in your mind! Ask Tahamina and Shamim. I never went more than ten kilometres over the speed limit. My honourable grandfather's orders are orders, are they not?"

"Don't be cheeky. It's very late. All of you go and wash and come to the dining room."

It suddenly occurred to Karim Saheb to ask anxiously, "Has Manish not yet returned from the office?"

"He's gone on business to Delhi," Rajmohan replied. "He'll come back after a week."

"In that case, we won't meet him."

After dinner Rajmohan took Karim Saheb up to his own room.

Parama had set two glasses of water on a small table. Raja took Tahamina, Shamim and Buna to his room for a good chat before going to bed.

Karim Saheb said fondly, "I see the four of them get on very well together."

"Birds of a feather," said Rajmohan. "Is it feather or flock?"

"Both," said Karim Saheb, enjoying himself.

For some time they chatted about this and that, lying alongside one another. They could hear the sound of a pop music record playing quietly and the joviality of the four young people. The two old men also could hear clearly what they were saying.

"There's no charm in third world cities," Raja was declaiming. "We have an uncle in West Germany. I want to go to him when I get my degree."

"You go first," said Buna, "and I'll come five years later."

Then Tahamina told them that her aunt was making arrangements for her and Shamim in Canada. Within one or two years they would go to Toronto.

Karim Saheb said, "Are you listening?"

"Yes," said Rajmohan.

And they fell asleep listening to the talk of their grand-children.

The next morning after breakfast the four young ones were ready to go out.

"Where are you four musketeers going this morning?" asked Karim Saheb.

"Buna and I are going to introduce Tahamina and Shamim to our friends," replied Raja. "We decided on our programme last night. Today we'll turn over the whole of Calcutta."

"But you have college. Buna has school."

"From today we have a four-day break from college. Buna has the same."

"When will you be back?"

"Tonight. We'll eat out."

"But I was thinking that today we would show Tahamina and Shamim over the house."

"We'll see it later, Grandad," said Tahamina, as the four of them swept outside like a sudden gust of wind.

Karim Saheb looked hurt and disappointed. For a while after that he looked around the house with Rajmohan. He recalled how his mother and father had the south room on the first floor, while he and his wife had the one beside it, the same room into which he took his new bride after their wedding. She was no longer alive, having lived only another fifteen years after going to Dhaka. His widowed aunt and his grandfather used to sleep on the ground floor. They too were now dead.

After wandering around like lost souls, the two old men came down and went straight into the back garden. Almost all the trees of forty one years ago were still standing. Karim, his parents and his wife had once brought a number of saplings from a fair in Shealdah and planted them – various kinds of mango, rose-apple, pomelo, star-apple and black cherry. Everyone in the family was especially fond of trees. Karim recognised each one of them, like someone recalling a previous life.

Karim Saheb was not even aware of Rajmohan wandering along behind him. He was overcome by the thought that he no longer had the slightest claim to his ancestral home.

Three days were spent looking about in which time Karim Saheb had not been able to properly show his grandchildren the house. They would go out with Raja each day and would not feel like it when they got back. For what little time they were at home they would be living it up. Troops of Raja and Buna's friends would invade the house in the morning, the afternoon and the evening, and whenever Rajmohan and Karim Saheb returned to their memories of forty one years ago, the young ones would be immersed in the computer, pop music, cricket, World Cup, West Germany, Japan, Canada, America and other such far-off, amazing parts of the world. The past had no claim on them.

Then, after five days, Rajmohan and his family all took Karim Saheb and his grandchildren to Dum Dum to catch their plane. Karim Saheb embraced Rajmohan and said most sincerely, "Don't leave it too long. As soon as you can, come and see your house in Dhaka."

"I will," said Rajmohan. "I certainly will."

"It's been a wonderful few days. But I have one great regret, Rajmohan-bhai."

"What is it?"

A little way off Raja, Tahamina, Shamim and Buna were talking and laughing exuberantly. Looking at his grandchildren Karim Saheb said, "They didn't have a good look at the house of their forefathers. They're not interested in their own origins. They are an utterly rootless lot."

Rajmohan could well sympathise with Karim Saheb's sadness. Indeed, a profound melancholy was now sweeping through him.

## STATELESS

## *deshnei*

The three of them – Asad, Jahura and Zorina – were sitting side by side on top of a rough hillock, at the bottom of which the waves were angrily crashing against the rocks. Before them was the Arabian Sea, dotted with countless fishing boats and variously coloured sailing boats. Flocks of seagulls all had their eyes trained on the water, and as soon as one of them caught sight of a fish it would swoop on it, clutch it in its sharp beak and lift it out of the water. Having nibbled it away in a moment the hunter would continue its raid on the sea with renewed earnest. The vast red ball of sun hung far off, fixed where the horizon marked off sea from sky. Yet here in Mumbai sunrise and sunset were both very late, so there were still a couple of hours before evening.

Behind the hill was a smooth road lined on both sides with coconut trees. On one side, further back from the trees, one had a view of big compounds and bungalows on the side of a large hill, like a picture in its frame. There were also numerous high-rise buildings, hotels, restaurants and fast food stalls. To one side, set at an angle, was the Church of Mount Mary with its steeple and shining cross reaching up to the sky. Altogether it was quite dream-like.

The place was called Band Stand.

But to return to Asad and company: Asad was thirty-five. He had prominent veins in his arms and legs, conspicuous knuckles and, on the palms of his hands, callouses like bits of burnt brick. He had always had to worry about managing to take care of himself, and his body bore clear signs of that. However, at this moment Asad was quite neatly dressed, wearing pressed pajamas and a long green shirt with vertical stripes. His face, with its strong jaw, was clean-shaven and his hair was parted and wavy.

Jahura was about thirty and had a dark complexion. She was quite good-looking, though not beautiful. She was a healthy girl, although there were some faint smallpox scars on her forehead, cheeks and chin. Her big eyes, highlighted with collyrium, gave her a bashful look. On her nose was set a red-stone nose-ring, on her wrists bunches of glass bangles, and around her neck a silver necklace. She was wearing a coloured salwar-kameez.

Zorina was Jahura's younger sister. She was eighteen or nineteen, a very lively and attractive girl, quite fair in comparison with her sister. She had a long, full face, and her thick hair was arranged in two braids hanging down behind her. She too was wearing a chintz salwar-kameez. Somewhere inside her was a hidden spring of laughter which was constantly overflowing. She was sitting between Jahura and Asad, chattering on continually. As well as laugh, Zorina could certainly talk.

Jahura and her family lived in a room in a slum that was like a quarter-kilometre long barrack, at one end of the city of Mumbai in the Cotton Green area. For many years Asad had lived in an even more lowly, makeshift slum beside the Mahim Creek. A few days back he had forked out ten thousand rupees in cash for a rented room in the Dharavi slum in Bandra East, a slum known throughout the world as the biggest in Asia. His other place was more appalling than hell; it was out of the question to take a new wife there – and in just a couple of weeks he would marry Jahura.

Jahura and her family hailed from Saharsa in Bihar, and Asad's home was originally in East Pakistan or, as it had become, Bangladesh. Of course, whether they hailed from Bihar or Bangladesh, Mumbai was indeed home to them now, as they had lived there for so many years and had set their roots deep in this city. They could not even think of leaving it for anywhere else.

The three of them had a good reason to be sitting on top of the Band Stand hillock overlooking the Arabian Sea. Both Asad's parents had died, leaving him alone, so the important responsibility for setting up home together with Jahura fell entirely on him. It was for this purpose that Jahura's father, Niyamat Ali, had agreed to Asad's taking the two sisters shopping. They – especially Jahura – wanted to choose a stove, some kitchen utensils and various other necessary items. After that, Asad would see them home to Cotton Green. But Asad was not one to let an opportunity pass when it presented itself. He did not take his future wife and sister-in-law to the market straightaway, but decided to spend a little time beside the sea, then to take them for a meal at some South Indian restaurant. After that they would go to the Linking Road market.

In all his thirty-five years Asad had never had the opportunity of being close to any young woman. In fact, he had to work so hard just to stay alive that he did not have the time for anything else. And yet, as he lay on his grubby bed in the slum after a day's unremitting toil, he thought so often of getting married and setting up a home with the girl of his choice on whom he would lavish all his loving care and affection. Yet even though he had wanted to marry, he had not done so, for want of money. Over so many years Asad had saved, little by little, to make his dream come true, and by now he had put together almost thirty-seven thousand. Out of that he had taken ten thousand for the room, and the rest would be spent on the wedding.

It all seemed a dream that in just a couple of weeks this attractive woman sitting only a couple of yards from him would be his.

Zorina was chatting on freely. "Asad-bhai," she said, "do you know that you'll be the first Bengali relation we've ever had?"

"I know," Asad replied. "Your father and mother told me the other day."

"My sister is as precious as the moon," she went on. "You must always remember that."

Asad turned around and said, "Oh, yes. Yes, that's true." And as he spoke he stole a glance at Jahura and saw that her big, dark and bashful eyes were looking at him. Their eye contact made Jahura blush and she quickly looked away.

Zorina was saying, "Make sure you take good care of my sister."

"Of course I will," laughed Asad. "And the girl who is as precious as the moon has a sister as precious as a diamond. I'll remember to treat her well, too."

Zorina took a moment or two to comprehend this. She frowned and said, "Oh, why should I take such flattery from you? That should come from another man."

"Has your father found that other man?"

"Not yet, but he will. Do you think I will stay in my father's house for the rest of my life?"

Asad smiled and said, "As long as your father does not find someone, I will take care of you."

Zorina said, "What an idea! Could you manage two women at once?"

"Just wait and see."

"Enough of this silliness. Now pay attention."

"To what?"

"Just be sure to respect my sister," Zorina said. "She will always take good care of your house."

Asad nodded his head slowly and said, "I'm sure she will."

"And one other thing."

"What's that?"

Zorina's tone became serious. "My sister has suffered a lot. Don't let her suffer any more."

Asad found his eyes straying to Jahura again. A little earlier she had looked extremely happy and vibrant, as though an immense gush of joy had welled up in her and set her face aglow, but now she looked quite melancholy, as though all the happiness, all the brightness, had just been snuffed out of her life.

Asad had no difficulty in understanding what Zorina had been hinting at. Niyamat Ali had never tried to conceal anything but had been quite candid in telling him that Jahura had been married before. However, that marriage had in no way at all been a happy one. Her previous husband, Javed Khan, worked in the Mumbai port and earned a lot of money, but the man was also a notorious villain. He was of poor character, bad-tempered and a drunkard. Whenever Javed had had a bellyful of his strong country liquor, Satan himself would take possession of him. He had a long list of misdemeanours with women, but should Jahura demur in any way, he would beat her brutally. It was impossible that she spend her whole life with such a low scoundrel as this, and on natural causes the marriage was dissolved.

After the divorce Niyamat brought his elder daughter back into his house and tried constantly to arrange her remarriage. After all, he and his wife were getting on in years and they had no son, only the two daughters. If anything should happen to them, what would become of the girls? This society was fraught with danger for unprotected young women. Therefore, Niyamat Ali had decided that once appropriate arrangements had been made for Jahura he would arrange for Zorina's marriage as soon as possible. By the grace of Allah a marriage for Jahura had at last been arranged with Asad, whose hand Niyamat had clasped as he told him earnestly that his daughter was very peaceable and tender, her needs were few, and she was very sweet-natured. Let Asad take care of her!

Zorina had said exactly the same things. With emphasis and reassurance, Asad said, "Don't you worry, Zorina. Your sister will never suffer at my hands."

Zorina's eyes lit up with gratitude.

When half the sun had sunk below the horizon of the Arabian Sea, Zorina said, "We should go now, Asad-bhai. Father will be very worried if we are late getting back."

"Yes, yes. Let's go," said Asad.

They came down the hill to the road. They had some *dosas, idlis, uttapam* and coffee at a South Indian restaurant, then took an autorickshaw straight to the vast market at Linking Road. They wandered about buying various things for their new home, packed it all on the roof of a taxi and went off to Cotton Green. Once Asad had got the two sisters home to their parents, he would take the taxi back to Dharavi.

Having left Linking Road and passed Bandra, Asad said to Zorina as they approached Dharavi, "Would you like to have a quick look at the place I have rented for your sister? It is very near." Asad would very much have liked Jahura to see where they were to set up home.

It had got very late when they had finished their shopping. Of course, the street lights of the Mumbai Municipal Corporation were on, and there were also the lights on either side of the road from the high-rise buildings reaching up to the sky as well as the neon lights in the rows of shopping arcades. Indeed, wherever one looked, as far as one could see, there was a mass of dazzling colour.

But Zorina was now starting to worry. "No, no, Asad-bhai," she said. "It's getting very late. You'll be married in fifteen days, and then I'll come many times."

Asad did not say any more. He dropped the sisters off at their place in Cotton Green and by the time he got back to Dharavi it was after ten.

The slum covered almost two-and-a-half kilometres, rows and rows of close set houses with tin, tiled or asbestos roofs, amongst which numerous tunnel-like alleys wound like a thousand snakes reaching out in all directions. It had no actual entrance as such. To get to Asad's place it was necessary to go down a southerly alley that was so narrow that the taxi could not get through it, so it had to wait on the wide road outside the slum.

There was no community – Hindu, Muslim, Sikh, Christian – that had no members at Dharavi. There were Bengalis, Biharis,

Goans, Tamils and Andhras, there were Oriyas, Sindhis and Gujaratis – the whole of India was represented here. The place was even called 'Little India'.

It was not an entirely innocent diversity. While there were countless hard-working and peace-loving people here, there was also a vast army of murderers, bootleggers and smugglers. For money – or 'betel nut' as they called it – many of them would even commit murder at the drop of a hat. They were what the newspapers refer to as 'contract killers'. There was an arsenal of weapons here ranging from knives and daggers and illegal country firearms to AK-47 rifles. Looked at in one way Dharavi was a school for a thousand kinds of crime. However, there was an unwritten rule that the criminals would not lay a finger on the ordinary, decent people of the locality, and because of this observance the law-abiding citizens could co-exist in the same environment as so many infamous crooks.

Asad got out of the taxi and was starting to get his things down from the roof when Rajibul Haq came out from under the awning of the teashop on the other side of the road. He was middle-aged, with sunken cheeks and a greying beard, and there were dark shadows under his eyes. He was wearing a shabby pajama, a long shirt of cheap cloth, and pointed slippers.

Rajibul and Asad worked for the same builder. When he had come from the state of Uttar Pradesh to what was then Bombay, Rajibul was just eighteen. Since then, the city had been his home. Like Asad, Rajibul had no one in the world. He had once had a wife and two children, but they had all died. Had he wanted to, he could certainly have remarried, but after the death of his wife and children he never had the mind to start up a new home and family. He had been renting his room in Dharavi for many years, and it was he who had arranged for Asad to move there.

A little way off Rajibul called to Asad, then said to him in a low voice, "I've been sitting waiting for you since evening in the teashop." He knew that Asad had gone shopping for his marriage and that he would return late.

Asad was somewhat alarmed by the tone of Rajibul's voice. He asked, "What's the matter, Uncle?" Asad called him 'Uncle' because he was such a fond friend and mentor.

"You're in a bit of bother."

"Meaning?"

"The police were looking for you at the slum in Mahim. There they learned your new whereabouts and came for you here.

Asad was an honest man in every inch of his body. He made his livelihood by the sweat of his brow and had never been involved in stealing or swindling or fraud or any kind of dirty deed at all. That the police were looking for him was extremely harrowing news for Asad, as he had never done anything at all reprehensible to cause them to be after him. Asad held his breath, then, in a shaky voice, he asked, "What have I done wrong? Why are they looking for me?"

Rajibul put his mouth up close to Asad's ear and said, "You are not an Indian. You came from Bangladesh. In which case –"

"But Uncle –"

"What?"

"I was only five years old when I came here. I'm now thirty-five. I've been in Mumbai for thirty years. You all know that."

Slowly nodding his head Rajibul said, with a sad look on his face, "I know, but so what? The police think you're an illegal immigrant."

There was a pause. Then Asad asked, "There are also many others who've come from Bangladesh. Are they looking for them too?"

"I've heard that they are," Rajibul said.

"What do they want to do?"

"I've no idea. But –"

"But what?"

Rajibul explained that they did not have good intentions; indeed, there was certainly some kind of sinister motive.

Asad asked, "Tell me, Uncle. What should I do now?"

"The police have got noses like dogs," Rajibul said. "As long as they've got a sniff of you, they'll keep on coming here after you."

The taxi driver was now getting impatient and tried to hurry things along. "Saheb, please pay me the fare. I can't wait around any longer."

Asad had been so stunned by the mention of the police that he could hardly think. He said, "Tell me what I should do, Uncle."

Rajibul was quite concerned. He told Asad to get his things down and to pay the taxi driver. Asad did that straightaway, then asked, "And now?"

"You'd better go away for a few days," said Rajibul. "I'll let you know when things seem to have got better. Till then go and stay somewhere else."

"Where will I stay?"

"There are some of your countrymen living in Ghatkopar. Go to them."

Asad looked at all the things he had bought for his marriage and asked, "What about all this?"

"You can leave it all in my place. Get it later."

"All right."

There was a pause, then Asad said, "Uncle, you know all my plans. In fifteen days –" His dejected, melancholy voice went silent, and his face was dark with worry.

It was not difficult for Rajibul to understand what it was that Asad was trying to say. "In fifteen days you'll be married, huh?"

"Yes." Asad slowly nodded.

Rajibul knew all about Asad's coming marriage. The date had been finalised by a few people, including Rajibul, at Niyamat Ali's Cotton Green home. He knew Niyamat Ali very well.

Rajibul said, "Wait and see for a few days. If the police are still being a nuisance, you'll have to explain the whole thing to Niyamat Ali and have him postpone the wedding for a little while."

Asad had come so close to fulfilling his dream that he never could have imagined that he would be set back in this way. Now he seemed to be enveloped in disappointment. He stood there looking downcast and saying nothing.

An idea struck Rajibul. "All right. You don't have to go to Niyamat Mian. I'll go some time and explain everything to him."

Asad slowly let his head hang down again. Not only had he suffered a blow to his own peace of mind, he knew that Jahura would certainly be devastated to hear that the wedding would have to be deferred, for she too had built up her own dreams around it.

With a glum look, Asad said, "You can't take all these things on your own. Come, we'll both take them to your place, then I'll go to Ghatkopar."

Rajibul thought for a moment, then said, "It's now very late. I don't think the police are likely to come back tonight. Stay the night in your own place and first thing in the morning we'll go off to work together. From there you can go straight to Ghatkopar."

"All right."

And the two of them went into the Dharavi slum carrying all the goods on their heads and shoulders.

Fear kept Asad from sleep the whole night. He racked his brains but could think of no reason why the police should be looking for him. He had no idea of how many terrible thoughts went racing through his mind. Was someone plotting against him in some way? Someone or other had got him into great trouble with the police, but who could this mortal enemy be? Yet he had never done anything to hurt anybody, ever.

There had been rumours that the police had been going about in search of certain people, but Asad had nothing at all to worry about so why was he worrying? He was not one of the ones the police were looking for, he was quite sure of that. Nevertheless, his life had been suddenly turned upside down.

As Mumbai is on the western side of India, dawn breaks very late there, and when Asad got up from his bed it was till quite dark. Yet no sooner had daybreak come than there were long lines at the taps on the road, and when Asad went there with his two plastic buckets there were already twenty or so waiting ahead of him.

Once he had completed his bath from his two full buckets the sun had come up. He went into his room and changed into some dry clothes, then took a cloth bag and put some extra pairs of trousers and shirts into it. Who could say how long he would have to stay in Ghatkopar? He also took the money left over from the marriage shopping of the day before. He would lock the room after Rajibul had come and then they would both go off to work for the labour contractor.

On other days Asad did not wake up before sunrise. After coming to Dharavi, or even when he was living in the slum at Mahim, Rajibul would have to call him. Today he was happy to see Asad already looking so clean and smart.

"Very good," he said. "Today I didn't have to call you. You're all ready." He said 'all ready' in English, for he used a few English words from time to time. So many people, not only from all over India but from so many other countries and races, lived in Mumbai, so English words were commonly heard here.

Asad said nothing. In silence he locked the door and gave the key to Rajibul. Then he said, "As long as there is still some chance of trouble from the police, you'd better keep this."

Rajibul turned his eyes from Asad's face. Even after his bath there were still dark shadows under his bloodshot eyes and the marks of worry were all over his face.

"My goodness, didn't you get any sleep?" asked Rajibul.

Asad shook his head slowly and said, "No. I couldn't sleep."

Rajibul laid a hand on his shoulder and said gently, "You're upset about the police looking for you, huh?"

Asad nodded slowly.

Rajibul said, "There's no need to worry so much. Everything will turn out all right. Now let's go, otherwise the train'll be so crowded that we won't be able to get on it. And if we're not there by nine-thirty, Tiwari-ji will get hot under the collar."

Tiwari-ji was the labour contractor's overseer. His job was to see that the labourers did their job properly and to take care that nothing was neglected. The man truly had the look of a vulture. There was no way of tricking him into making the work a little easier or of allowing a little time to relax and have a smoke. His mouth was a filthy sewer and the intent of his obscene language was to damn fourteen generations of one's forebears. Although the firm paid more than other builders, every penny demanded its full quota of blood and sweat.

Rajibul and Asad set off side by side. From the Dharavi slum it would take them about three minutes to walk up to the main road. From there they would take a bus to Bandra station where they would catch the train to Andheri. When they got to Bandra, a huge crowd had already started to form. Except for about three hours in the night this city was in a continual and impatient hustle and bustle. The two men bought their tickets and joined the pushing and shoving throng that was cramming into the train.

When they got down at Andheri station, they caught a bus. They had to go to Mahakhali, east of Andheri, where a noted Sindhi construction company called Ramani Associates was building a huge housing complex of altogether twenty four seventeen-storey blocks. Included in it all would be a park, swimming pool, bank, post office, primary and secondary schools, community hall and various entertainment facilities. Some two thousand labourers under twenty five labour contractors worked there from nine-thirty in the morning until six at night. If everything went to plan, the complex would be completed within three years.

Two of the buildings that were close to finished were where Asad and Rajibul were working. They got to the site at nine-twenty-five and by that time countless labourers had already arrived. Their supervisor, Tiwari-ji, was sitting jammed into a huge chair. In front of him was a square table on which a thick attendance register lay open.

He was a man of about a hundred and fifty kilograms, with brown skin and a short, fat neck and hardly any throat to speak of, for his great head sat squat against his torso and there were three rolls of fat under his chin. His hands were like those of Bhima's club as seen in the television serial, *Mahabharata*. His hair was cropped very close to his scalp, except for a thick tuft at the back into which a rose had been tied. His round, reddish eyes were all the time darting from one side to the other. He wore a finely woven dhoti tucked in at the back and a silk short-sleeve panjabi over a red net-woven singlet.

There was a gold chain around his neck, on his left wrist was an imposing watch with a wide steel band, and on his feet were thick leather slippers. Tiwari-ji was originally from Benares. He was about fifty and his hair had gone grey from supervising labour since he was very young. At this complex he had eighty labourers working under him and he knew the names of every one.

As usual all the labourers were standing in a line in front of their supervisor. Asad and Rajibul were right at the end of it. Tiwari-ji asked no one anything. He would take one look at a man's face and then tick his name in the attendance register. The men would move away as soon as their names were ticked off.

Marking the register did not take very long. Then, in a deep, harsh voice, Tiwari-ji would bark out his order, "Get to work now!"

And so the day's toil would begin.

In all the buildings of the complex the work of concrete pouring was now going on, in some buildings up to the fifth storey, in others up to the sixth. Today in Asad and Rajibul's two buildings it would go up to the seventh where, over the past few days, the whole floor had been covered with a strong decking of timber pillars over which a framework of iron rods had been placed, and the concrete would be poured into this.

It was Rajibul's job to operate the concrete mixer, a steel container that was like a giant pot run by electricity into which were poured stone chips, sand, water and cement. When the mixture was ready it was sent up in big metal dishes to be poured over the iron framework. This job was done by Asad and many others. The same kind of work was also being done in all the other buildings and at any one time fifty or sixty mixers might be running, making a constant, deafening noise.

Standing with their dishes in front of Rajibul as he operated the mixer were Asad, Rafik, Fakira, Mujib and many others. Once the concrete was ready they filled their dishes and took them up to pour them. Like Asad, Rafik, Fakira and Mujib had been brought by their parents from East Pakistan into India some thirty or so years back. Having wandered about living here and there they finally settled in what was then Bombay. Rafik, Fakira and Mujib now lived in a slum beside the railway line near Mulund.

Looking furtively here and there, Rafik asked Asad in a suppressed voice, "Have you heard any news?"

"What sort of news?"

"About the police looking for people who came from Pakistan or Bangladesh."

Asad's heart started to thump. His voice shook as he said, "Who told you about it?"

Rafik mentioned a few names. Of course, they were not names included in the building contractor's register. Some of them worked in clothing or small plastics factories, some in roadside teashops or restaurants, others sold coconut milk at Juhu Beach. They were spread throughout various parts of Mumbai. Most of them lived in the poorest of slums, some even slept on the pavements, on the beach or in parks. Rafik lived in a slum near Sion station.

"What have the police said to them?" asked Asad.

The concrete was ready, and the other labourers were starting to move towards the buildings with their dishes now full. Sitting nearby in his own chair Tiwari-ji kept watch over everything like a vulture. Seeing Rafik and Asad chatting together he flared up. "Hey, you sons of dogs! What's all this standing around talking? Isn't there any work to be done?"

Asad and Rafik were greatly alarmed by this, for they knew that Tiwari-ji would come down hard on them if he caught them slacking on the job. It was not just all the obscenity and abuse, it was also the threat that at the end of the day, at pay time, they might be dealt short. "I'll fine you, you bastards!" he shouted.

Frightened, Rafik said to Asad, "We'll talk at lunch-time. That jackal's likely to dock our pay." They hurried to the mixer and then to their never-ending labour. Their first shift was from nine-thirty until one-thirty, when they had a forty-five-minute lunch break. After lunch they worked without a break until six-thirty. The concrete pouring had to be continuous.

A bell rang to end the first shift.

Asad and his friends washed their hands and faces and cleaned themselves up. On the roadside nearby there were rows of cheap South Indian restaurants where everything from rice, chapatis, puris, idlis, dosas and the like to bread and vegetables were available. In addition there were also Gujarati dishes comprising some rice, about six puris, dal, three or four kinds of vegetable, pickles and sour curd arranged in the various compartments of a stainless steel tray or *thali.*

In front of each restaurant there were long benches to sit on and eat at. Asad, Rafik Fakira and Mujib bought some Gujarati thalis and sat facing one another. Pouring dal over his rice Asad reminded Rafik of what he had been talking about earlier. Who had told him that people of the former East Pakistan were being hunted by the police?

"I can't say," said Rafik. "But they're being hunted, I know that much."

The other two, Fakira and Mujib, said that they too had heard of the police raiding various places.

Fakira said, "Last night I had to go to Goregaon to meet Hamid. He said that the police had been to their slum." Hamid had come from East Pakistan at the time of the Bangladesh War. His home had been in Sylhet.

"Why did they go to Hamid's, did he say?" Asad was anxious to know.

"Yes," said Fakira, slowly nodding his head.

"What, then?"

"They wanted to see their ration cards."

"And then?"

"They looked at the ration cards and left. They made no more fuss."

Rafik and Fakira lived in the same place. Rafik said to him, "You didn't tell me the police had gone to Hamid's."

"I didn't get back till very late," said Fakira. "You were asleep then. And then this morning after getting up and washing we had to catch the train. What chance did I have to tell you anything?"

Asad had been listening to Fakira and Rafik with bated breath. He asked, "Why did the police want to see their ration cards?"

"I don't know," said Fakira.

They all looked extremely worried. They could not work out why after all this time the police should be seeking out people who had come from East Pakistan thirty and forty years ago.

Asad ate, but he had no taste for whatever it was that he was eating. As he sat there with his friends, he heard them tell of the police raiding various places, although the police had not come to any of theirs yet. Nevertheless, Asad felt the threat weighing heavily upon him.

Asad thought for a moment then said, "I'm in some serious bother, brothers."

Fakira and Mujib were surprised. Mujib asked, "What kind of bother?"

Asad told them all that had happened the night before, about the police looking for him at Mahim and then going to Dharavi. They were alarmed by what he said.

"But you're getting married in fifteen days!" said Fakira.

Asad nodded slowly. "Yes. I've done a whole lot of shopping for our new place. And now I'm very worried."

A numbness seemed to fall over the South Indian restaurant. A few moments later, Fakira tried to offer Asad some encouragement. "Worried about what!" he said. "About the police going to Hamid's? But he had no problem, nor will you."

"But –"

"But what?"

"Uncle Rajibul told me to go and stay somewhere else for a few days. He said once this police fuss has died down, then I can go back to Dharavi."

Rajibul was regarded as a prudent, experienced man, so it was felt that his advice to stay away from Dharavi for the time being should not be ignored but taken very seriously.

Mujib asked, "What are you going to do, then?"

"There are three or four people from my village at Ghatkopar. I'll go to them."

"Today?"

"Yes. After work. I'll have to come and go between there and Andheri. I'll have to take two trains and a change of bus, so the fares will add up to quite a bit. But what choice do I have?" Asad smiled sadly.

Mujib suddenly remembered something. With great concern, he asked, "What about your wedding in fifteen days' time?" He and the others knew all about Asad's wedding, to which they had all been invited. The conventional grand feast had been arranged too – biryani, chili chicken, and the usual sweets such as *rasagullas* and *firni* – and there would be singing all night long. But now, all that was uncertain.

Asad said, "Uncle Rajibul has said to postpone the wedding."

Mujib thought for a moment, then said, "That's a good idea." Fakira nodded in agreement.

The bell had sounded for the next shift over at the construction site. Asad and the others had not realised that their forty-five minutes had gone so quickly. They hurriedly finished their meal, rinsed their mouths, paid the bill and ran back to the site.

Rajibul had said that he would go himself to Niyamat Ali and explain the need to postpone the wedding. But at six-thirty, when work had finished and payment was being made, he said to Asad, "I'm going now to meet Niyamat Mian. I think you'd better come with me."

Niyamat Ali and his family, especially Jahura, had been looking forward with such high hopes to the wedding day. For Jahura and Zorina the previous afternoon on the hill beside the sea at Band Stand had been like a dream. Then the three of them had gone about choosing the things they wanted to buy. They would set up such a happy home. Now what would Jahura's reaction be to being told that they should postpone the wedding? Asad felt terrible as he thought of how upset she would be. He asked hesitantly, "Do I have to go, Uncle?"

"Yes," answered Rajibul. "If I go alone and tell them, maybe they'll understand. But it will be a lot more convincing if they hear it from your own mouth. They won't suspect any ulterior motive in wanting to postpone the wedding. Just explain to them carefully about the police."

Asad had not considered before that it would be more persuasive for him to go himself rather than to send someone else. "All right, Uncle," he said.

They caught a train from Andheri to Bandra where they changed for Cotton Green. Niyamat Ali lived about five minutes from the station by bus or about twenty five to thirty minutes on foot. The two of them had spent so much on fares that they decided to save a little money and walk.

The two-storey slum with its tiled roof in which Niyamat Ali and his family lived was like a barracks. There were about two hundred rooms on both floors, one family to each room. Like the Dharavi slum, this one too was a mini-India with its representatives from provinces all over the country.

Niyamat Ali's family lived in a corner room on the first floor. Niyamat worked in a cotton mill nearby. He had already got home from the mill after work and was extremely excited to see Rajibul and Asad, whom he received very warmly.

They sat down close to Niyamat Ali and Zorina. Niyamat's wife, Ruksana, brought tea and sweets for her future son-in-law and his respected mentor, set it all down in front of them, then sat a little way apart from them. Jahura, of course, was not present but was behind the door to the little kitchen. Asad could feel her dark, bashful eyes peeping out from behind the door.

Niyamat and his family were as surprised as they were happy at the unexpected visit of Asad and Rajibul. Niyamat and Ruksana perhaps wondered at it, given that the marriage would be in just two weeks and that only the day before Asad had spent so much time with Jahura. Maybe their future son-in-law could not go a day without seeing their daughter. This marriage would bring such happiness to Jahura, not bitterness like the last one.

Niyamat said, “This is a surprise, Rajibul-bhai.”

“There’s something we have to tell you.”

“First drink your tea and have some sweets. Then we’ll hear what you have to say.”

“No. Let’s talk now.”

But Niyamat would not hear of it. He entreated them to eat and drink but Rajibul and Asad had no appetite at all. Nevertheless, Niyamat and Ruksana were so insistent that they had to at least pick at what was there. When they had eaten a little, Niyamat asked, “Now. What have you come to tell me?”

Rajibul cleared his throat. With a melancholy look, he said, “You’re not going to like hearing this.”

“What do you mean?” Niyamat asked. They were all a bit taken aback.

Rajibul looked down as he said, “The date of the wedding will have to be postponed.” Suddenly everyone was stock-still, like wooden puppets.

After a few moments Niyamat said with great concern, “But everything has been arranged. All the people of the locality have been informed. How can we postpone the wedding now? What will we tell people? It’s a question of family honour, Rajibul-bhai.”

“I understand that,” said Rajibul. “But we have no alternative.”

Clasping Rajibul’s hands, Niyamat asked, “Why is there no alternative? What has happened?” His voice had become even more worried.

Rajibul said to Asad, “You tell them.”

Asad related the matter about the police.

"Why are the police after you?" cried Niyamat. "Have you done something wrong?"

Asad insisted that never in his life had he done anything dishonest or hurtful to anybody.

"Then why are the police after you?"

Asad was nonplussed. Had the mention of the police sown seeds of suspicion of something else in Niyamat's mind? He noticed that Zorina's face had gone quite ashen and that Ruksana was holding her veil to her face and sobbing. And his heart missed a beat when he caught a glimpse of the dark and bashful eyes looking out from behind the kitchen door. With his hands to his face Asad shook his head emphatically as he said, "I don't know. I don't know. I don't know! I've never done a bad thing in all my life!"

Rajibul said, "I've known Asad since he was very young. You'll never find as a good a man as he is."

Niyamat just sat there awhile, stunned. Then he said, "Tell me, then. What will I tell our neighbours and relatives now?"

Rajibul had not thought that Niyamat might ask this kind of question. He said, "Just tell them that some kind of inconvenience has arisen and that the date has to be deferred. Such unforeseen things happen in people's lives. We have to be prepared for everything."

This kind of philosophical approach was of little consolation to Niyamat. Dejected, he asked, "For how long must the wedding be put off?"

"Don't be so worried," said Rajibul. "Not long. In six or seven days I'll let you know." As he spoke he laid a hand encouragingly on Niyamat's shoulder, though he was unsure as to whether or not Niyamat had been reassured.

His voice now thick with doubt and disappointment, Niyamat said, "All right."

"We'd better be going now."

Niyamat walked some of the way with them. At the station Rajibul took the train to Bandra. A little later Asad's train arrived. He would go to Ghatkopar.

Right alongside the railway line at Ghatkopar was the makeshift slum in which Ainul, Jabbar and Kalimuddin lived with their wives and children. Along with Asad and his parents they too had once come with their mothers and fathers to this city, and like Asad they too had lost their parents long ago. Ainul and the others had set up home here when they had got married. One of them washed dishes at a small roadside restaurant, one was a hawker, the other delivered lunches to offices.

They all seemed very worried by Asad's story. Kalimuddin said that they too had heard some talk about the police raiding various places, but as yet they had not come to Ghatkopar.

They were three good men, and they did not turn Asad away but made arrangements for him to stay with them. Asad would have to commute from there to Andheri until the police had finished creating a fuss; if they returned to Dharavi, he would hear of it from Rajibul.

Asad commuted between Ghatkopar and his work for about six

days. As soon as he arrived at the site each day, the first thing he did was to take Rajibul aside and ask, "Have they been back, Uncle?"

And Rajibul would slowly shake his head and say, "No."

After six days had passed, Asad's worry had eased off considerably and he started to breathe more easily. He asked, "What do you think? Will the police come back?"

Rajibul thought awhile, then said, "Seeing they haven't come in all this time, maybe they won't come back at all."

"It's really difficult coming all that way from Ghatkopar each day. I'm also spending so much on fares. Will I come back to Dharavi, then? Tell me."

"Don't come just yet. Let's see in a few more days."

In other words Rajibul wanted to be absolutely sure about the police. As they had still not come back, then they might indeed not come again, so dispelling Asad's worries – but one could never be sure. In a few more days it would be clearer as to whether Asad could wash his hands of the whole affair or not. It was necessary to proceed cautiously.

Asad hung his head and said, "All right, then." He understood why Rajibul had told him to stay yet a few more days at Ghatkopar.

In these six days Niyamat Ali had come to the Andheri site three times seeking news. With the responsibility of his daughter's marriage on his shoulders could he just sit idly by and do nothing? He had been picking up snippets of information about the police which had led him to feel that Asad might now be out of danger, and so he was a little confident when he asked Rajibul, "So now I can make the arrangements for the wedding?"

Rajibul counselled Niyamat Ali against excessive haste as he had done to Asad. "Wait a few more days," he said. A prudent and experienced man, he had not lost his suspicions about the police.

Niyamat asked anxiously, "How many days?"

Rajibul thought a moment and said, "Ten or twelve."

If nothing happened within the next ten or twelve days, it could be assumed that the affair had blown over. The police had probably come after Asad on some flimsy word or other floating about, and once they realised that he had done nothing wrong, that their suspicions of him were unfounded, they would stop pursuing him.

Unworried now, Rajibul said, "The trouble's passed. You can come back to Dharavi."

Asad felt so relieved that the whole nightmare that had weighed on his mind like a mountain had at last been lifted. Beset by intense fear day and night, he had suffered such terrible anxiety for almost a month! Now he could think of nothing other than his marriage. Rajibul had advised him to finalise the date as quickly as possible, and his former wonderful dreams of Jahura came back to him. Niyamat Ali would have to be told too, so that the wedding preparations could go ahead again, and this time nothing would be allowed to stand in their way.

So at Rajibul's suggestion Asad returned to Dharavi. When he got back there after work, he tidied and cleaned the place up. While he was living alone, the windows and the doors had been totally bare, but his new wife would have to have privacy, so he had the tailor make some curtains for her.

He had an old, three-legged bedstead with bricks doing the job of the fourth leg, but in a couple of days he would get rid of it, as he had seen a bed which he had decided to buy at the cheap furniture shop at the Dadar Market. Asad would do everything possible for the comfort and pleasure of Jahura, even if it sent him into debt.

Nevertheless, although he had come so close to his dream, its fulfilment was not to be eventuate.

Two days later, having just returned to Dharavi from Andheri, Asad was lying down. In the last month, having finished the pouring on one floor, work had now started on the floor above, and each day after work his body ached all over. He decided that he would have a little rest, take a bath and then go out and have some tea.

It was almost eight o'clock and from the distant Bandra overpass or the Mahim church opposite everything looked like a dream with nothing but light coming from the rows of high-rise buildings along the shore and the sodium lamps beside the road. Asad let his eyes close. Suddenly he heard the sound of several pairs of booted feet, then the sound of loud, hurried movement. At the same time came a rough voice, "Open the door! Open the door!"

Asad's doze was shattered and in a flash he was off the bed and opening the door to be confronted by a sub-inspector of police and four constables bearing rifles.

The officer inquired, "Are you Asadul Mian?"

For a moment Asad's heart seemed to stop beating. No, he could not escape them. Like hunting dogs they had got his scent and were now covering their prey, just like so many police, with a look of dumb emptiness on their faces. Asad watched them with bated breath. He choked, "Yes, sir."

"We've been looking for you for a few days. Did you think that you could throw dust in the eyes of the police and go on hiding somewhere in Mumbai?"

Asad said apprehensively, "No, sir. I was just spending a few days with some friends. Sir, would you kindly tell me why you have been looking for me?"

"We've heard that you're not an Indian national. That you're an illegal Bangladeshi immigrant."

By now Rajibul had heard of the arrival of the police and had come running, and many of the Dharavi slum people too were forming quite a crowd in front of Asad's house. All of them looked extremely worried.

With his hands clasped Asad said, "No, sir, no –"

Rajibul had now pushed through the crowd and said solicitously, "Sir, Asad is a good man. Thirty years he has been in India. He is one of us."

The officer turned his dull eyes on Rajibul and asked, "Who are you?"

"I have no relations at all, sir. But he is like a son to me. He calls me Uncle."

The officer turned back to Asad and said, "He says he's your uncle. That you've been in India thirty years. Where were you before that? And tell the truth."

Asad's throat was as dry as wood. He explained that as a five-year-old boy his parents had brought him to India and that since then this had been his home.

Furiously the officer rebuffed him. "Liar! You've come to India only recently!"

Rajibul was now desperate. He said, "No, sir. Asad has been here since he was a child."

The officer roared at him, "Don't you say another word! Just shut up!" And he turned back to Asad and asked, "How do I know that you've been here for thirty years?"

"I've been in Dharavi only a month, a month and a half," said Asad. "I stayed in a number of places before that. You can ask the people there. And I've also worked with many men in many places. They will tell you."

"I'm not interested in any of them. Have you got a ration card?"

"No, sir."

"Any other document that will say you're an Indian?"

For some time now Asad had been hearing of the police going from house to house wanting to see ration cards, the reason for which he had only recently come to know. Asad's parents had died when he was fifteen or sixteen, and since then he had managed to survive by whatever means he could find. For the last few years he had worked for real estate labour contractors, finding somewhere to lay down his head wherever he could. He never had a permanent address so how could he have got a ration card? Moreover, he had never thought that it was sufficiently important; as time went by, he had always managed well enough. Yet how was he to know that one day the lack of a ration card or some other kind of identity document would land him in such trouble? He had lived almost all his life in this country without one, but now it seemed that he did not belong here at all.

Asad's face went pale with fear. He said, "Sir – sir – " but he could not get any more words out.

The officer went on, "You were saying you've lived here for many years. Have you ever voted?"

Asad slowly shook his head. "No."

"You know you had to have your photo taken to be eligible to vote?"

"I did hear that."

"So did you have your photo taken?"

"No, sir. I was living in a makeshift slum. No one told me anything about getting my photo taken."

Though the officer had been speaking somewhat courteously, his words interspersed with his rebuffs, now he suddenly became fierce. He shouted, "You're a bastard illegal immigrant! No ration card, no photo identity card, and you say you're an Indian! Take him to the station!"

"Believe me, sir," pleaded Asad, clasping the feet of the officer, "I came to India when I was five years old! India is my home."

Rajibul was terrified. He said, "Sir, Asad has no ration card. That is his mistake. But he really has been here for thirty years –"

"Didn't I tell you to shut up?" snarled the officer through clenched teeth. "There's nothing you can do for him, you bastard son of a pig!"

"No, sir, I'm telling the truth. Please have mercy. He's getting married in a few days –"

But all of Rajibul's pleas fell on deaf ears. The officer said to the constables, "Take this Asadul Mian away."

Asad would not go. The constables had to drag him to the jeep. Then they took him to the station.

Asad was not the only one. There were many others without proof of identity who were being held at the police station as illegal immigrants. Asad knew many of them. Long ago they had come to India from East Pakistan, but why they were being held by the police so many years later was something no one could understand. They were all extremely worried.

The next evening Rajibul came to the station with Niyamat Ali to visit Asad. Niyamat was terribly upset. Striking his head with his hands he muttered continually, "What will become of my daughter?"

Rajibul was usually a man of great strength of mind who did not succumb easily to misfortune, but now that was no longer so. He suddenly looked much older. His eyes had heavy shadows, his cheeks were drawn and he looked utterly defeated.

Shaking his head emphatically he said with profound dejection, "I was unable to do anything for you, Asad." He told him that that day he had not gone to work at Andheri but had gone in the morning to Niyamat Ali's place at Cotton Green. They then went to see many people, telling them of Asad's plight and asking if a ration card could be issued in his name, for such an identity document would allow him to stay in India. However, Rajibul and Niyamat were only little people, as worthless as insects, and no one had ears for them. Indeed, they were all suspicious of what they thought were their ulterior motives in so urgently seeking a ration card and they chased Rajibul and Niyamat out onto the road as though they were dogs.

After some three days those who had been brought to the police station were put on a train and taken by a party of police to the West Bengal border where they were handed over to the Border Police with the words, "These are illegal immigrants. They entered India against the law. Take them back to Bangladesh."

How far away had Mumbai now become! Asad suddenly felt as though he had left a familiar world and had landed on some unknown planet. Again and again that pair of dark, bashful eyes appeared before him. No! he would never in his life see Jahura again, and his heart felt shattered.

The Border Police sent Asad and the others across to the other side. But there was a Border Patrol over there, too, and they commenced a cross-examination of all those men who were now seeking access. Asad could not hear what the others were saying, but in answer to an officer's questions he said that he had heard from his parents that their original home was in some village near Munshiganj.

"What is the name of the village?" demanded the officer.

"I don't remember," answered Asad. "I was so very young when we left the village."

"Who do you have in the village?"

"I don't know, sir."

The officer put many more probing questions, but none of Asad's answers seemed to satisfy him. Moreover, the Bengali that Asad spoke was broken and inflected with a peculiar mix of Hindi, Urdu and Marathi.

The officer had some whispered discussion with his colleagues, then said to Asad, "You don't belong to this country. Get back to India."

"But, sir –"

However, no one listened to anything Asad had to say. He and those who had come with him were pushed towards the border, but he knew that as soon as he got there he would be sent back.

Asad was born an East Pakistani. Then for thirty years he was an Indian, during which time East Pakistan became Bangladesh. After all these years it was determined that he was not an Indian, nor was he a Bangladeshi. He was stateless.

Confused and distracted he walked towards the border.